M000040051

BOBBY AND THE GOLDEN CROWN

MITCHELL BOLNICK

AND

ELLA MAVIS

Bob and the Golden Crown LLC

Bob and the Golden Crown LLC
Peoria, AZ, 85382

For more information go to:
bobbyandthegoldencrown.com

Cover design by Carlo Majuta

ISBN: 978-0-692-65072-1 (Trade Paper)

Printed in the United States of America

THIS BOOK is for my family. To me, the meaning of life is family.

—*Mitchell*

THIS BOOK is for all the authors and writers who put wonderful works of art into our world.

—*Ella*

WE WOULD like to thank the amazing Sally J. Smith and the awesome Christine Jeffries for editing this book. Also, thank you to the Eliances family for your support. This book would have never happened if we didn't have all of you!

BOBBY WALKER AND THE GOLDEN CROWN

Prologue

In 2000, I went for a hike with my wife, Christine, and our nine-year-old daughter, Katelyn, and our seven-year-old son, Matthew. We were avid hikers, back road drivers, and campers who just loved being in the outdoors. This particular weekend, we chose to go to one of our favorite towns, Sedona, Arizona. We had two main objectives: first, hike somewhere we had not been before, and secondly, to have a great meal at our favorite Mexican restaurant in town, El Rincon. While accomplishing both, we had an experience we never expected....

My wife and I had been to the Sedona area many times since moving to Arizona in 1988. We spent time exploring north of town into Oak Creek Canyon, and the many canyons southwest of town. Along the way, we had done many short hikes, including a couple of the "harmonic conversion" areas that many believed held special spirits and forces. We always respected the areas but never felt anything and thought the whole concept a bit silly, if the truth were to be told.

On this trip, we chose Bell Rock for our adventure. There really was no path up the rock, so we did some climbing and walking wherever we felt comfortable. Being bell-shaped, hence the name, the rock had huge rounded rocks to climb up that led to level spots perfect for resting now and then. There were crevices and cracks all over with vegetation growing here and there where it could find a foothold and some water. At one point, we rested and Matthew noticed something strange above us shoved into a crevice in the rocks. It was a crown! Yes, a real crown, like you would put on your head. It had skulls and bones and other symbols on it.

Of course Matthew wanted to climb up and get the relic, but Chris and I held him back. We felt that someone had placed the crown there for a reason and that it should be left alone. Neither child bought into our thinking, but being the adults, we prevailed and moved on. Matt and Katelyn wouldn't let us live it down. We really did not win anything, least of all peace and quiet.

The rest of the day, throughout dinner and the two hour trip home to Peoria, all Matthew could talk about was *his* crown and what terrible parents we were for not letting him have his treasure. It was not common for one to find a true treasure and we had just let it slip through our hands—like it was nothing special. In fact, for years, every time we went to Sedona, Matthew wanted to go hike Bell Rock to find *his* crown.

Matthew never really let us forget our faux paux and failure for him to gain his fortune and the glory that would be according to him. Throughout the years, we would talk about whose crown we thought it was and whether or not it had any special powers. As time passed, a story began to develop and as other events in our lives combined with the telling of the story, it grew and grew and grew. Eventually, we had a pretty lengthy telling of a fun, mysterious futuristic story. We transformed this experience into the book you are holding, Bobby and the Golden Crown, and the trilogy yet to come.

CHAPTER 1: THE DRIFTER

The inquiring group of locals and tourists chased the man through the red rocks scattered across the pitch-black desert floor. Thirty or so strong men, holding flashlights far from their bodies, hunted this unusual stranger as he crouched behind the tallest rock he could find. He had been seen by so many, but yet no one knew a thing about him. His presence around Sedona, Arizona created a frenzy that wouldn't die down until his identity was discovered and exploited.

He ran quickly, kicking up absolutely no dust behind him. The drifter fled from the curious crowd and into the darkness of a nearby rocky cove. He held onto his only possession and chanted a few subtle words before relaxing against the solid wall behind him. As the flashlights grew nearer, he let out a sigh of relief. His troubles would soon be over. The deed had been done, and he would be rewarded for escaping the clutches of the nosy people closing in on him.

The drifter calmed his nerves. Suddenly, a flashlight blinded him. He took a step back causing his treasured artifact to fall from his grasp and into a crevice below the cliff where he stood. Time was up. He couldn't go back to get his valuable possession. Afraid of the harsh reprimand he was destined to face, the drifter kept this dire mistake a secret until it was unearthed by an unsuspecting adversary...

1

CHAPTER 2: ROBERT DAVID WALKER

Robert David Walker, Bobby to everyone who knew him, never thought of himself as anything special or extraordinary. Born to an upper middle-class family in Phoenix, Arizona, Bobby entered our world at the most ideal time that any parent could ask for. The United States economy was booming. Phoenix, one of the epicenters of the boom, was the perfect metropolis to raise a family. Bobby's father, Gordon Joseph Walker, Faja to his kids and Gordy to everyone else, owned a small business that employed thirty people. Bobby's mother, Kimberly Roosevelt Walker, worked for a large insurance company.

At six years old, Bobby was the perfect mixture of Kim's tall brothers and Gordy's big-footed relatives. He was very athletic, for a six-year-old. His olive-colored complexion blended in with his blue eyes and floppy blondish hair. Bobby's young, big-nosed face looked just like Gordy when he was younger. Handsome for a young boy, but not remarkable, Bobby was never the kind of kid who obsessed over his weak knees or abundant allergies (also another wonderful attribute from Gordy's side of the family). Even with his awkward body and oversized feet and hands, Bobby managed to speed down the court, making him an outstanding player during any youth basketball game.

"Look at him go!" one of Bobby's basketball opponents announced as Bobby charged down the court at full speed. His teammates watched on in amusement which gave Bobby the determination he would need to sink the winning shot. Springing in the air like a grasshopper, Bobby threw the ball toward the backboard, scoring the final two points. The crowd roared on. His team celebrated their win. Bobby was a hero. Everything was perfect.

Bobby's unique control over his far-reaching arms and flagpole legs made him the first pick for starting point guard. He lived in nothing but basketball shorts and T-shirts, and played every game with dedication and a lot of heart. He dreamed of joining the Duke University basketball team before getting drafted by a pro team. The future was bright for big-footed Bobby—he would succeed, just like he always did.

A few games after his latest basketball victory Bobby was back in action, ready to win another game for his team. Racing down the court, dribbling the ball in perfect rhythm, Bobby prepared to take his shot.

"You're gonna miss!" Nicole, Bobby's older sister by two years, shouted just as the ball left his fingertips.

The ball sailed through the air, bounced off the corner of the rim and headed straight for Bobby's nose. There was no time to react. Bobby closed his eyes and absorbed the impact as everyone around him let out a massive, "Ouch!" Bobby was dazed, his body landing on the wooden court floor with a thud.

Bobby opened his eyes and watched Martin Andrews, his quick-footed best friend, recover the ball. His eyes shut again. Even though Bobby was down, he listened carefully to stay connected to the game. The buzzer rang out and the crowd's concern for him quickly turned into cheering for Martin's victory. Martin had done the impossible—taking the team from last place the year before to the top contender for the championship. Bobby was no longer the hero.

Why? Bobby thought. Nicole rarely came to his basketball games, but every time she did, she seemed eager to ruin his big moment. *Why on Earth did she get so much satisfaction from tormenting me?* Bobby's eyes fluttered open to Nicole towering over him.

"I told ya!" she said. On his other side, Coach Shea leaned into him, asking what day it was.

Bobby sat up, pressing his hand to the bridge of his nose. The team checked on Bobby as Martin kneeled next to him. He looked up at the stands and the quiet audience where everyone seemed anxious to see how he was doing. He gave everyone thumbs up. It was all over, and Bobby did everything he could to keep himself from strangling his sister.

Kim and Gordy came rushing to Bobby's side. "What happened, Son? You had that shot. You should have nailed it," Gordy asked as Kim and Coach Shea helped Bobby to his feet.

Bobby merely looked over at Nicole, giving her a stare that could have set her on fire. "Someone distracted me," he hissed. Nicole seemed to ignore him as Coach Shea asked Kim if Bobby's nose was broken.

"Probably," Kim responded. "We'll take him to urgent care." She and Gordy checked Bobby's head and face for additional injuries. "I don't think he has a concussion," Kim added, "but sometimes with teenage boys it can be hard to tell," she smiled.

Bobby continued to glare at Nicole as Kim and Gordy helped him walk out of the gym. This wasn't the first time Nicole had unleashed her big sister taunting on Bobby. Even though Kim worked from home, Bobby was frequently subjected to the evil doings of Nicole Christine Walker. But Bobby was a worthy adversary. He stood his ground and refused to let his older sister boss him around. However, Bobby let her get to him, and ruin his basketball victory.

A few days had passed, but the trauma from Bobby's injury had left his nose a bright red. He looked like a clown. Bobby tried everything to get the swelling to go down, but nothing worked. He sighed loudly, hoping that Nicole would feel a tiny bit of regret for causing his injuries.

"Bobby, are you listening to me?" Nicole stomped her foot as she snapped her long, skinny fingers in his face.

"No, Nicole, I never listen to you. Now leave me alone so I can get ready." Bobby looked at his red, swollen nose in the bathroom mirror.

She pinched his scrawny arm. "Just because we're going out of town to Sedona for your birthday doesn't mean you have the right to act like you know me!"

Bobby placed a cold towel on his face. "It's my birthday, Nicole. Shouldn't you be focusing on making the day special for me?" He turned to face her, pointing at his nose. "Besides, you should apologize for what *you* did to me."

"Me? Apologize to you—no way!" She shook her head allowing her long blonde hair to fall to her shoulders. "Listen, this is important. I can't have you pretending that we know each other."

"I wish I didn't know you! You're ruining my life!"

Nicole curled her lips into a sinister grin before skipping off to her room.

Kim knocked on the bathroom door. "Bobby, stop playing with your nose and get ready to go." He nodded. "Did your dad give you your allergy pill?"

Bobby sighed. "Yes, Mom."

"Don't forget to put on sunscreen," Kim instructed.

Sunscreen! he thought. He pulled a bottle from the cabinet, squeezed a hefty amount onto his hand and carefully covered his entire nose. He looked into the mirror for a final time and smiled. The redness was mostly gone. Bobby put the bottle of sunscreen and a first aid kit into his backpack and headed downstairs to the living room.

He looked around the house, hunting for a clue as to his family's whereabouts. Through the sheer living room curtains, he spied the grainy outlines of Gordy and Kim as they raced around the front yard. Bobby exited the house and jumped straight into the action. Gordy stuffed various hiking supplies into the back of the SUV. Nicole sat in the backseat of the truck with her door open and her portable CD player blasting The Spice Girls. Kim whizzed by Bobby and headed back into the house.

Bobby took a moment to enjoy the chaos. Gordy stopped long enough to say, "You didn't have to put the sunscreen on your nose yet, Bobby."

"It's big and red. I don't want anyone to see it."

Gordy came down eye-level with him. "It's not that bad."

Bobby smiled. Gordy's simple, encouraging words was all he needed to feel better. Before Gordy straightened, Bobby examined his face. Something wasn't right. Before he could ask a question, Gordy was back on his feet and helping Kim with another bag.

Bobby had sensed that this weekend trip to Sedona seemed uncomfortable for both Gordy and Kim. Gordy had taken the week off from work to prepare for Bobby's birthday, but he seemed preoccupied the entire week. Bobby begged his father to shoot hoops in the backyard one day—Gordy said no, explaining that he had some important business to take care of. Kim spent the week dabbing her eyes and ordering pizza every night before putting he and Nicole to bed early. Normally, Bobby surrendered to cheesy, pepperoni pizza without a second thought. But this past week, Bobby couldn't shake his parent's strange, absent behavior.

Bobby thought about what had happened the night before. He was giddy and wide awake. Craving a cold slice of pizza, he snuck downstairs to see what he could find. A conversation between Gordy and Kim at the kitchen table stopped him in his tracks. Gordy said that Meg, one of his sisters, would have wanted it this way. Bobby barely knew of his Aunt Meg, but he found the conversation intriguing. He crouched down next to the stairs and listened further.

"Are you sure about this?" Kim said.

Gordy sighed. "It makes sense. Bell Rock was her favorite place. She'd be happy to know that we carried out her final wishes."

Kim placed her hand on his. "Poor Bobby. I wish the memorial service wasn't on the same weekend as his birthday."

"It's okay, Kim," Gordy stood. "We'll do some hiking on Saturday to celebrate Bobby's birthday. I think he'll enjoy it." He left the kitchen and neared the stairs.

Bobby raced back up the steps and dove into his bed. Minutes later, Kim poked her head in. "Happy birthday, Bobby." She whispered before quietly shutting the door. He glanced over at the clock—it was 12:01 am. *What happened to Aunt Meg?* Bobby held onto his basketball-shaped pillow and stared at the ceiling.

"Kim, leave the office behind." Bobby heard Gordy say to his mother as he pulled the hatch down on the back of the SUV with a loud slam, bringing Bobby back into the present. He looked up at the morning sun. It was going to be a beautiful day.

Kim opened the rear passenger door for Bobby to climb in next to Nicole. "I can't," she replied. "The Andersons have found yet *another* issue with their policy. I can't afford to lose them as clients." Once Bobby and Nicole were safely strapped in, she shut the door and got into the front passenger's seat. Gordy gave Kim an encouraging smile as she pulled out a pen and yellow highlighter.

Gordy started the truck and looked into the rearview mirror. "Okay, kids. Are you ready for some fun and another Walker adventure?" Bobby and Nicole cheered. Nicole turned off her CD player and put it away.

Gordy closed the garage door, and they were off on their adventure. Ten feet away from their driveway, Bobby's eyes widened. "We forgot to feed Chivas and Dab!"

"It's okay, Bobby. Your mom asked the Thompsons to watch them." Gordy replied.

"The Thompsons can't feed the dogs today," Kim refuted. "I told them I would leave food and water out for the day. We have to go back."

Gordy put the SUV in reverse and backed up to the house so Bobby could feed the family dogs. After Bobby returned and the truck had made it to the stop sign at the end of the block, Bobby made another startling discovery. "I forgot to give them water!" Turning around for a second time, Gordy parked the truck in the driveway, again.

"Is there anything else you forgot, Bobby?" Nicole hissed when Bobby had returned from his tasks.

Kimberly turned around in her seat, "Nicole! Be nice to your brother. It's his birthday." Bobby smiled at his mother.

Gordy pulled out of the driveway for a third time. Inching the truck to the stop sign again, he put on his turn signal and came to a complete stop. "Is there *anything* else we need to do before we start our trip?" Bobby, Nicole, and Kim shook their heads, giving Gordy the green light to travel away from the house and toward Interstate 17.

Nicole poked her head up front. "Why are we having a funeral for Aunt Meg if she didn't die?" Bobby gasped. How did Nicole know what was going on?

Gordy looked over at Kim. "It's not a funeral, Nicole. We're having a special ceremony to remember the amazing person she was," Kim replied.

"Sounds like a funeral," Nicole added.

"Well, it seems like a funeral, but it's not." Gordy sighed. "Anyways, the service isn't until tomorrow, so let's focus on the fun hike we have planned for the day."

Nicole grabbed her CD player, but Bobby stopped her. "Aunt Meg died?"

She rolled her eyes. "Didn't you hear a word Mom and Faja just said? She didn't die."

He shrugged. "If she didn't die, why are we going to a memorial service tomorrow?"

Bobby waited patiently as Nicole opened her mouth and closed it promptly. She tapped Kim's shoulder. "Mom, you need to explain this again. Funerals are for people who die. If Aunt Meg didn't die, why are we going to her *memorial* service?"

Bobby paid careful attention. "Nicole, when someone is missing for a long time, their family might hold a memorial service for them. Now let's just leave it at that." Kim turned another page in the policy.

Nicole turned to Bobby, "That's why we're having a funeral." She placed her headphones on and turned up the volume.

Bobby gazed out the window wondering what happened to his Aunt Meg. He knew very little about her, but he had heard great things about her lively spirit. The SUV passed building after building, heading away from the busy streets of Phoenix and into the changing elevation of northern Arizona. Gordy tried to carry on a conversation with Kim as she read each line of the Anderson's policy word for word while classic music played on the stereo. Bobby listened in as his parents discussed various family matters including financial concerns and the upcoming school year.

Gordy seemed to notice Bobby's interest in the grown-up matters and asked, "What movie do you guys want to watch on the way up?" Both Bobby and Nicole agreed upon a fun cartoon movie Gordy had recently picked up for them.

Kim put on the movie, "Please use your headphones so we can listen to our music." Bobby put his headphones on and caught a smile cross Gordy's lips.

Once the movie ended, Bobby turned his attention back in his dad's direction. They had already passed Bell Rock, South of Sedona, and were coming into town. He stuck his head forward. "Faja, when we get to Sedona, can we eat at El Rincon?" he asked, eager to eat at his favorite Sedona restaurant.

Gordy smiled. "Sure thing, buddy."

Kim looked up from her papers. "We're already here?" The landscape had changed from tall buildings to red rock formations.

"Yep!" Gordy answered. "Time to relax and enjoy ourselves."

"You're right, Gordy." Kim shoved the stack of insurance policies deep into her briefcase before dropping it at her feet.

Gordy smiled at his wife, "I'm happy to see that you've finally checked out of the office, Kim."

Kim rolled down her window, allowing the cool Sedona air to fill the car. "It's vacation time!" she shouted in excitement.

Bobby enjoyed seeing his mother happy. He again looked forward to his birthday trip out of the hot, searing Phoenix sun and into the cool air of Northern Arizona. Even if he would have to attend a memorial service for his missing Aunt Meg the very next day.

"Mom, we're going to a memorial service. We're not really on vacation." Nicole said. Kim rolled up her window and peered over at Gordy.

Bobby despised his sister for ruining the family's fun with her rude observations. Nicole at nine years old had recently entered into her know-it-all phase, making it almost impossible for Bobby to relate to her. But even with their constant bickering, Bobby looked up to Nicole, appreciating her strong will and intellect. Nicole, on the other hand, made it clear that she didn't want to be seen associating with her weird and awkward younger brother. Folding her arms and leaning back into the seat, Nicole glared at Bobby. He knew exactly what this meant—she was waiting for the perfect opportunity to ditch him. He smiled, not minding at all if she magically disappeared.

Bobby leaned forward and tried to salvage the moment, "Hey, Dad, why are the rocks red up here?"

Gordy scanned the landscape across the horizon in front of the truck, "They are all from an old volcano, Bobby. A long time ago, the San Francisco Peaks in Flagstaff exploded, and the lava flowed down into this valley."

Bobby frowned. "I think it's weird that we have red rocks in Arizona—and volcanoes."

Kim laughed. "Weird? Are you worried it will explode again?"

"I don't know."

Nicole rolled her eyes. "If you're so worried, why are we spending your birthday up here?"

Bobby shook his head. "I never said I was afraid. I just think it's weird, that's all."

Gordy let out a loud laugh as he slowed the truck down. They cruised into the streets of the old Spanish village replica of Sedona known as Tlaquepaque, packed with tourists visiting shops and travelers coming for the great food at El Rincon, the Walker's favorite restaurant. Glued to the window, Bobby admired the "weird" red rocks covering the landscape for miles. He impatiently waited as Gordy hunted for a good place to park. Once the vehicle came to a stop, the family flung their car doors open and greeted the sweet Sedona air.

"Let's get lunch, and then we'll head back down to Bell Rock." Gordy advised the family as they headed toward their favorite Mexican restaurant.

Bobby jetted down the sidewalk, leaving Nicole behind. He approached a small shop and stopped at the front window. An advertisement for a UFO tour caught his eye. When Gordy caught up, Bobby pointed to the poster and asked, "Faja, can we go on a UFO hunt?"

Gordy chuckled. "Bobby, how many times do I have to tell you? UFOs are fake. So is all that mumbo jumbo about the vortices." He corralled Bobby forward toward the restaurant.

Bobby took a special interest into his father's statement. He continued to ask questions about UFOs and the vortices over lunch. Gordy explained that Sedona, known by many travelers and locals as a spiritual place, was labeled as a location for positive energy vortices. The UFOs were a hoax, plain and simple. Bobby's attention quickly moved from the paranormal hotspots and onto his upcoming birthday hike.

The Walkers dined on chimichangas with machaca beef, spicy chicken enchiladas, and Bobby's favorite, beef burrito with beans smothered in cheese. To celebrate Bobby's birthday they split a pair of fruit burritos, one filled with blueberries and the other with apples, both with a side of ice cream. The waiters and waitresses sang Happy Birthday to Bobby along with the family and other nearby restaurant patrons as he blew out a candle sitting in the ice cream.

Bobby gushed over what type of adventures they would find on their hike up Bell Rock. Once the bill was paid, they headed out to their favorite hiking trail and into an adventure they would never forget.

CHAPTER 3: THE COUNCIL

Jonathan studied the reports recently gathered about his latest experiments. These types of experiments had been initiated after World War II, and conducted in a bio-dome called "The Universe" as a way to better understand humanity and how to improve it. Nearly fifty years after World War II ended, Jonathan and his team of advanced scientists were in charge of monitoring these experiments and sharing their findings with the world's leadership.

Jonathan pushed his eyeglasses to their proper place on his nose, and looked over the numbers again. The time had come for him to make a motion before the Council regarding his observations. Even though he had made previous motions in the past, this motion would be the most important and for the first time in a long time, he was a little nervous. Standing to his feet, he retrieved his white lab coat from its hook and exited his office.

The Council, a collection of senators representing countries throughout the world, was the governing body of the world's leadership. The senators, also referred to as Council members, gathered on a semi-frequent basis to discuss world issues. This group had the power to vote on important issues that would significantly impact all of mankind. Jonathan, one of the group's youngest members, was not a senator, but rather the Ambassador for Science, one of the most important positions within the Council.

A tall, dark skinned man in a white suit met Jonathan at the door. "Sir, the car will be here momentarily."

Jonathan nodded to his assistant. "Thank you, Gerald," He clutched his file folders. "Has Sabrina provided any additional substantial information I'll need for the meeting?"

Gerald shook his head. "No, she didn't leave any additional documents at my desk." He opened the heavy glass door for Jonathan, "Shall I have your driver retrieve you at the Depot hall later today?"

"I'll take the Sun Train back." Jonathan stepped out of the clear glass building. The smell of delicious treats made his stomach growl.

The driver opened the rear door of a black sedan. Jonathan climbed in and rolled down the window. He enjoyed the sweet air for a moment. *Maybe it won't be that bad.* He thought. The vehicle pulled away from the curb and made an immediate left. The festival for the Universe Summit was already under way. The rumbles of the crowd grew louder. Jonathan placed his file folders next to him and prepared for the first sights of the celebration.

The sedan slowly pushed forward as Jonathan spotted a few lone people sitting on the sidewalk. He raised his hand, put on a crooked smile, and waved. A white man and a black woman huddled together and eating cotton candy, waved back. Jonathan looked down the street. More and more people had gathered. He continued waving at the growing crowd.

The entire street had been invaded by giant balloons swaying in the wind, multi-colored streamers hanging from lively green trees, food carts, and townspeople. Children chased each other around as their parents attempted to get them to sit still. Ice cream and berry filled cakes were devoured. Various individuals with different cultures aligned the street, cheering for Jonathan. Overwhelmed, he smiled at a few groups before sitting back in his seat.

He watched his fellow citizens enjoy the festival. As a Council member, it was his job to greet each party-goer with a smile. Secretly, the celebration was Jonathan's favorite part. He remembered racing down these streets as a child, looking for a sweet tart or a piece of cheesy bread to taste. He locked eyes with a Council member—an older gentlemen with firm, white eyebrows and sparkling teeth. The man winked at Jonathan, sharing the magic of the Summit festival with him. Jonathan was thrilled. He wanted to become a Council member and participate in the same parade one day. Now, it was him winking at a future Council member. He had come a long way.

But Jonathan was well into his thirties now. The dazzling allure of the Universe Summit festival had passed. Awaiting him was an important business meeting that would steer the direction of his current scientific studies. He exhaled sharply and waited for the sedan to stop outside the main doors of the Depot Hall, an extension of the Institution Complex. This is where the key developmental ideas were born.

The moment it did, the driver raced around and opened the car door. "Your destination, sir."

Jonathan exited and smoothed out his lab coat. He retrieved his file folder and walked through the Depot Hall entrance.

Traveling among the other members of the Council, he entered the Main room. Made of solid, spotless glass, the Main room was giant and had a large round desk and black high back chairs. Each station at the table had a name-plate for each representative present at the day's meeting. As the Controller, the oldest man in the Council, and his cabinet of five men took their seats at the head of the table Jonathan darted for his chair, hoping no one would strike up a conversation with him.

The Controller banged his gavel several times, bringing the meeting to order. "Council members, welcome to the fifty-first annual Universe Summit. Since the inception of The Universe in 1942, we continue to ascertain the exact information needed to move our world forward. Each of you has been selected to be here based on your scholastic and scientific input into our latest experiment. I thank you for your commitment to carrying on our mission."

The room erupted into loud applause. Jonathan studied the Controller, looking for any evidence as to the direction of the meeting. The Controller was the liaison between the Council and the Ministry—he knew all pertinent information before anyone else. His stoic demeanor made it impossible for anyone to read his mind. His eyes fell on Jonathan, allowing him to make an assessment of the man in charge. *Here we go,* Jonathan thought. He sat up straight in his chair.

The Controller read his minutes from the latest Ministry meeting which Jonathan found incredibly dull. The Ministry, composed of three men and three women from different countries on a rotating basis, was the governing board of directors who oversaw the actions of the Council. Two ministers were replaced every five years and the balance between men and women was vigorously maintained. Each change was referred to as the *Changing of the Ministry* as the makeup of the Council also would change. As the Council monitored the day-to-day events happening in the world, the Ministry made major decisions on what actions needed to be taken for the future. The Controller was in charge of sharing with the Ministry everything that the Council discussed so decisions could be made. Once the Ministry made a decision, the Controller announced it to the Council who then enforced it. No one ever got an audience with the Ministry directly without going through the Controller.

Every member of the Council trusted every decision the Ministry made—every member except one, Jonathan. Each time the Ministry had a meeting, nothing of interest was shared with the Council. Jonathan shifted his weight in his seat, trying to find a comfortable spot. These types of meetings were rather boring but useful if the necessary action items were ever addressed. Since this was a Universe Summit Jonathan maintained his focus on the Controller, waiting for the opportune moment to figure out what was going on inside the Controller's head.

The Controller continued. "So, as you can see, the Ministry is pleased with our progress," He looked up from his notes. "However, there is one thing."

Senator Preston Churchill of England stood. "Pardon my interruption, Mr. Controller. Has the Ministry shared any information with you regarding our concerns with another flu epidemic?"

"The last epidemic was more than forty years ago," the Controller replied. "Why do you ask?"

"England has been struck with a super influenza strain. Over two hundred cases have been reported. I'm concerned for my people." Senator Churchill took his seat.

"I understand," the Controller relaxed his shoulders. "I'll make sure the Ministry approves emergency relief for your people." The Senator seemed satisfied.

"I read in one of the founding member's journals that the fourth Ministry thought the Universe Initiative wouldn't make it past the initial ten-year trial period." the Controller said. The room erupted into light laughter. "We all know today what a great miscalculation that was. Nevertheless, one of our council members made it a point to enlighten me on the viable nature of this project. After the death of Alexander, the prior Ambassador for Science, he has taken it upon himself to spend the last seven years becoming very acquainted with the Universe Initiative and its vast components. At this time, he would like to share a motion with the group." He turned to face Jonathan. "I introduce to you all our Ambassador of Science, Jonathan. My fellow Council member and friend, you have the floor."

Smoothing out his lab coat, Jonathan rose to his feet and grabbed the note cards from his file folders. He walked to the head of the table and greeted the Controller before facing the room. Several pairs of eyes, both young and old, stared at him, waiting to hear his motion. Hands shaking and short of breath, Jonathan fumbled through his note cards.

"You shouldn't be nervous, Jonathan. No one here is your enemy," the Controller whispered to him before taking his seat.

Jonathan cleared his throat. "Thank you for this amazing and yet rare opportunity to address you today. As an adjunct member of the Council, I wanted to bring forth a motion regarding the Universe Initiative. As we all know very well, this project has offered a wealth of knowledge and resources we use every day over its long tenure. As we examine these contributions on a deeper level, you'll find that there are still many things yet to be studied."

Senator Ivana Sergeev of Russia stood. "I apologize for inserting myself into your speech, Jonathan, but I think we should get straight to the issue at hand. It is my recommendation that we take action as a council and restructure the Universe Initiative. Countless years of research and time have been spent on this project with diminishing returns."

A roar of murmuring voices filled the room. Jonathan glanced over at the Controller. He whispered a few words to the member next to him before readdressing the Council.

"Senator Sergeev of Russia, it is rude to take the floor from another council member during his motion. Please hold all your comments for the discussion session."

Senator Sergeev, a short woman with broad shoulders and large arms, shook her head. "Mr. Controller, I mean neither you nor Jonathan any disrespect. But we have studied this matter for several years and believe it is in our best interest to move on. This initiative has run its course. It's costing us far too much money. Perhaps we could create a new initiative that is established from a new, more modern base."

"But it has been such a boon to our lives! Without this initiative, we wouldn't be where we are today!" shouted George Marren, Senator from the United States of America. "If we abandon this project we will have to create a brand new plan, a costly and timely undertaking. Is that something this Council is looking to do?"

Low voices bickered back and forth amongst the members seated at the table. The Controller stood and slammed his heavy gavel down several times. "This uproar regarding the Universe Initiative will stop at this moment!" The room slowly grew quiet. "Now, the Ambassador has a motion we need to consider. If any of you interrupt his speech with another outburst, you will be removed from the Council chambers and will be required to approach the Ministry for reprimand!"

This was not an empty threat. Jonathan appreciated having the Controller's support, however, something didn't seem right. Normally, a council member had the right to voice a concern over a motion regarding the Universe, but there was more to the Controller's dismay with Senator Sergeev's outcry. *I hope I'm not being set up,* Jonathan thought to himself. The Controller nodded for Jonathan to continue.

Jonathan waited a few moments before proceeding with his presentation. "As I was stating earlier, this initiative has created a great wealth of knowledge and resources for us. Within my short years of doing research on the Universe's responses to our experiments, I have experienced many amazing scientific discoveries of my own." Jonathan looked around the room at the motionless audience. "I personally have learned a lot from watching these…" Jonathan paused mid-sentence. Taking a deep breath, he placed his note cards on the table. "I'm sure everyone present is ready to hear my motion."

Senator Sergeev nodded. Jonathan glanced over at the Controller who gave him an approving nod. "I move that the Council and the Ministry approve the Universe Initiative for another thirty years."

Several members around the table rose, yelling their frustrations loudly at Jonathan. Senator Sergeev stood again, "Now, now, we shouldn't let this issue get out of our control!" Jonathan had a mind to interrupt her but missed the perfect opportunity. "Young Jonathan is new to the Council. He doesn't have the knowledge or insight that we have. We must take his motion into consideration."

The Controller's eyes grew dark. "Senator Sergeev, I do not know what you are scheming, so I'm issuing you a final warning regarding your conduct."

Senator Sergeev smiled. "I mean no harm to Jonathan. I'm not here to create any type of scheme or charade. My sole objective is to express my concern regarding the initiative. I, like many others in this room, believe that thirty years is way too long. Some members of the Council won't even be alive at that time!" The room applauded Senator Sergeev's response.

Jonathan shook his head. "That is what the previous Ministry stated forty years ago, and look where we are today.

If it weren't for the latest innovations brought on by this initiative, many of you wouldn't be here. Senator Nguno, we know now that your country of Nigeria would have been devastated by an Ebola outbreak had it not been for the experiments we did. AIDS would have impacted not only Africa, but the entire world. Because of our experiments these perils were avoided. In addition, the technology that we have tested over the years has had a great impact on our world. If we abandon this project we will throw away an opportunity to learn even more!" Jonathan stared at Senator Sergeev.

The Controller cleared his throat. "Thank you, Jonathan, for your motion. You may take your seat." Jonathan quickly left the front of the room and sat down in his chair. "As we can see, the Council has an issue with extending the project for another thirty years. I, however, am in favor of the motion. In an effort to keep the peace amongst us Council members, I will accept the motion under the following terms. Term number one—we will extend the Universe Initiative for a timeframe of ten years. At the end of this ten year period, we will revisit the matter and take further actions at that time." The room nodded in consent.

Senator Sergeev gave Jonathan a slight nod. The Controller continued. "Term number two—Jonathan will be reassigned as the head scientist and observer on this initiative. Any persons or parties who partake in this program will report directly to him and him alone." He looked Jonathan in the eyes. "Because of your dedication and thoroughness in this project, I hereby grant you complete access to the Council and the Ministry. From this day forward, you have earned a permanent seat at the Council table and can request a meeting with myself and the Ministry as you need."

Jonathan froze as he received a standing ovation. In the history of the Council, an observer was never appointed to a permanent seat within the Council or approved for an open invitation to request an audience with the Ministry. Or at least the idea of an audience with the Ministry. In order to speak with any member of the Ministry, Jonathan had to request a meeting with the Controller first. The top tier of leadership was still off limits. The Controller advised the Council members to take their seats as he continued the rest of the meeting. Once the summit had adjourned, Senator Sergeev pulled Jonathan aside.

"Congratulations, kid." Senator Sergeev extended her hand. Jonathan reached out for a handshake. The moment their fingers touched the Senator pulled Jonathan into a hug. "You may want to keep a better hold on your property."

Releasing Jonathan from the hug, the Senator continued to converse back and forth with other members standing close by. Jonathan's heart sank. He had hoped no one knew his secret.

CHAPTER 4: AN UNUSUAL FIND

Bobby jumped from rock to rock, leaving his family behind him. "Come on, you slow pokes!" He hurried up the narrow path, his sneakers kicking up red dust behind him.

The moderate hike up Bell Rock was a fun adventure for Bobby and the Walker family. The "trail" followed along the base of the bell before spiraling up the side of the rock. On this beautiful, sunny day, several other families and hikers had hit the trails. Since the rock didn't have any formal pathways upward, Bobby led the family from the end of the trail and up the rocky wilderness.

"It looks like a spaceship!" Bobby said. He stared at the dome-shaped top with tiered cascades of smooth, red rock below it.

"Yeah, it kinda," Gordy walked up next to Bobby. "Let's take a rest, buddy."

Bobby ignored him. "I wanna go all the way to the top."

"It tops out at just under 5,000 feet, so that's only about five hundred feet, but the last half is straight up with a lot of climbing required! I don't think we'll be able to make it that far."

Bobby wasn't buying it. "Anything's possible if you just try." He quickly took the lead again, jetting past Gordy and farther up the smooth rising rocks ahead.

The hike required stepping around chaparral shrubs that covered the mountain's surface. Bobby managed that part with complete ease. He pressed forward. The Walkers followed closely behind Bobby. He led the way until the ledges grew taller than he could climb. Gordy offered his assistance and helped Bobby conquer each obstacle.

"How far do you think we have to hike to reach the top, Faja?" Nicole whined. She picked up a couple of lava rocks and put them in her backpack.

Gordy took a deep breath and wiped his brow. "It all depends on the path we take. If we stay low and go around and around while we wind upwards, it's a minimum three-mile hike. If we head straight up from here, it's less than a mile."

"Let's go straight up!" Bobby chanted as he hoisted himself on top of a rock. Gordy stood close by. "I got it, Faja."

"My feet hurt!" Nicole shouted from a short distance behind Kim.

"Wimp!" Bobby hurried up the trail, determined to be the first one to reach the top.

After an hour of intense rock climbing, Gordy demanded that everyone stop to rest before entering the summit of Bell Rock. Bobby reluctantly complied. He took a seat on a big flat rock next to Nicole.

Nicole untied the laces of her new hiking boots and freed her feet. "Happy birthday, *Bobby.*" She hissed while her toes stretched.

"Thank you, big sister," He said with a smirk. "I hope we make it to the top."

"I'm fine right here." Nicole sighed.

Bobby pointed to her backpack. "Can I have one of your lava rocks?" She shook her head. "Please, it's my birthday."

"Carry my backpack for me?"

"No way!" Bobby rose. "I'll get my own rocks."

"Bobby, you should rest and save your energy for the rest of the way up." Kim advised from the perfect shady spot underneath.

Nicole stuck her swollen feet in her boots and joined Kim. Bobby looked at the rocks and cliffs ahead. He retreated back to his family just in time to hear Nicole negotiating with Gordy for a piggyback ride. Kim handed Bobby a cold bottle of ice water from her backpack.

"Honey, please stay close until we all catch our breath." She pleaded.

Bobby nodded and plopped down again. He daydreamed about cowboys roaming the terrain below while Native Americans sat camouflaged on the rocks up high. He wondered how many times the Indians sat right where he perched, taking aim against their enemies. Looking around the tall boulders above him, a flickering object caught his eye. He jumped up and ran toward the rocks.

"Where are you going, Bobby?" Kim stood and shouted after him.

"There's something up here!" Bobby shouted. He stopped once he had a clear view of the shiny object. Gordy and Kim approached him.

"Bobby, what's up?" Gordy placed his hand over his eyes to shield the sun.

Bobby pointed at a crevice in the rocks. "I think it's a crown."

Gordy took a few steps closer to the crevice. "I don't see anything, buddy."

Bobby walked past his father and climbed up to the crevice. Before anyone could protest, he put his hand in and pulled out a golden crown.

The golden crown, covered in blackened spots, was a rare relic to find out in the Arizona desert. Strange markings of skulls, crosses, stars, and other symbols Bobby had never seen before covered the outside rim of the crown. Smooth stones and jewels were imbedded in the multi-pointed top. Running his fingers across the metal, Bobby felt a burst of energy flow throughout his body. He admired his treasure, an accidental birthday present.

"It really is a crown," Nicole said as she took it out of Bobby's hands. "I wonder what this thing is doing all the way up here."

Bobby took it back from Nicole. "It doesn't matter. I'm keeping it."

"No!" Kim and Gordy shouted in unison.

"But it's my birthday!"

"Sorry, buddy. We can't let you keep it." Gordy said, reaching for the crown.

Bobby pulled the crown into his chest. "Why not?"

"Because we don't know who owns it, who left it here, and most importantly, why they left it here," Kim said.

"Besides, it might have some special purpose or meaning." Gordy motioned for Bobby to hand him the crown. Reluctantly, Bobby handed it over. The moment it grazed Gordy's hand, he dropped it. "Ouch! That's hot!"

Bobby scrunched his eyebrows before picking it up. "No, it isn't."

"Don't be so dramatic," Kim said to Gordy. She picked up the crown and admired it. "These symbols are really weird." She put it down on a rock. "I think we should leave it here."

Bobby picked it up. Gordy seemed shocked. "It didn't burn either of you?"

Bobby tucked the crown under his arm and turned his hands palm side up. "It's not hot, see," Both Kim and Gordy looked over Bobby's cool, uninjured fingers. "Told ya."

Kim snatched the crown from Bobby's body. She wrapped it in a bandana, climbed up as high as he could and placed it far into a crevice where Bobby couldn't reach it. "I've had enough weird and unusual for one day. Let's keep hiking."

Bobby sat down on a rock and folded his arms. "I'm not going anywhere until I get that crown."

"The answer is no and that's final." Kim said.

Bobby never heard his mother tell him no unless she was serious. He knew she meant business. She sat down next to him, placing her arm over his shoulder as he sulked. "Fine." he said in a low voice.

"Bobby, I know you want that crown, but there's just something weird about it. You have to understand that we're doing this to protect you." Kim kissed his forehead.

"But I found it. And it's my birthday. Don't you think that's a sign?" He pouted.

She sighed. "Bobby, I don't think that crown was meant for us to find. Besides, your dad and I will get you another crown that's not covered in black spots and scary symbols."

"But it's not the same. I want that one."

"Come on, Bobby. It's not the end of the world. We have the rest of this amazing hike left." She leaned into his ear. "Your dad has a special surprise waiting for you at home."

Bobby smiled as he jumped to his feet. "Well, come on then!" He looked into the crevice one last time.

Gordy led the way until Bobby rushed to the front of the Walker pack. Bobby did everything he could to refocus on their beautiful hike. Together, they reached the top of Bell Rock. It didn't take Bobby long to get upset over missing a chance to take the hidden treasure home. He couldn't explain it, but it felt like he was meant to find the golden crown wedged deep inside that crevice. With no path to follow they did not pass the crown on their way down the mountain. Gordy was thankful for that. On the way back to the hotel for the night, Bobby folded his arms tightly around his body, and stayed quiet for the whole ride.

Gordy remained quiet as well. He examined his hands several times. Bobby noticed his father's strange behavior, but decided not to bring it up. Looking down at his own fingers, he didn't see any swelling.

Kim looked back at Nicole and Bobby. "Hey, guys, how about some pizza for dinner?" Nicole was asleep, but Bobby was wide awake.

"Sure." He replied with a shrug.

Kim sighed. "Bobby, please understand that I'm doing this because I love you."

Bobby shifted in his seat. "I like pizza," he smiled. "Thanks, Mom."

She returned his smile and faced forward. Bobby rested his head against the seat. He closed his eyes and dozed off. He dreamed of putting on the golden crown as a surge of energy took over his body and seemed to carry him away.

CHAPTER 5: THOSE AWKWARD TEENAGE YEARS

Nine years passed and Bobby forgot all about the golden crown. Puberty came and went, leaving Bobby with even bigger feet, longer arms and flagpole legs. He cut his blond hair short into a buzz cut, making him feel manlier. He traded in his T-shirts and basketball shorts for nice pants and button-down shirts. On special occasions, he'd wear a fedora and tie with a clasp. Bobby thought sixteen looked good on him.

Hiding behind a pair of sunglasses, he waited for Nicole to park her car. He liked catching rides to school with her, even if she didn't enjoy her little brother tagging along. Nicole had no choice—when Gordy and Kim bought her the car, the agreement was that she had to take Bobby to school, period. Every morning followed the same pattern: both teenagers woke up, dragged themselves out of bed, fought over which of them could shower first, and made their way to school, still fighting along the way. During the entire car ride, Nicole lectured Bobby about their respective social statuses among the other classmates, and her expectations of him.

Nicole, now an eighteen-year-old and even more of a straight A know-it-all, had grown into a beautiful, petite firecracker. She had long blonde hair and straight, pearly-white teeth. All the guys in her senior class fought for a chance to date with her. With the homecoming dance just around the corner, she was in a particular kind of mood. She slammed her car door which confirmed Bobby's suspicion.

"Look, Nicole, it doesn't matter what you wear to that dumb dance. You'll still beat all the other girls," Bobby said, flinging his backpack over his shoulder and placing his sunglasses on the back collar of his shirt.

Nicole put her purse on her arm. "Bobby, you know the drill. Once we get to school, we don't know each other!"

Bobby rolled his eyes. "Everyone hangs out at our house after school. They know we're related."

Nicole checked her hair one last time in the car mirror. "Whatever! Just don't talk to me until the final bell rings. Got it?" Bobby drifted off into space like he normally did when Nicole spoke to him. She punched his arm. "Got it?"

He rubbed his arm. "Yeah, yeah, I got it."

She smiled. "Good." Within a few minutes Nicole had joined her friends, leaving Bobby completely alone.

Martin, Bobby's childhood best friend, threw his arm over Bobby's shoulder. "Has Nicole picked a date for homecoming?" he asked.

"She's not going with you, Martin." Bobby tossed Martin's arm off, and they proceeded to walk to class.

"Who's she going with?" Martin asked.

Bobby shrugged. "I have no idea, and I don't care. I've gotta focus on basketball."

"I hear ya," Martin said as he reached his class. The two friends said goodbye as Bobby proceeded down the hall.

Ashley Lincoln walked toward him. Bobby had to stop and admire her silky brown hair and large, white smile. He loved her since the fifth grade. Ashley hurried past a few grey lockers and into their first period class. Bobby followed her. He would follow her anywhere.

The moment his foot touched the classroom floor, Mrs. Jensen, his history teacher, informed Bobby that the school's basketball coach, Mr. Jackson, wanted to see him. Bobby cautiously walked from his classroom to the coach's office.

"Bobby, please have a seat." He pointed to a chair facing his desk. Bobby slowly sat down. "As you know, I've seen you play at almost all the school's basketball games."

A knot grew in Bobby's throat. "Oh, yeah?"

Coach Jackson nodded. "Bobby, you've got some real talent. The head coach has been getting calls from a couple universities and scouts."

A smile spread across Bobby's face. "That's great! Do any of them happen to be Duke University? I really want to go there."

Coach Jackson paused. "I'm not sure, but ASU and U of A are looking at you."

"That's great, but I don't really want to go to school here. I really want to go to Duke."

Coach Jackson folded his hands and placed them on his desk. "Now if you want to play for these teams or go to Duke, you're gonna have to keep your grades up." He paused. "Including your history grade. You're pulling in a solid D right now. What's going on?"

Bobby, normally a straight A student, despised everything about his history class. Except for Ashley Lincoln. "I don't know."

"Why not?" Coach Jackson leaned back in his chair.

Bobby shrugged. "I've been working on my three-point shot. I haven't had time to read the material."

"You're a smart kid, Bobby. I'm sure you can find the time to get your grade up."

"Coach Jackson, I'll do my best. Maybe Ms. Jensen sill let me do extra credit." Bobby smiled.

"Your sister, Nicole, was a stellar student when she was in Mrs. Jensen's class. Perhaps she can tutor you."

"Yeah, right." Bobby blurted. He quickly recovered. "I mean, she's busy at the moment. But if you can get me some extra credit, I'm sure I'll be able to raise my grade."

"Talk to Mrs. Jensen and see if she'll agree to let you redo one of your major projects."

Bobby smiled and jumped out of his chair. Before he left the room Principal Jackson stopped him. "Bobby, next year you're gonna be a senior. Don't let that stop you from finishing strong and heading off to a good school, even if it isn't Duke."

Bobby nodded. "I'll do anything to get into Duke. And I'll keep my head in the game and in my books." Bobby headed back to class.

He slipped into his seat behind Ashley. *If only she knew I existed,* he thought. Ashley never came to any of the basketball games—she only attended football games. Bobby was convinced that she had no idea how talented he was. This was all for good reason. He hardly said two words to her since the fifth grade. Bobby was convinced that she didn't know he existed.

Today, Ashley turned around for the very first time, muttering the words, "Mrs. Jensen told me to share my notes with you." She smiled and placed a half sheet of paper on his desk. That was all Bobby needed.

This was his one and only chance. "Will you go to homecoming with me?" he blurted. *What are you doing?* he shouted inside his head.

Ashley's brows scrunched together. Mrs. Jenson clapped her hands and Ashley turned back around. "Bobby, the lost colony of Roanoke. What do you think happened to them?"

He regained his focus, and avoided staring at Ashley's beautiful hair. "I have no idea. They could have disappeared for so many reasons."

"Name one reason."

Bobby paused for a moment only to say, "I could name three good reason—they all died, they were captured by Native Americans, or something spooked them and they fled the area. No matter what happened, we can all be sure that no one lived to tell about it."

Mrs. Jensen seemed intrigued by Bobby's answers. She began pacing the front of the room. "What could have spooked them?"

Bobby glanced down at the notes that Ashley had laid on his desk. Amongst her lovely scribbles, the word *disappearance* was circled. A flood of emotions came over him. Mrs. Jensen called his name a few times. "Oh, sorry," he said. "Maybe they had an encounter with a group of unfamiliar people. Maybe the Spanish caught up to them."

"Good observations." Mrs. Jensen moved away from Bobby and continued the lesson.

Bobby couldn't stop staring at Ashley's notes. Disappearance. Aunt Meg. Years had passed since his aunt's mysterious disappearance. How many years had she been missing—Bobby wasn't sure. Gordy never went into detail about Meg's last known whereabouts. When Bobby asked questions about Meg's case, Gordy and Kim shut him down, begging him to drop the subject. Bobby saw the hurt in their eyes so he always did.

The class bell finally rang. Ashley stood, grabbed her backpack, and flung her hair back. Bobby rose. "I have a boyfriend." She said before scurrying into the hallway filled with chattering students. Bobby helplessly watched her leave.

Mrs. Jensen tapped his shoulder. "Can I help you with something, Bobby?"

Bobby pushed his hurt feelings aside and got down to business. "I need extra credit in order to get into Duke and play basketball. Is there anything I can do to bring my grade up?"

Mrs. Jensen, a tall, slender woman in a bright floral dress, took a pencil from her tangled black hair. "Bobby, all you have to do is complete the homework on time," she tapped the pencil's erase against his temple. "Everything you need to pass this class is up here."

Bobby sighed. "I know," he pleaded. "I'm having trouble focusing. All this history stuff doesn't seem relevant."

Her eyes lit up. She retracted her pencil. "I have an unusual project for you." Bobby knew all his teachers were fond of his curious nature. He hoped her project would be intriguing.

"Bobby, I want you to write about something of great importance from your childhood."

"What does that have to do with history?" Bobby was convinced that his history teacher had gone mad.

She smiled. "I know you and your family take regular trips around Arizona. I want you to write about the history of any historical site you've come across."

Bobby thought about Sedona and the golden crown came to his mind. "I'm sure you're gonna say no to this, but I'm going to ask anyway. On one family trip, I found this rare golden crown in Sedona. If I can find some information on that, can I write about it?"

Mrs. Jensen nodded. "Sure. If that doesn't work out just let me know, and we'll pick something else."

The moment school let out, Bobby rushed home and sat down at his computer. He dove into his project, not allowing a single second for reflecting on his broken dream of taking Ashley Lincoln to the school dance. Bobby searched the Internet for clues regarding the golden crown or its possible owners. *Golden crown found in Sedona? Missing crown in Sedona? Golden crown and Sedona?* Bobby's searches for the golden crown turned up nothing. He stared at the blank computer screen, trying to think of any other words he could use to get a hit.

Strange things found in Sedona. Once Bobby typed in these words, a listing of websites containing the word *vortex* popped up. Bobby let out a huge sigh and closed the page. Pulling up a new window, Bobby settled on Montezuma's Castle for his school project. It took him less than an hour to finish the entire report including the references.

Bobby pulled a sheet of notebook paper from his backpack. Slouching in his desk chair, Bobby attempted to draw a sketch of the crown to jog his memory. He drew an image of the pointy crown embellished with strange symbols. His mind wandered back to his seventh birthday. As he gazed at the drawing, he got excited, just like he did when he was a little boy.

***

The hike up Bell Rock had never really left Bobby's mind. Thoughts of Aunt Meg's memorial service usually followed shortly after. Everyone had worn hiking boots and black attire on that beautiful Sedona day. One of Bobby's female cousins sang a melancholy ballad about a life lost too soon. Nicole clung to Kim's side while Gordy read a poem he had written about his free spirited younger sister. Young Bobby felt guilty for daydreaming about the golden crown the entire time.

His remorse for being so selfish grew. But his drive to retrieve the golden crown deepened as well. Bobby had wanted to go back up to Sedona and search for the golden crown. And Meg. Bobby knew Meg was a sore subject in the Walker household so he focused on the crown. Time after time, Gordy insisted that no one living under his roof should attempt to retrieve it. As Bobby got older, his determination to solve the mystery of his Aunt Meg's disappearance and reclaim his golden crown persisted. He discreetly brought up these important topics constantly.

"Aren't you the least bit curious about it?" Bobby asked Gordy one night during dinner. Bobby's thirteenth birthday was around the corner, and he had a plan to retrieve his long-lost birthday present. Nicole was at a sleepover, giving him a chance to pour his heart out to his parents without her mocking him. "At the very least we can go back up there and see if it's still where I left it."

Gordy shook his head. "Bobby, that crown was probably found a long time ago."

Kim nodded, agreeing with Gordy. "Your dad's right. It's probably not there anymore." Bobby stabbed his broccoli with his fork. Kim patted his back. "That crown was really creepy, Bobby. I assumed you had better taste." She teased him.

Bobby sank into his seat, disappointed that he missed out on a chance to go back to Bell Rock. He watched Gordy look down at his fingertips. "Listen, Bobby, I'd love to take you back up to Sedona so we can do more exploring. But I'm not going back up to Bell Rock to look for that creepy thing. Why don't we just leave it in the past where it belongs?"

Bobby protested. "Come on, Faja! Where's your sense of adventure?"

Gordy let out a loud snort. "Bobby, your mom said it best. I thought you'd be caught dead before putting that gaudy hunk of junk on your head."

Bobby rolled his eyes. "Faja, I'm not going to wear it. I want to study it." Bobby's eyes widened to the size of saucers. He was unable to contain his excitement at the prospect of finding the crown again. "There was something special about that crown. I could feel it."

"The answer's no, Bobby." Gordy said as he finished up his dinner.

Bobby gave Kim a pathetic look. "Maybe we'll go back up there in a couple years," Kim promised. Gordy darted his eyes in her direction. Kim smiled. "I mean, what's the harm, Gordy? It's not like he'll ever find it again."

"I hate to do this, but I think it's in everyone's best interest if we just forget about that crown. It causes nothing but fighting and arguments when we discuss it," Gordy said.

Bobby tore his dinner roll with his fingers. "I promise I won't touch it. I just want to see if we can find it again, that's all."

Kim seemed to cave in. "Gordy, maybe we can take Bobby back up there for his birthday. I mean it can't hurt if he doesn't touch it."

Gordy placed his fork down. "Bobby, I'll make you a promise. Once you turn eighteen, you can go get your crown."

"I can't wait that long! Why can't we go this year?" Bobby shouted.

Gordy stood. "Because we have an even better surprise for your birthday." He paused. "We're going on a road trip to California!"

Bobby jumped to his feet, wrapping his arms around his father. "Cali? Thanks, Faja!" he looked over at Kim. Her face was void of the normal sparkling smile he always saw. "Aren't you excited, Mom?"

Her eyes shot over to Gordy then back to Bobby. "Of course," she smiled. "It's gonna be a fun trip!"

Sleeping peacefully in his room that night, Bobby envisioned himself climbing over the red rocks, heading toward the golden crown shining in the sunlight. He placed the black-spotted relic on top of his head.

***

"What are you doing?" Nicole asked, shaking Bobby until he awoke the next morning. She looked at his drawing of the golden crown. "Why are you drawing the crown?"

Bobby sat up. "It was for a school project." He gathered all his papers and shoved them into his notebook before depositing them into his backpack. "I went on the Internet to see what I could find out."

Nicole scrunched her eyebrows together. "Did you find anything?" Bobby shook his head. Nicole pointed to his computer. "Can I look something up real quick?"

She placed her hands on the keyboard. Bobby swatted them away. "Use your own computer!"

"It'll only take a minute!" Nicole said as she struggled to strike the keys. Bobby blocked her, making sure she couldn't type. The fight continued back and forth until she pulled out her long nails, ready to scratch her way to freedom.

"Fine! Use it!" Bobby got up and headed downstairs to watch TV.

Nicole sat down and placed her hands on the keyboard. Bobby snuck back into his room. Before she started typing, Nicole clicked on a link about Sedona vortices and read several articles on the connection between different galaxies through these desert portals.

"What are you looking at?" Bobby said which startled her.

She grabbed a pillow and tossed it at his face. "Stop spying on me!" she rolled her eyes and left the page, on a quest to do some online shopping.

Bobby continued to pester her until she gave up and retreated to her room. Sometime during that night, Bobby had another dream about the crown. He placed it on his head. This time, Bobby wasn't a big-nosed seven-year-old.

CHAPTER 6: THE OBSERVER

Jonathan woke up early every morning right as the sun rose. He had worked late into the night, and had gone to bed only three hours earlier. The moment his alarm clock rang, he jumped up and headed to the kitchen. Rubbing his eyes vigorously, Jonathan boiled a hot pot of fresh coffee. His wife, Meg, woke up shortly after he did. Travelling down the stairs of their small wooden bungalow, she smiled at Jonathan once she reached the kitchen. Jonathan kissed her cheek and poured the two a cup of coffee. He looked out across the vast jungle in front of him, barely able to see the crystal blue pond in front of their home.

***

Shortly after they married, Jonathan and Meg built the home themselves. As a child, Jonathan had always dreamed of constructing an energy-efficient house. He designed the structure to consist of one-hundred percent all natural building supplies and a solar roof. It sat close to an aging tree that crept into the pond. The home was their haven.

After settling down with his new wife, Jonathan focused all his skills and intellect into getting a stable job. This was a fairly easy task. His superior talents in math and science made him a primary candidate for a career as an observer.

Observers, an elite collective of scientists and researchers, were the backbone of the Universe Initiative. Their job was to observe "test subjects" being used as a means to understand more about human behavior and technological/scientific advancement. As these subjects were being exposed to the tests, the observers would use this information to resolve important issues with impacts on society. Jonathan, the head observer, used direct observation methods to gain the most detailed data possible. It was important to not only understand the impacts and changes that resulted from the experiments but the reasons for the changes and the human impact. Having direct contact with the test subjects allowed him to gain better insights.

Many of Jonathan's experiments resulted in key advancements in his community. Within the last ten years, Jonathan had reengineered ocean water into a source of electricity. This revelation created a fully sustainable way to produce energy without creating poisonous greenhouse gases or deadly nuclear byproducts. The Ministry, pleased with his contribution, awarded Jonathan by allowing him to conduct an experiment of his choosing. Once he got the approval, he embarked on a social experiment to cure the conflicts between man and religion. As he completed each test, Jonathan noticed something interesting about his findings.

The strife amongst his collective of test subjects wasn't necessarily related to religious oppression, but rather the perceived oppression of a group controlling them. "People do not want to be controlled by religion or a group of self-made leaders. They want peace amongst all people. They *deserve* peace amongst all people." Jonathan had explained during one of the many meetings of The Council.

Jonathan continued performing tests in an effort to cure mankind of the need to fight over the right entity or person to worship. As Jonathan brought more and more enlightenment to The Council through his studies, some of the other members of the group began to embrace his ideology. They welcomed his thoughts on the proper function of leadership and the need to allow a person to embrace whatever lifestyle he or she had chosen.

"We are a collective of free-thinking people. Let us not live in the constraints of what others might think of us, but rather the truths that we embody. The objective is to believe what you want, as long as peace remains amongst us. Our ultimate goal is to create and maintain a society where none of us will be subjected to any religious wars, political persecution, or anything that may create oppression amongst our citizens." Jonathan shared these words everyday when he addressed his team at his lab.

Jonathan's eloquent way of weaving the needs of his people into the expectations of the Council was unheard of. He created an understanding between leadership and the common man. The Controller was proud of his achievements. The Ministry took special notice of Jonathan and requested that The Council find more funding for the Universe. When Alexander Kingsley, the prior Ambassador of Science got ill with liver cancer, Jonathan was the natural choice for his replacement.

Jonathan was able to foster a new order where conflict didn't play a role in everyday life. There were no holy wars or fanatical groups trying to conquer others through spirituality. Terrorists no longer existed. Everyone respected one another, living in unison with an open mind and an open heart. That year, Jonathan won the prestigious *Innovator of the Year* award. The Controller ordered that Jonathan proceed with more tests, the bigger the better.

But success was short lived after that point. Jonathan's ability to bring forth stunning results began to deteriorate. Each project he created in the lab was ineffective. His attempts to eradicate nuclear threats between his test subjects had failed. Pretty soon the test subjects were at odds with one another again, destroying all of Jonathan's hard work. The world surrounding the test subjects was diverging away from the world Jonathan lived in. The Controller, as well as the rest of the Ministry, pulled back most of their support and funding for The Universe Initiative. This decision crippled Jonathan, leaving him desperate for another experiment that would make a huge impact.

***

Jonathan grabbed his cup of coffee, piled three of Meg's famous apple cinnamon strudels on a plate, and headed for the kitchen table. A tall slender fellow, Jonathan never indulged in sweets or fatty foods unless he was stressed or worried. Over the past several weeks, he had only survived on high calorie delicacies including strudels, shortbread, cheesy pastas, and coffee, of course. Meg's concern for him grew, prompting a conversation regarding the dangerous side effects of a poor diet and exhaustion.

"I wish you would let me make you a healthy breakfast." She muttered as she sipped her coffee. "You're going to get fat."

"I've got it under control." He took another satisfying bite of his sugary pastries.

A few months earlier, Jonathan's team had created an elixir that was being administered to combat the adverse effects of sugar and high fat foods. This small step for his research team appeased the Council, but it wasn't the breakthrough they had hoped for. Jonathan feared that the Controller would relinquish him from the Council. *I have to keep my seat in the Council if I have any chance of making a difference,* Jonathan thought every night before attempting to concoct more amazing results for the Ministry.

"Did you get any sleep last night?" Meg asked. Jonathan took a seat at the table, coffee in one hand, his other hand sifting through a stack of papers he had abandoned the night before. She sat down next to him. "Maybe you could take a break from all your research. We can spend the whole day together."

Jonathan placed his cup down so he could use both hands to riffle through the papers. "Meg, you know how important this initiative is to everyone here. I can't just take a day off." He rubbed his temples.

She leaned in close to him. "You've been working hard on this thing for the last ten years." She pointed to the gray hairs tucked into his curly black mane. "I don't think one day will make that big of a difference."

Meg, a petite red-head, frowned at Jonathan's intense concern for his job. She was a free spirit, always looking for opportunities to enjoy the beautiful island where they lived. Dressed in a white sundress, she sipped her coffee and waited for her husband to look up from his work.

Jonathan concentrated further on his stack of documents, desperately searching for a key sheet of paper. He pushed massive stacks across the table, mumbling a few choice words under his breath.

Meg tossed her long hair to the side. "Jonathan. Are you listening to me?"

He looked up at her. "Meg, I don't have time this morning to argue with you about my job. I'm on the brink of a potentially lifesaving discovery."

She threw her hands in the air. "You say that about everything you work on! How am I supposed to know that you mean it this time?"

"The work I do protects lives and creates stable communities." He paused. "But today, I'm working on another project."

Jonathan frantically rummaged through his piles again. Moving one stack to the other side of the table, his coffee cup spilled all over his strudels. He looked up at Meg. She seemed to wait patiently, ready for him to explode. Calmly, he placed the cup upright and continued on his quest. Meg threw her hand on Jonathan's, causing him to stop moving. "Honey, you need rest. You can always save the world tomorrow."

He gently pulled his hand away from hers and moved a few more sheets onto another pile. Jonathan's somber face was overshadowed by a massive grin. "I've got it!" He jumped up from the table. "I've found the missing piece to this problem I've been encountering for the last eight months!" Clenching the document in his fist, he raced upstairs to get dressed for work.

Meg followed him. "Jonathan, we're worried about you. Kathleen and Emily would love to spend more time with you."

Kathleen, the couple's eldest daughter, had just turned eleven. She was just like Meg, a sweet person with a heart for helping animals. Emily, the couple's nine-year-old daughter, wanted to be an observer, just like her father. Late at night, Emily would sit at the table with Jonathan, watching him hunt through pages filled with letters and numbers. Jonathan enjoyed his daughter's company and often allowed her to ask him questions about the project.

Last night, Emily had snuck downstairs to do some investigating. Jonathan greeted her with a tired smile. "Honey, shouldn't you be sleeping?"

She tucked a section of her strawberry blond hair behind her ear and sat down at the table. "You should be sleeping too, Daddy."

He picked up a plate of brownies. "Want one?" she nodded and retrieved a square and took a large bit. Frosting covered her nose and cheeks. "Good, huh?"

Emily chewed a few times before laughing. "The best." She picked up a wrinkled notebook, "What's all this?"

"It's one of my many books on the Universe." Jonathan replied.

Emily flipped through the pages. "What's the Universe?"
A loud cough came from the staircase. Both Jonathan
and Emily looked up to see Meg standing at the foot of the
stairs. Emily quickly rose and ran past her mother and to her
room.

Meg never approved of Emily's interest in the Universe
Initiative. Meg's disapproval created tension in the household,
which wasn't Jonathan's intention. He kept the peace by
limiting his work hours to his office at the lab, unless an issue
arose that required his immediate attention. Lately, the
Controller requested that Jonathan and the other observers
work more hours on the Universe Initiative. With the
project's renewal date coming up, the Ministry put a great
deal of pressure on Jonathan's entire team to complete their
research before the next summit.

It was morning now, and Jonathan was running out of
time. "Meg, you have no idea what this information means!"
he held up the document. "I have the proof I need to extend
my experiments for the next ten years!" He pulled his button-
down shirt, a pair of slacks and his lab coat from the closet.

Meg folded her arms. "Great! Then Emily can take your
place and continue those experiments." Jonathan laid the
paper down so he could change out of his pajamas. Meg
grabbed the document, her eyes widening. "What exactly
does this mean?"

After he completed his wardrobe change, he grabbed the
paper. "It'll take too long to explain." He rushed back
downstairs, his items in hand and Meg on his heels. Once he
turned to face Meg, his eyes lit up. "Meg, this is it! This is the
breakthrough the Controller has been waiting for. Every wish
we've ever had is about to come true!"

Meg laughed. "We live in Utopia. Because of all your
hard work, we don't have to worry about a thing."

Jonathan shook his head. "You don't understand. Just ten more years and I'll have the keys to the entire world!"

Meg put her hand on Jonathan's face. "You already have the keys to the entire world."

He kissed her cheek. "I'll see you later tonight." Clutching his document tightly, Jonathan rushed back to his lab so he could reconstruct his key to the portal.

CHAPTER 7: THE FIRE STARTS

Another year passed and Bobby turned seventeen. Nicole graduated high school and got accepted to Arizona State University, ASU, to study journalism. The only time the Walkers saw her was during Phoenix Suns basketball games at the arena. Bobby convinced Gordy and Kim to let him turn her room into a home for his basketball trophies. Every night, he would admire them, and dream big about his future basketball success. His grades were up—Duke would be foolish not to accept him.

And Ashley Lincoln was now single. Rumors around the senior class was saying Ashley didn't have a date for homecoming yet. Bobby decided to strike while the iron was hot. Now seniors in high school, they shared sociology class together. Bobby strutted into class with his sun glasses dangling from his back collar. Instead of gazing at Ashley from several rows away, he would take the seat right next to her.

Bobby watched her enter the classroom and sit down without looking in his direction. *What should I do now?* Bobby thought. Say something. He opened his mouth but nothing happened. "Anything's possible if you just try." He mumbled to no one in particular.

Ashley turned to him. This was his moment. Her beautiful lips formed each word perfectly followed by a dazzling smile.

"Yes, I'll go with you to homecoming." Bobby replied.

She started giggling. "Bobby, I asked if you had a pencil I could borrow."

Mortified, Bobby sluggishly retrieved a pencil from his backpack and handed it to her without making eye contact. "Here."

"Thank you," She grasped it. "And yes, *I'll* go with you to homecoming."

Bobby pinched himself to make sure he was fully awake. Mr. Bates call the class to order. Ashley turned toward the front of the classroom, flipping her hair in the process. Eventually, Bobby managed to look up at the chalkboard. *She said yes!* He screamed inside.

Mr. Bates slammed a yardstick against his desk, scarring the life out of Bobby and several other students. Bobby calmed down and waited patiently for the lesson to begin.

"Mar—tin And—drews." Mr. Bates pronounced each syllable of his name slowly. "What year did World War II begin?"

Martin looked in Bobby's direction for help. Bobby tried to mouth out the year, but Martin missed it completely. "1977?"

The class erupted in laughter. Mr. Bates shook his head. "If you don't learn about past social conflicts, history is bound to repeat itself."

"This isn't history class." Martin muttered. Mr. Bates narrowed his eyes at Martin, observing him like a predator watching its prey.

Bobby held up his hand. "World War II began in 1939. Even though the war started that year, conflicts between a few nations involved in that war were believed to have begun before that year."

Mr. Bates turned to face Bobby. "That is correct, Mr. Walker. And when did World War II end?"

"1945." Bobby paused. "It was also believed to be one of the deadliest wars in history."

Mr. Bates nodded. "Very good, Bobby. It's been several decades since World War II, but it seems like we haven't learned a thing. Violence is being used all around the world to suppress and conquer people and countries."

Martin raised his hand. "But isn't war necessary to keep the bad countries from taking over the world?"

"Violence isn't the answer. If each country declares war on one another, there will be nothing left. However, in some cases, war can be used to promote peace. America has declared war against countries with weapons of mass destruction, like Iraq and Iran, but it had been for a good reason." Mr. Bates answered. "Can anyone tell me why the US would make such a move?"

Bobby put up his hand. "Iran started participating in nuclear testing, a result of the *Atom's for Peace* program. Prior to the peace program, nuclear exploitation was used solely for building bombs. After World War II ended in 1945, the United States and other countries around the world didn't want to abandon their nuclear capabilities or give up this amazing source of power. So, after several failed and deadly tests, scientists found a safe way to convert nuclear power into an energy source we use every day." He stopped to take a breath.

Mr. Bates nodded. "See, nuclear power can be used for good."

Bobby wasn't convinced. "But some countries are using nuclear power to build weapons.

Our government believes North Korea has a stockpile of weapons of mass destruction. The worst part is North Korea doesn't belong to the Non-proliferation treaty, meaning they don't support the use of nuclear energy for peace."

Mr. Bates cleared his throat. "Mr. Walker, you have raised a lot of very important points, but I'm not sure we have much to worry about. North Korea hasn't made a move yet, and nuclear power is safer than ever."

Bobby was ready for a debate. "What about Chernobyl? When Reactor Number Four blew up, it cast 50 million tons of radioactive fuel and particles over a mile high into the Earth's atmosphere. That was about ten times the force of the Hiroshima bomb. That one mistake created over 25,000 cancer cases worldwide, mostly in children. If a nuclear war breaks out, our entire planet and its inhabitants would be devastated."

Mr. Bates let out a small chuckle. "Bobby, none of our nuclear reactors are susceptible to a situation like that. Nor are we in danger of a nuclear war."

"Every day, it seems like some terrorist group is threatening our country with some sort of nuclear attack." Bobby retorted. "It could happen."

"You should run for President of the United States, and then you can convince the global community to relinquish this powerful energy," Mr. Bates seemed to brush off Bobby's concerns. "Until then, keep praying for a miracle."

Bobby shook his head. "If I was President, I would end world hunger, global warming, wars and nuclear energy. I would invite all the countries worldwide to come together every year for a summit so we could talk out our issues. I would do my best to protect humans from being persecuted for their religious beliefs or ideologies. If I were President, the entire planet would be saved, and there would be no more conflict."

Martin and a few other students rose, clapping and cheering for Bobby. He looked over at Ashley. She had made a paper crown from a yellow colored sheet of paper. Softly, she placed the crown on Bobby's head. "Maybe you should be king—homecoming king to start."

The bell rang, releasing the students from class. Ashley waved goodbye, and row by row, everyone, except Bobby, retreated for the halls. Mr. Bates approached him with a wide smile. "Bobby, you did an outstanding job today. Are you sure you want to go to Duke University? You seem more suited for MIT." He patted Bobby on the back.

"What's MIT got that Duke doesn't?"

"Bobby, I know you're caught up in the basketball dream, but at heart I think you're a science person."

Bobby gave Mr. Bates a crooked grin and said, "Going to Duke has been my goal since I was a kid." He stood and threw his backpack on. "It feels right." Mr. Bates chuckled and said "You are seventeen and have a long life left to live. You don't have to make a final decision right now.

***

The night of the homecoming dance finally arrived. Bobby entrusted Nicole with picking out his suit. It was laying on his bed, securely wrapped in a garment bag. Gordy and Kim washed the SUV for him. Ashley's corsage was resting in the fridge. Everything was perfect. After getting a haircut, Bobby showered, and stepped into his room. He eyed the yellow paper crown Ashley had made for him sitting on top of his desk. Bobby picked it up. He smiled—only one more year and then he'd be able to retrieve the real golden crown.

As hard as it was, Bobby respected Gordy's wishes to keep his promise about going back to Sedona. It wasn't easy, but he felt having his parent's respect was worth it. Bobby placed the crown down, got dressed and headed downstairs. Kim started crying instantly. Gordy fought with his Nikon camera as he held it up at eyelevel to get a few pictures of Bobby and Nicole posing. Nicole pinched Bobby's cheeks and made jokes

51

about him being *the belle of the ball.* Bobby was completely annoyed, but grateful to have his family there to see him off.

He climbed into the SUV, and waved goodbye to his family. Bobby hit the I-17 North, headed to pick up his beautiful princess. He glanced up at a freeway sign—*I-17 North... Flagstaff.* Flagstaff was close to Sedona. The golden crown. He looked down at the gas gage. He had a full tank. Bobby's hands gripped the steering wheel.

"Don't be an idiot, Bobby." He said out loud. It was homecoming night with Ashley Lincoln. Ashley Lincoln! Moments like these never came around twice. Bobby took the next exit and stopped at a stoplight. It turned green and he entered the intersection. A flash of bright lights startled him.

***

Bobby's eyes fluttered open. A pinch in his arm was the first thing he noticed followed by stiffness in his right leg. Gordy and Kim, sitting in two chairs in the corner of the room, jumped up.

"Mom?" Bobby asked before coughing hard. Kim handed him a glass of water.

"Bobby, how are ya feeling?" Gordy placed his hand on Kim's shoulder.

Bobby gulped the water, but it didn't seem to help. He motioned for another cup full. Kim poured him another glass. Her eyes were red and sad. She looked down at his leg. Bobby refused to.

"Buddy, you were in a car accident. Some jerk ran a red light and T-boned you." Gordy paused. "The doctor says you managed to come out of it with only a few minor cuts on your left arm, a broken leg, and a dislocated knee."

Bobby ignored the pain throbbing in his lower left leg and knee. *This can't be happening to me,* he thought.

"Good news is, you only have a hairline fracture in your lower leg. You should be able to walk in about two months at the most." Gordy smiled.

Bobby watched Kim closely. Something else was wrong. A knot grew in his stomach. "Faja, what's the bad news?" he looked over at Gordy. The smile had been wiped off his face. "Please, tell me before I have a heart attack."

Gordy reached out and put his hand on Bobby's shoulder. "The ligaments in your knee are torn which means…"

"I can't play basketball. Can I?" Bobby held his breath. Kim shook her head. He exhaled loudly and wished the world away. A glimmer of hope sparked inside him. "Anything's possible if I just try, right?"

"Absolutely!" Nicole walked through the door with three cups of Starbucks coffee. Bobby took an inventory of his hospital room as she scrambled to find a place for her purse—two chairs, several machines, a wall-mounted television and a privacy curtain. Everything was real. It wasn't a dream.

Bobby closed his eyes. Gordy and Kim gave Nicole an update on Bobby's progress before heading to the hospital cafeteria for a late breakfast. He opened his eyes. Nicole pulled a chair next to his hospital bed.

"I missed the homecoming dance, huh?"

Nicole sipped her cup. "Yep. Ashley was crushed. She came by afterwards to see you, but you were still out like a light."

"How long have I been here?"

"Three days. You had a concussion. Mom said that you might be able to go home this afternoon." Nicole clicked her tongue a few times. She set her cup down. "Bobby, I'm sorry this happened to you."

Bobby rustled with his blankets. An object rustled with the fabric before falling onto the floor. Nicole bent forward and retrieved it. Bobby smiled and opened his hand. "Give it here."

Nicole handed him the paper crown Ashley had made. He placed it on his head. She smiled. "Looks good on ya."

That was it. Bobby looked down at the cast consuming his ankle up to his thigh. His emotions were heavy. His dream date with Ashley was ruined. Duke University would no longer want him on their star basketball team. Bobby pulled the crown from his head.

If only he had kept going down the I-17 away from that intersection. Everything would have been different. Bobby wished that he had followed his heart to Flagstaff—to Sedona. To the golden crown.

"Mom and Faja are worried about the SUV and all your medical bills. Apparently Mom's company might have to let her go in the next couple weeks. It's a shame—I really like living on campus in Tempe." Nicole carried on. She sighed. "Oh well, we all have to make sacrifices, I guess."

Bobby turned to her, staring her in the eyes. "Nicole, I'm going to Sedona. I'm going to Bell Rock to get the golden crown."

Nicole shifted her wait in the chair. "What do you mean you're going to get the golden crown?"

"Look at me. My basketball career is over. Our family is falling apart." Bobby inhaled sharply and held the breath in for a moment. His chest hurt too. He exhaled slowly as Nicole rolled her eyes. She obviously found his performance completely overdramatic and unnecessary.

"What does any of this have to do with the golden crown?"

"Think about it. Finding that crown was the last really happy memory I have of our family. It was right before we had the funeral for Aunt Meg." Bobby said. Nicole looked into her lap. "Things are changing fast, and not for the better. We should go back and get the crown."

She grabbed his hand. "I love ya, baby brother, but this makes no sense. Mom and Faja don't want you anywhere near that gold, jeweled, creepy..."

Bobby tuned her out. He imagined finding the crown again and recapturing his most valued treasure.

"...unless we were to sell it." Nicole's eyes widened. "Bobby, you're a genius! We should get the crown and pawn it! That will bring enough money to soften the financial blow your car accident caused."

"What are you talking about? That's not at all what I was saying."

"It should be," said Nicole. Bobby folded his arms tightly against his bruised chest. "Get it together, Bobby! You have to understand that this is a necessary evil."

"I'm not selling it, Nicole!"

She leaned in. "The other guy didn't have insurance. Mom only got liability on the SUV since they were planning on buying a new one next year when you graduated. We need the money."

Bobby's heart was pierced. She had a point, but he wasn't going to give up that easy. "Once I get better, I'll get a job."

Nicole shot up. "Robert Walker, stop being so selfish!" Tears welled in the corners of her eyes. "I know you really want the golden crown for yourself, but you have to think big picture. Mom and Faja have slaved away for us to have everything we could have ever wanted. This is our chance to do something for them."

Bobby read the hurt on her face. She wanted what was best for the Walker family. Bobby did too. The decision weighed him down. He could feel his thoughts crushing the bones in his body. It had to be done. Bobby gave her a nod. "Okay, let's go get the crown."

CHAPTER 8: ROAD TRIP

"Let's take the road trip this weekend." Bobby told Nicole
the moment she walked through the door.

It was Christmas break and Bobby's leg was finally
healed. Nicole, home for winter break, motioned for him to
follow her upstairs to her room. She shut the door quietly.
"Okay, how are we gonna make this happen?"

His plan was simple—take all the money he had saved
up over the years for college ($500) and apply it to getting
the golden crown. Nicole would be in charge of
transportation and securing the hotel room. Bobby would
handle logistics and the treasure hunt. The more Bobby
plotted and schemed, the less certain he was about selling the
crown. The golden crown still represented everything good in
his life—Ashley Lincoln saying yes to homecoming, the
Walker family's hike on his seventh birthday, and the dream
of playing for Duke's basketball team.

Nicole seemed to sense his apprehension. "Bobby, I know
this is hard for you. You're doing the right thing." She
retrieved a bottle of cobalt blue nail polish and painted her
nails.

"Can I at least spend some time with the crown before we
sell it?" He begged even though he had no intention of
selling it.

She nodded. "What's the itinerary look like?"

"I'd like to head out on Friday and come back Sunday.
That will give us two days to comb over Bell Rock."

Nicole blew on her nails. "Sounds good. How's the leg feeling?"

"It gets stiff occasionally, but I'm able to run and walk at a decent pace. The doctor says I might be able to play a game or two in a few months." Bobby touched one of his first place basketball trophies on Nicole's desk. "I'll have to take my time during the hike."

"We don't have to do this, Bobby." Nicole muttered.

Bobby couldn't abandon the idea. He understood the seriousness and sadness behind Gordy and Kim's fight to provide for both he and Nicole. Kim had been unemployed for over a month. Bobby watched her scour the internet for job after job. She held onto the insurance payout check just in case they needed the money for bills. Gordy worked long hours and often left before Bobby woke up.

But through it all, Gordy and Kim cleared their schedules to attend Bobby's physical therapy appointments. They had sacrificed so much for his recovery. Cashing in the crown was the least he could do.

"I don't mind. They deserve it." Bobby put on a genuine smile. "Now let's get everything together."

He pulled out a map of northern Arizona and sat down on the bed next to Nicole. They discussed in great detail every idea that popped into their heads. Nicole's interest in Bobby's travel plans further encouraged him. If Nicole didn't find the plan or the information interesting, she usually stopped listening after the first sixty seconds. Bobby tried to remain calm as he watched her deliberate silently.

"What are you planning on telling Mom and Faja?" she asked.

"I'm not sure."

Nicole's brows drew together in a frown. "How do expect this to work if you don't tell them anything?"

"I'm going to tell them something, Nicole. I just haven't figured it out yet." Bobby's big foot began to tap against the bed frame. Sweat beaded on his forehead as he let out a short cough.

"Robert Walker, I know you better than you think." She snapped. "You want me to tell Mom and Faja. Just admit it!"

Bobby let out an undetectable sign of relief. "Okay, fine. Yes, can you tell them?"

Nicole grinned. "Why of course, baby brother." She paused. "Here's the thing. I have a date Friday night so we'll have to leave Saturday morning."

Bobby nodded. "I'm okay with that."

He shot up from her bed and turned to the door. Before he could move an inch, Nicole's blue cobalt fingernails grabbed onto his arm. "Wait a minute, Bobby. Why are we staying in a hotel? Why not just camp out in Sedona?"

Bobby chuckled. "It's freezing in Sedona right now."

"Got it." Nicole rolled her eyes. "I'll go online tonight and book the room."

"Thanks, Nicole." Bobby retreated for the door.

"Hey, Bobby?" He placed his hand on the door handle and slowly turned back to face her. "Don't worry about anything when it comes to Mom and Faja. I'll take care of it." Bobby smiled before opening her door and rushing to his room.

Inside the privacy of his room, Bobby lowered himself into his bed—his throbbing knee was killing him. He took a few deep breaths and stared at the ceiling. *This is what you get for lying to your parents*, he thought. His guilty conscience continued weighing him down. He sat up and focused on his trip—the trip that would solve the Walker's financial problems.

Bobby set his sights on taking advantage of his entire stay in Sedona. He figured that it wouldn't hurt to check out a

couple shops for more information on the golden crown. First
he would start by getting the crown. Looking down at the
map, he grabbed a marker from his desk and drew a large X
on Bell Rock. X marked the spot.

***

Saturday morning couldn't come fast enough for Bobby.
He woke up well before his 6am alarm. Running downstairs
in a flash, he double-checked Nicole's Jeep as it rested in the
garage. He had packed it the night before so they could get a
head start in the morning. After making sure everything was
securely positioned, Bobby rushed back to his room and
threw on a tee-shirt, cargo pants and a sweatshirt.

"You're up early, Bobby." Gordy said as he pushed
Bobby's door open, holding a coffee cup in one hand and the
newspaper in the other.

"I'm so excited for this trip, Faja!" Bobby tucked one foot
into a hiking boot and then the other.

Nicole had told Gordy and Kim that she was taking
Bobby camping in the Superstition Mountains. The plan
worked out great—Gordy had already made arrangements to
meet a wealthy investor that weekend while Kim prepared
for an important job interview set for that Monday. Bobby felt
confident that he and Nicole could sneak up to Sedona
undetected.

Gordy sipped his coffee. "I'll bet. Listen, Bobby, take it
easy out there. If your knee starts to act up, you two head
straight home."

Bobby nodded his head. "Of course, Faja." He scanned the
room for his sunglasses. He finally spotted them on his desk.

Gordy watched Bobby race to the desk to grab his
glasses. "Now onto the more important thing…the golden
crown."

Bobby stopped mid-step, almost falling on his face. *Why
is he bringing up the golden crown? What did Nicole tell*

them? He thought. He recovered quickly and placed his sunglasses on his back collar. "Oh, that thing? I forgot all about that hunk of junk."

"Oh, really?" Gordy's voice was exaggerated. This wasn't good. "Remember, Bobby, I told you I'd let you kill yourself for that crown after you turned eighteen. The last time I checked, you were still seventeen and some change."

Bobby laughed nervously. "You're funny, Faja. I don't plan to look for—"

Gordy cut him off. "The Lost Dutchman mine is in the Superstitions. You seem to have a knack for finding treasure," he paused. "Don't bring anything back that doesn't belong to you."

It took Bobby a second to realize what Gordy was implying. He chuckled. "I'm not looking for the Lost Dutchman gold, Faja. Seriously, my treasure hunting days are over. Besides, you said it best—the golden crown up in Sedona was probably found a long time ago." *Oh no! I've said too much.*

Gordy took another sip of his coffee. "Robert Walker, consider yourself warned. If you come back with as much as a tiny piece of mica, you'll be grounded for so long you won't be able to attend your kids' weddings."

Bobby scrunched his eyebrows. "How would I have kids if I was grounded?"

Gordy put the newspaper under his arm and placed his hand on Bobby's shoulder. "I mean it, Bobby. No more treasure hunting."

Bobby studied his father's concerned look. "But when I turn eighteen, I can still go back and get the golden crown, right?"

Gordy gave a slightly nervous laugh. "I prefer that you change your mind about the whole thing before then." Bobby laughed. That wasn't going to happen. "But once your eighteenth birthday comes around, you'll be an adult. You get to make your own decisions."

Bobby nodded somberly, and Gordy patted his back. He hushed the guilty feeling rising in his belly. Bobby left his room and pestered Nicole until she woke up. The two planned to pull out of the driveway at 7am sharp. At 7:01, Bobby was ushering Nicole to the driver's seat. Annoyed and sleepy, she gave Gordy and Kim a hug and asked them to say a prayer so she wouldn't kill her brother. Bobby gave his parents a wave, and they were off on their adventure. Right as Nicole hit the stop sign down the street from their house, she received a text from Gordy. She turned the phone screen so Bobby could read it. *Make sure Bobby doesn't come back with any treasure!*

CHAPTER 9: STARTING OVER

One year had passed since Jonathan had uncovered what he needed to create another golden crown, his key to the Universe. In the beginning, he was full of energy and excitement over his idea to make another key. The task would not be easy, but he was willing to try. He had to try. Each night, after all his colleagues left the lab, Jonathan quickly got to work. He hid behind a cloak of secrecy, afraid that someone would find out that his original key had been misplaced.

Senator Sergeev's admission of knowing about Jonathan's missing key was merely a scare tactic. He figured this out after she had arrived at the lab one afternoon, unannounced. As she pried through a few file folders regarding the Universe Initiative, her eyes grew dark.

"The Universe has reached the end of the ten year extension period," she said. "A decision will be made at the next summit. You only have one week to get everything in order."

To Jonathan, this sounded like a threat. "That's increasingly difficult since we no longer have access to travel to the Universe."

Sergeev nodded. "That's right. The Ministry has confiscated your key, and forced you to remain here. It's a shame really—I was looking forward to your next set of findings." She gave him a sinister smile.

Jonathan stood tall, unaffected by her jab. "You had mentioned a lost possession of mine. To what were you referring?"

She reached inside her black briefcase and pulled out a tiny note card. "This fell out of your file folder on the day you asked for an extension for the Universe." Sergeev paused as Jonathan read a combination of numbers on the card.

He opened his lab coat and secured the card inside his pocket. "That was not intended for you to see." The note card was a reminder that Jonathan needed to work harder. He needed to make that key.

Sergeev tilted her head. "It's only a matter of time before the Council finds out that your lovely initiative is losing them so much money." She grabbed her briefcase and opened the door. "See you next week."

Jonathan slammed the closed door. He refocused on the task at hand.

A week passed and Jonathan wasn't any closer to resolving his main design issues. He couldn't overcome the main hurdles that kept him grounded. But he never gave up—he had to find a way. The summit was only in two days time, and he needed to finish the key.

Jonathan had memorized the entire process. Each key was specifically made for the person using it. The golden crown, in Jonathan's case, was programmed to align with his DNA to open up the portal so he could travel throughout the Universe. When transport time came, Jonathan only needed to type in a three digit code, a pass code, into his computer, and replicate it on the tiny keypad inside the crown. Once completed, Jonathan would put the crown on his head and focus on where he wanted to travel. He would arrive there within seconds.

Lately, transporting seemed impossible. It took almost a year for Jonathan to construct the exact dimensions of the original golden crown. Once completed, he finally got the sensors and microns reengineered to work simultaneously during the transportation process. Things were looking up. It was time for the last step—syncing the crown with his computer to rewrite the pass code. He could barely control himself. Nothing would stand between him and his safe passage to the Universe.

Jonathan snuck the golden crown replica into his office and locked the door. He opened up a blank command screen and typed in the necessary binary codes. Nothing happened. He reentered the information a second time only to have the computer reject it. He closed down the programs, rebooted the computer, and retried for a third time. Access denied. The golden crown, the key to the Universe, was worthless unless he could obtain a new pass code to program it.

This is probably the doing of the Controller, he thought. Jonathan looked up at the clock—1:30 PM. The Controller was more than likely in his office.

Removing his lab coat, he clutched his documents on the golden crown, his lifeline, in his hand. Jonathan was on a mission for some answers.

The moment he entered the reception area, Gerald stood at his desk. "The Controller sent someone over to see you." Gerald's voice shook.

Jonathan froze. "Did he leave a message?"

Gerald nodded. "A meeting is taking place in exactly one hour in the Main room. The Controller expects you as well as the rest of the Council to be there. Apparently the Ministry has a very important issue to discuss."

Jonathan nodded and decided to go back to the lab and gather his latest findings on the Universe. He ventured back into the hallway, passing several white computers on top of glass desks. He turned the corner and arrived at his office. Jonathan pressed his hand against a black box next to the

64

door and pushed it open once a tiny light on the black box turned from red to green. He entered his office, a mid-sized room with a large glass desk, white computer, and a wall full of filing cabinets. Jonathan placed his document on the desk and sat down in his white high-backed chair.

As he held his hand three inches above the bottom right-hand corner of his desk, a small, illuminated square appeared on the glass. Pressing his index finger to five separate places on the square caused the filing cabinets to part and move toward the white ceiling and into the floor.

A massive opening appeared, leading the way to a large room covered in bright fluorescent lights. Men and women dressed in white lab coats held clear tablets electronically powered by the lights above. The workers travelled around the room, hovering for a few minutes over samples placed in separate stations before taking notes. Once completed, they rotated to the right and repeated the process. As they input their data into the tablets, four large screens on each wall displayed the information for Jonathan to see.

Jonathan took a couple of steps inside and glanced over the large monitors. There was nothing noteworthy to report. He took a deep breath and stepped out of the lab, he proceeded to make his way out of his office as the cabinet wall closed behind him. It was time to face the Controller.

***

Jonathan rode in silence as the solar train sped him away from his office and to the Ministry complex. During the entire ride, he contemplated what issues the Controller had flagged for review. The Universe Summit was still a few days away. Jonathan still had time to develop another amazing innovation that his team could use. Craving an apple cinnamon strudel and large cup of coffee, he tried to contain his nerves as the train slowed to a stop at the Institution complex.

Jonathan walked across the prestigious Depot Hall to join the rest of the Council in the Main room. Each step inside the Depot Hall always felt daunting to him. The pictures and shrines of the Ministry seemed to glare at him as he hurried to take his seat inside the Main room. Normally, Jonathan played each move over and over in his head but not today. He was overcome with fear. Two Asian men in white suits stood in front of the Main room's metal doors.

"I have a meeting with The Council today," Jonathan announced.

The men bowed their heads as each one placed a hand on the long steel handle and pulled the doors open for Jonathan.

Light rumbling of men and women chattering greeted Jonathan as he stepped onto the white carpet. He looked around, noticing that only half of the Council was in attendance. He spotted the Controller nodding his head as a young woman in a white dress handed him a black folder. He gave her a smile before locking eyes with Jonathan. Clearing his mind and dropping into deep concentration, Jonathan tried to decipher what the Controller was thinking. The Controller merely gave Jonathan a half smile before moving onto another group of Council members to converse with.

"I wonder what's on the agenda for this secret meeting," Senator Sergeev said, walking up next to Jonathan.

"I bet it'll be quite interesting," Jonathan replied blandly.

"Remember our conversation, Jonathan," she whispered.

Senator Churchill patted Jonathan's back. "I'm happy to see you, Jonathan." The man moved farther into the room and sat down in a black high-back chair.

Jonathan wasted no time taking his seat at the round, glass table. "I'm sure you'll be fine, pal." Senator Marcus Swanson of Canada said as he sat down next to him.

The Controller took his place at the head of the round table. The other Council members took his lead and proceeded to their positions at the table where they remained standing. Jonathan and Marcus stood, giving reverence to the Controller.

"Thank you everyone, you may be seated." the Controller smiled. In unison, the Council members sat down. "I have called this meeting today to discuss an issue that has been plaguing the Ministry for some time now. Over the past eighteen months, the Ministry has examined the effectiveness and growth potential of key components of our society. As a collective, we have struggled to come to terms with the fate of a few projects we've licensed. After careful consideration, we've formed the following conclusions."

The Controller opened up the black folder and scanned a single white sheet of paper. The senator from France, an elderly black woman, glanced over at Jonathan. He looked over at her and they held a stare until she gazed elsewhere. Jonathan was silent, waiting for the Controller to divulge his bad news. *Please, don't do this to me,* he thought.

The Controller looked up. "Where are the members representing The X Project Initiative?" Two men seated at the far end of the table stood. "My fellow Council members, I regret to inform you that the Ministry has decided to discontinue your efforts. We no longer see the cost benefits of intergalactic exploration in other cosmic galaxies similar to our own. Perhaps once we have proof that other nonhuman life forms reside within a reasonable distance from our world, we can reassess the project and relicense it."

The two short men in white suits stood completely still. The table erupted into quiet murmuring as the men slowly collected their belongings and proceeded for the metal doors. A knot grew in Jonathan's throat.

The Controller continued. "Where are the representatives from the Sustainability Project?" One man wearing a black suit slowly rose. "Because of the importance of your project and its focus on capturing our many vast achievements, you have been granted licensing for a period of ten years. I personally appreciate your team's willingness to insist that we look unto ourselves for the answers to the future, not someone else."

The Council members clapped for the man in the black suit as he took his seat. Jonathan remained quiet—he knew what was going to happen next.

The Controller stared him directly in the eyes. "Ambassador Jonathan from the Universe Initiative, please rise to your feet." The clapping stopped all at once. Jonathan got up slowly, running his hands down the front of black suit. The Controller closed his black folder. "My dear friend, Jonathan, I wish you and I were meeting today under other circumstances. The Ministry and I know how hard you have worked to keep your project viable…"

"Then why are you doing this?" Jonathan asked out of turn. The room engulfed in a stream of chatter resulting from Jonathan's malfeasance.

The Controller brought his gavel down onto the table once. The Council members quieted their voices. "I'm not here to make an enemy out of you, Jonathan. The Ministry had a very long discussion about the Universe Initiative, and we all agreed that it should come to an end."

Jonathan slammed his fists on the table. "You cannot do this! You cannot prohibit the continuation of this project!"

The Controller didn't budge. "The Universe has digressed too much from our society. As a result, the value of your experiments has been greatly diminished. The main focus of this project was to use the Universe for the benefit of our world. It's time to terminate the project."

"What about the test subjects? We have destroyed parts of their world, creating conflicts, and exposing them to long-term problems that have shaped their minds, bodies, and souls. We are responsible for them!" Jonathan's voice roared.

"Oh no, a bleeding heart pleading his case of the *test subjects*," Senator Sergeev joked. "They created their own world" she retorted. A few of the Council members gave a quick chuckle. "The Universe costs too much. We can no longer justify it."

Jonathan directed his attention to Senator Sergeev. "Those *test subjects* are not rats in a maze. They are no less human then you and I. They have defined personalities and free thoughts, just like us. We deserve to give them a chance to redeem themselves and complete the tasks I've laid out for them."

The Council members didn't say anything in support of Jonathan's plea. Everyone focused on The Controller. "Jonathan, your time is up. The project has come to an end. The Ministry has made its decision, and we are not going to decide against it. You will not receive an extension."

"You should grant me more time! Give me until the next summit to bring information or data that will show the importance of this initiative." Jonathan demanded.

The Controller sighed. "Jonathan, you are an observer. You see the unfavorable results more than anyone else in this room. You and I both know that the Universe Initiative has run its course. It's not a good use of our resources. I can't allow us to delegate funds to this project anymore. Effective immediately, destruction of the Universe will commence. In its place, we will begin construction on the Universe II."

Applause filled the room. Jonathan shook his head. "You are making a mistake!" he shouted over the noise. "Why spend time and money on a new one? We can continue with what we already have."

The Controller pulled out a small device from his coat pocket. As he touched varies parts on the object, the lights lowered. A giant, holographic sphere dropped down from an opening in the ceiling. "This is the Universe II. Senator Sergeev has been working very closely with Russian scientists to develop another suitable field for our tests. This habitat, or *world* as you call it, is ten times smaller than the current Universe. It requires less maintenance."

"Where will the sample of test subjects come from? If you put the entire population of the current Universe in this location, there will be over-crowding." Jonathan pointed out.

"We'll conduct a lottery selection of the Universe's current population. In total, only one million test subjects will be transported over." The Controller continued tapping the device. The Universe II floated over to a small platform in the corner of the room. "With this new initiative, the Council will be able to see what's going on down there through this hologram. This will help us reduce the size and the cost of your lab by thirty percent, Jonathan."

Senator Sergeev stood. "As we can all see, this version of the Universe is smaller and on the cutting edge of modern science. We will have the capability to accelerate test results while maintaining full control of the subjects."

"We never wanted to have control of them. The goal was to observe and influence, never to interfere. Every decision made must come from the test subject. We cannot take that away! It's unethical!"

The Controller banged his gavel down. "Jonathan, enough! You had several years to reform your project, and you were unable to do so effectively. Destruction of the Universe is non-negotiable." He paused. "Even though you have strong feelings regarding our decision, I hope you'll accept our offer. Since you are the greatest scientist and observer the current Ministry board has ever seen, we are allowing you to maintain your position as Ambassador of Science and the Lead Scientist and Observer over the Universe II." Jonathan's face remained hard like marble. "I hope you will take this opportunity as a chance to redeem yourself."

The Council remained still. Jonathan threw his body down in his chair, pressing his fingertips to his temples. "How long do I have until you destroy the Universe?" he muttered to the Controller.

"Thirty days," the Controller replied to Jonathan before returning his attention to the rest of the room.

Jonathan looked up. "I want another year," He paused. "If we plan to reap the test subjects from the current Universe, my team will need time to finish up our experiments and prepare the subjects for transport."

Sergeev opened her mouth. "I think—"

"We'll revisit this subject later. I will give you thirty days to develop a detailed reasonable plan to move forward and present it to the Council" The Controller informed Jonathan. "With these three pieces of business completed, I hereby announce the meeting adjourned."

The Council members stood and carried on conversations with one another. Jonathan stomped out the metal doors. The moment he entered the hallway a hand grabbed his arm. Jonathan turned around and faced the Controller.

"You have to understand that this decision is for the best, Jonathan." The Controller's eyes softened.

Jonathan forcefully pulled his arm away. "I've worked so hard to please you! And still it isn't enough!"

"The project has run its course. It's time to start new and explore new options." The Controller sighed. "Once the Universe Initiative II is in effect, you'll see it my way."

Jonathan got close to the Controller's face. "You should have just let me complete my research! I believe in the test subjects, and I know they'll make it through! They're strong and intelligent."

The Controller shrugged. "I'm sorry, Jonathan, but I don't share the same faith you do."

"I'm not surprised, Father." Jonathan stormed off, leaving the Controller behind.

CHAPTER 10: DESTINY

Bobby had sensed something different about Nicole the moment they merged onto the I-17 freeway at New River road from their Peoria home. He peppered her with questions until she revealed her well-kept secret.

"Bobby, I was gonna wait until Christmas to announce. But since you keep *bugging* me, I guess I'll tell you." One hand on the steering wheel and the other on the gear-shift, she glanced over at him. "Since your car accident, I've been working with Principal Jackson, Mrs. Jensen, Mr. Bates, and pretty much your entire senior class to tell people about what happened to you. We've reached out to media companies too."

Bobby was taken aback. "Why did you do that?"

Her eyebrows narrowed. "Your dreams of playing college basketball were shattered the moment that idiot hit you! You shouldn't have to suffer because of him." Nicole regained her composure. "Anyways, we were on a mission to get a few universities to consider allowing you to apply for some tuition relief so you can attend next fall. And it worked! ASU, U of A, MIT, and a few others accepted our offer. Bobby, they're gonna help you pay for school, except for books and stuff."

Bobby threw his arms around Nicole causing her to swerve. She smiled and pried him off her. "Was Duke on the list?" he asked.

Her smile fell, "No. I wasn't able to get all my paperwork in on time for fall of next year. The lady I spoke to said I should try again once the program reopens."

Bobby thought he'd be crushed. Instead he smirked. "That's okay. Everything happens for a reason."

"Here, here," chimed in Nicole. "Which school are you thinking of attending?"

Bobby reflected on his conversation with Mr. Bates. "MIT, maybe." Nicole sighed and wiped something from her face. A tear maybe. He put his head on her shoulder. "Unless you really want me to go to ASU with you!"

Nicole squirmed. "Yeah right, nerd! The further away you are the better!" She rolled her eyes and shifted gears. "Us coming up to Sedona and getting the golden crown will help with sending you far, far away, perhaps I should contact Moscow University?"

Bobby sunk down in his seat. "I really don't want to sell it unless we have to."

"I know," Nicole cleared her throat. "Let's talk about the plan again."

Bobby went over every detail. They would check into the hotel first, change clothes and get out to Bell Rock to begin the search. Once they pulled into Sedona, Nicole offered to buy lunch at El Rincon. Bobby's stomach was in knots so he declined. Nicole drove straight to the hotel and they dropped off their stuff. And then the journey began.

***

Bobby folded his arms after he changed his clothes. "I need you to pick up the pace, Nicole." He leaned next to the jeep massaging his knee. Bell Rock sat close by.

Nicole brushed her fingers through her long hair before pulling it up into a ponytail. "I figured you wouldn't be in such a hurry to find the crown. You know, because of the fact that you'll have to pawn it in the end."

74

She had a point. Bobby thought things through for a moment. "I'm still excited to find it again. Even if at the very end of this journey, you'll pry it from my hands, and sell it on EBay."

"Oh, brother." Nicole hoisted her backpack onto her body. "For what it's worth, I'll apologize in advance for ripping you away from your long lost childhood toy. I'll also apologize for crushing your dreams of putting the crown on your head and declaring yourself as king of the Universe." She laughed.

Bobby reflected on her words. "I know the crown probably belongs to someone else, but I always felt like it was supposed to be mine." Nicole seemed to have stopped paying attention to him. While Bobby waited for Nicole to finish filling her water bottle, he took out a map of Bell Rock. "I can't remember exactly where the golden crown was, but I think we'll be able to get a pretty good idea once we get out there and things start to look familiar to us."

"The only problem is all the rocks look alike! It's like trying to find a needle in a *needle* stack. How on Earth are we supposed to find the crown if we can't even find the right set of rocks?" Nicole said as she secured the lid on her water bottle.

Bobby laid the map out on the hood of the jeep so she could see it. He pulled out a pen and proceeded to points to various places on the page. "I remember that we parked over here." He pointed to the North of Bell Rock parking area, "and we walked along this path here to the far side of Bell Rock and around the Southern side."

"I remember that, too." Nicole interjected.

"So, the question really is, at what point did we start heading up and around?"

Nicole paused. "I recall Faja saying he wanted to get as far away from the *tourists* as possible, so, I think we walked around almost to the Eastern side, maybe somewhere in between." She studied the map further. "Well, let's assume that we started from the Southeastern base and spiraled our way up this way. That's what we did when we came out here the first time with Mom and Faja." Bobby nodded in agreement. She covered her eyes with sunglasses. "Let's do this!"

***

Bobby and Nicole arrived at the base of Bell Rock by late morning. Just like when they were kids, a stream of giddiness travelled through their stomachs as they began the hike. The calm, quiet of Sedona's red landscape brought them both comfort. Kicking up red dust under their hiking boots, they easily stepped across the rocks in front of them. Bobby took the lead, hunting for clues or signs that would jog his memory.

Bobby scanned the vast desert floor filled with different-sized red rocks and boulders. He let out a loud sigh. "This is going to take a lot longer than I thought."

Nicole stopped and took a long drink of water. "It could literally be anywhere." she sat down on a rock and put her hand out. "Let me see the map."

Bobby walked over and handed it to her. He watched Nicole's eyes examine it from behind her oversized sunglasses. She held the paper extremely close to her face, straining her eyes for a better view. Bobby smiled. "You look like Faja."

Nicole looked up at him. "What do you mean?"

"The way you study the map, it reminds me of Faja." Bobby grabbed the map from her and imitated Gordy. When Gordy read maps his eyes became human lasers, checking every single line on the page with precision. Since the lines were so small, Gordy would place the map about an inch from his face, which always caused Bobby to laugh.

Nicole swatted Bobby with her hand. "I'm trying to help you, you fool! If you keep making fun of me, I'll leave you up here!"

Bobby let out a loud laugh. "Okay, fine, you win. Just hurry up, so we can keep moving."

Nicole sat quietly for a few more minutes before handing the map back to Bobby. "It's pretty much anyone's guess at this point." She looked along the cylinder portion of the rock. "Bobby, I think we should take our chances and go straight up."

Bobby glanced at the map again. The path they had selected would either cut down or prolong their search by several hours. As a desperate measure, Bobby put down the map and closed his eyes. He relaxed his mind and focused on the last time he and his family had come to Bell Rock. He imagined the surrounding rocks he had climbed on during his seventh birthday, the day his life had changed forever.

"What are you doing, weirdo?" Nicole asked.

"Ssshhh! I'm trying to focus on my seventh birthday and our last trip up here." Bobby kept his eyes closed. He narrowed his search down, picturing the first few hours of the trip. The family had made it around the entire base and then began hiking into some of the steeper rock formations. Bobby opened his eyes and jumped to his feet. A sharp pain radiated through his knee.

"Are you alright?" Nicole asked. Bobby figured that she saw him wince.

He rubbed his knee. "Yeah, I'll be fine." He pointed into the distance. "We were on this side but further that way."

Nicole pulled her sunglasses to her forehead. "Which way?"

Bobby pointed upward. "That way."

Without hesitation, Nicole stood. Bobby led the way for the first hour. They climbed up the crevice they had travelled years earlier. Bobby paused again to reflect on the previous trip. He remembered Gordy and Kim asking him to slow down and Nicole complaining about her feet hurting. He pictured himself rushing over the "giant" rocks and being proud of scaling them by himself. Bobby pointed his finger down a long, winding, rocky path. "It's this way."

Bobby continued with this crown hunting process for about a couple of hours and then stopped so he could "meditate." By late afternoon, the two were beginning to get worried. They had traversed over the easy terrain and completed several steeper areas. With the sun making its way toward the horizon, Bobby kicked it into high gear. "We're gonna have to find it soon if we want to get it and get back before dark."

Nicole nodded. "You're right." She looked around at all the medium size rocks. "All the rocks seem the same. How on Earth are we going to find it?"

Bobby motioned further up the mountainside. "The boulders were a lot bigger. We need to continue climbing up." He wasted no time waiting for Nicole. Bobby climbed onto several rocks and hoisted himself up. Nicole followed suit.

An hour and a half later, Bobby and Nicole were exhausted and sunburned. The sun was beginning to set in the distance. Starving to death, Nicole pulled out two peanut butter sandwiches and handed Bobby one. Reluctantly he ate it as he glared at the orange and red sky forming in front of him. "Well, we did all the hiking we could for today. I think we have to head back and try again in the morning," he muttered.

Nicole nodded. "You're right. It'll be way too dark soon." She stood. "I've got to use the restroom. I'm gonna find a bush. I'll be back in a few minutes."

"Okay," Bobby said as he turned to face her. Just then, as the sun hit a crevice in the rocks behind Nicole, something began to sparkle. Bobby's heart skipped a beat.

CHAPTER 11: DISAPPOINTMENT

Jonathan clenched his fists and walked onto the solar train, throwing his body down on the first available seat. The Ministry had crushed him in one single vote. He had poured his life into the Universe Initiative and couldn't imagine starting over. Senator Sergeev was wrong—creating the Universe II wasn't a viable alternative, definitely not in the timeframe the Council envisioned. Jonathan just had to prove it. He pulled himself together only to fall apart again soon after. What was he going to tell Meg?

***

The Controller never approved of Meg. The moment Jonathan laid eyes on her he knew she was the one. He was barely twenty-five years old with a heart of gold and a love for the desert. Meg had arrived in Flagstaff at the age of eighteen and graduated from Northern Arizona University four years later with a degree in Geology. Instead of heading back to Ohio after school, Meg stayed in Flagstaff and moved to Sedona shortly afterward. She had climbed up Bell Rock over a dozen times, each time hunting for a new find or friend.

On one such trip, she came across a golden object sparkling in the sunlight. Meg studied the crown sitting on top of the rock and climbed up several boulders to retrieve it. She reached out and placed her hand on top of it only to find another hand resting under hers. "Excuse me, that doesn't belong to you." The man spoke. Meg looked up at the tall, black-haired man with a kind smile and athletic build.

Meg kept her hand firmly on the crown and on top of his hand. "Why isn't the crown on the king's head?" she joked. "If it was laid here for just anyone to find, he must not be much of a king."

Jonathan smirked. "I guess I lost my kingdom." He waited for Meg to remove her hand, but she didn't.

Jonathan couldn't afford this extreme inconvenience. Handpicked by his father, the Controller, Jonathan had recently begun his service with the Exploration team. The Exploration team's task was to travel throughout the Universe, collecting data on the subjects from the experiments the Ministry had authorized. This information was given to the observers who used it in their experiments in the lab. As the Controller's son, Jonathan was picked first by the Ministry as a means to keep their legacy intact.

The Ministry had high hopes for Jonathan. The youngest and the brightest of the bunch, Jonathan took this opportunity as a chance to prove to his father and the Ministry that he could be trusted to do an outstanding job. He joined the Exploration team and began setting his sights on learning as much as he could about the places he had visited. Jonathan desired to use this knowledge to better his own people.

Once the Exploration team was established, their first task was to create a key that would open the portals used for travel. Jonathan enjoyed creating his key, making sure it reflected so many things about himself and his dreams. The key was gold, his favorite color. The black tint and stars represented the galaxy and space. Each jewel represented all the multitudes of places he wanted to travel. He fashioned the key into a crown, reminding himself that he, not the Controller, was the king of his destiny.

Seeing Meg's soft hand on Jonathan's crown made his heart skip a beat. The Controller would banish him from the project if he knew that some unprivileged person touched the power to return to his home. Besides, Jonathan had engineered the crown to burn the skin of anyone other than himself who touched it. This effective safety feature was quite simple to make, but apparently was not working making this young lady a fascinating study.

The keypad inside the crown acted as an alarm. Once the crown was picked up, the recipient had only had ten seconds to put in the correct pass code. If time elapsed before the correct pass code was entered, the sensors covering the crown would heat up. The only person immune to his defense mechanism was Jonathan, since he had programmed the crown to recognize his DNA.

Before Meg, no one had ever attempted to touch his crown. He wondered how far should he let her take things. Meg released the crown. "I'm sorry, I was only kidding."

Jonathan quickly scooped it up and placed it back in his backpack. He dusted off his cargo pants and T-shirt before holding his hand out to help her up. "I'm Jonathan. What's your name?"

Meg stood without his assistance. "Meg. Meg Walker. Can I interest you in a cold drink in town?"

Jonathan smiled at her kindness and took her up on the offer. They hiked down Bell Rock and met up in town later that day. Several cold drinks later, Jonathan knew everything there was to know about Meg. Her warm smile comforted him as she expressed her need to adventure all over Arizona and the world. He enjoyed listening to her share her dreams of travelling for the rest of her life, never setting up home in one place for too long. Meg's attractive smile and open nature was the perfect companion for Jonathan and his restless spirit.

Jonathan made regular visits to Sedona to see Meg. Every time they met, he fell deeper in love with her. She felt the same way about him, only Meg knew very little about Jonathan. She asked him numerous questions about his past, and he always shut down, making absolutely no comments about where he was from or what he was planning to do. After six months together, Meg broke it off with Jonathan, telling him that she wanted to move away from Arizona and travel across Europe.

This was Jonathan's only chance. He begged Meg to understand his situation and why he couldn't be completely forthcoming with her. She rejected him, demanding that he come clean or she would leave him behind. With their love hanging on the line, Jonathan made a desperate move and told her about the Exploration team and his assignment. After he made a full confession, Meg smiled at him.

"I want to go back with you. I want to be a part of this amazing place you live in." Meg said as she put her hands on Jonathan's. "I've always dreamed of having an adventure like that! Please take me with you!"

Jonathan searched her eyes. "Meg, I can't take you with me. I shouldn't have told you about my project. If my father finds out, he'll banish me."

She smiled at him. "Jonathan, quit hiding behind your father's shadow and make a decision for yourself. If you love me and want to spend the rest of your life with me, you'll make a way for us to be together." Jonathan knew she was right, even though Meg's dream was next to impossible.

That day Jonathan and Meg risked it all and took the big step. Jonathan grabbed Meg's hand. He put the crown on his head, and closed his eyes, hoping that the crown would carry them both to the other side. The moment they crossed over together the Controller summoned his son for a conversation. The Controller made it simple. Jonathan had to give up Meg or his future with the Council and the Ministry would come to an end. Jonathan chose Meg, and they lived with the consequences of his *poor choice* for some time.

Jonathan considered his decision to give up a future with the Ministry a necessity if he wanted to have a full, adventurous life. Once he invited Meg into his world, they married, started a family, and accomplished their goals. Meg taught him how to paint and to live simply and full of spirit like their children did. He encouraged her to look past her passions and hunt for logic and truth in every experience she had. Over time the pair grew closer and closer together.

Eventually, Jonathan concentrated on learning more about Meg as a test subject instead of the woman he shared his life with. Seeing the Universe through Meg's eyes brought new challenges to him. She had exposed him to the plight of the human condition through the things she had observed throughout the Universe—war, violence, starvation, fear, greed, manipulation, division, the list continued to grow. The test subjects needed someone to work in their best interest. They needed Jonathan.

After several years Jonathan stopped roaming free. He set out to rejoin the Council and asked the Controller to give him a second chance. Jonathan's father was happy to have his son back and made a special motion to have Jonathan added to the Council as an adjunct member. Jonathan joined the lab and became an observer. Since Jonathan had a special interest in Meg's kind, he was put in charge of the Universe Initiative.

***

Jonathan didn't know how to tell Meg about the fate of her people. He knew she had family that would be severely affected by the Ministry's decision to destroy the Universe. The solar train slowed down in front of the lab, and Jonathan slowly got off. He headed straight for his office, not saying a word to any of his colleagues. As the door to his office closed, Sabrina, a senior observer and one of Jonathan's closest associates, knocked on the door.

"I'm not available at the moment." Jonathan yelled.

She knocked again. "I think you'll find the information I have uncovered very interesting."

Jonathan sighed. "Come in."

Sabrina opened the door with a stack of papers under her arm and a tablet in her hand. She looked over the dark bags under Jonathan's eyes and the grim look on his face. "Jonathan, I'm sorry I disturbed you, but I found something I think you'd like to see."

Jonathan ran his hands down the front of his face. "Sabrina, it doesn't matter. Whatever you have to show me won't change a thing."

Sabrina sat across from him and placed the papers and tablet down. "I don't know what that means, but this might make a difference."

He looked her in the eyes. "It's over, Sabrina. The Ministry is going to destroy our project and make way for a new one. I have thirty days to develop a plan to move forward with The Universe II."

Sabrina bit her lip and nodded. "I see." She powered on her tablet. "I was observing a place near the desert that you liked, you know, the one where you met your wife?"

Jonathan nodded. "Of course." He exhaled deeply. "What did you find, Sabrina?"

Sabrina pressed several keys. "I was observing a few locations in that place they call *Bell Rock*, and I came across this." She set down the tablet down and blew up an image for him to see. "I think that's your key."

Sabrina was the only person besides Jonathan who knew the golden crown was missing. Her observation brought him great joy. He zoomed in on the picture of his crown wedged between a few boulders. He let out a sigh of relief. "I knew it had to be there!" He pulled the replica from his desk. "The system's blocked me from creating a pass code for this one. If you can help me override it, I'll go down there and bring this one back."

Sabrina nodded. "I'll see what I can do."

Jonathan keyed his code into his desk, and the doors to the lab opened. He rose from his desk and walked into the massive room. Sabrina followed. Jonathan looked down at each station—war, disease, famine, religion, greed, politics and several others. He watched the observers stop at each station and key in a few numbers, wait for a response and then move on to the next station. Sabrina walked up next to Jonathan.

"The Controller sent over his formal notice advising us that the Universe is going to be destroyed. I'm sorry, Jonathan." Sabrina said.

Jonathan smiled. "Look at these results. We have made so much progress because of these test subjects! I have learned so much from Meg about their problems and how I can help our world advance. Now that I know where the key is, I know they have not advanced to the place of becoming a threat."

Sabrina put her hand on Jonathan's forehead. "Are you feeling okay? You're not making any sense."

Jonathan was exhausted, but he wasn't sick. "Sabrina, I was always afraid that the crown would be discovered, and our world would be found out. This is proof that the test subjects are harmless. They are worth saving. We can't let them destroy the Universe. "

The entire lab grew silent. Sabrina put her hand to her mouth. "The Controller's notice warned us about this. It said you would do anything to convince us to keep the Universe up and running." She lowered her hand. "Our involvement with your rebellion against the Ministry would be considered an act of treason."

Jonathan's eyes widened. "Rebellion? Treason?" He chuckled at the absurd thoughts. "Have they gone mad? I am a member of the Council in good standing and that has not changed. What makes them think that my simple desires to save my life's work are considered an act of treason?"

Sabrina stepped up close to him. "I'm not sure. Soon after the notice arrived, the Ministry sent several officers over to assess our work. We were informed that Senator Sergeev would oversee our transition to the Universe II. I'm sorry but we can't help you preserve it." Jonathan put his head in his hands. She leaned into his ear. "Don't worry, Jonathan, the Universe still has it's failsafe in place," she whispered.

Jonathan pulled his hands from his face. "What failsafe?" he asked in a low tone.

"Your key. As long as the crown is embedded somewhere in the Universe, it cannot be destroyed. The Controller initiated that protocol as a safety measure for all observers. He wanted to make sure that if you got lost, nothing could be done to harm you. He has no idea that you are here while your crown is over there."

Jonathan shook his head. "I can't rely on that. I'm sure the Ministry has found a way to decommission the failsafe. After all, they managed to control all the other keys to the Universe. Who knows what else they're capable of. We need to figure out another plan."

Sabrina nodded. "I don't agree with your plea to preserve the Universe, but as your friend I can't sit back and watch you suffer." She sighed.

"I understand. I appreciate whatever support you're willing to give me." Jonathan spoke from the heart.

Sabrina remained quiet while Jonathan looked over several of the stations in the room. The Universe wasn't cost-effective, that observation was true, but the test subjects were evolving. Jonathan admired their resilience most. They impressed him. Mankind had found a way to overcome many obstacles in its path.   He believed no one could put a price tag on that.

"Please don't take this the wrong way, but I wish you'd change your mind about all this." Sabrina said as she broke his concentration.

Jonathan turned to her. "You don't have to help me."

She sighed. "I still don't agree with your logic, however, I'm here for you."

He shook his head. "Sabrina, I can't tell if you're trying to assist me or convince me that I should give up." He smirked.

"You've always taught me to be subjective. I can't go against the Ministry, but I also can't condone the extinction of any species." She thought for a moment. "However, they are only test subjects."

"They are *people*." He pleaded.

"Then I am on your side." Her smile quickly turned to a frown. "Well, as much as I can be." Sabrina seemed on edge.

He put his hand on her shoulder and smiled. "Take a deep breath."

As Jonathan continued persuading Sabrina to accept his view on the Universe, they were didn't see Bobby place the crown on his head and disappear.

CHAPTER 12: LOST AND FOUND

At first Bobby was shocked to see the golden crown resting in between the rocks. The thought it remained untouched for ten years baffled him completely. The sun setting in the distance brought his attention back to the task at hand. He shook his head and took a long, deep breath. Bobby climbed the short distance to place himself directly below the crown. He looked down, searching for Nicole. She was nowhere to be found.

Bobby surveyed the ledge above and measured the amount of effort it would take to reach his prize. Gordy had done a good job of jamming it into the back of the crevice. He needed to get higher up. He massaged his aching knee. Bobby scrunched his eyebrows—it was harder than he thought.

Cautiously, Bobby stepped onto a rock and gripped the ledge above him for support. He pulled himself up carefully. Bobby's eyes hit the crown, and he smiled, realizing it was closer than he had originally thought. Foolishly, Bobby let go of the ledge and reached out for the crown. In a split second, Bobby fell backward, losing sight of the crown and hitting the ground with a loud *thud.* He took a few seconds to catch his breath before hopping back onto his feet, brushing himself off, and resuming his position on the rock.

Bobby grabbed onto the pointy rocks and pulled himself up with a great deal of effort. Looking upward, he found another small ledge that could be used to balance his weight.

Bobby went for it, thrusting his hand forward and grabbing the second ledge. Comfortable with his success, Bobby pulled himself up until he was completely supported by the ledge and directly in front of the crown.

He took a brief break to gaze down at his mountain climbing victory. As Bobby's eyes met the ground below, he realized that the crown was a lot further up than before. *How could that be?* When his family abandoned the crown last time they never managed to place it so far up. By all accounts, it made no sense for the crown to change locations... unless someone had moved it. Bobby's eyes scanned the landscape, fearful that the owner was close by, ready to take the crown back. Throwing logic to the wind, Bobby wasted no time plucking it from its resting place.

The golden crown was exactly how Bobby had last seen it. He marveled over it and ran his fingers over the jewels, stars, and skulls. His mouth cracked into a full smile. Slowly, Bobby put the crown high above his head and laid it upon his sweaty, dusty hair. Bobby closed his eyes and relished in the moment.

A warm sense of comfort and appreciation came over him as he meditated on his small achievement. Everything felt right, like things had finally fallen into place, the way they were always supposed to be. Bobby opened his eyes and grabbed his chest. The air around him had cooled to a comfortable 72 degrees. The red dusty earth he was previously sitting upon was now a white, high-backed office chair. He placed his shaking hands onto the glass desk in front of him and stared at his reflection bouncing off the computer monitor.

"Where the heck am I?" Bobby asked himself as he scrambled to control his breath. He ran his hands over his hair and yanked the golden crown from his head. "Did you do this?" He asked while looking at it.

Bobby looked from right to left, only finding white walls and filing cabinets around him. He gently placed the crown on the desk and rose to his feet. Without giving it much thought, Bobby raced to the office door and yanked it open. The sterile halls and bright lights beaming from above gave him reason to pause. He closed the door shut and looked back at the crown. "Okay, I'm not sure what or *who* you are, but I'm a little freaked out!" He said to the crown. He grabbed his head and began pacing the room. "This can't be happening! I mean, these things don't really happen to people, do they?"

Bobby's mind was twisted. He felt crazy and unsure about what to do next. He nodded. "This has to be a dream." He snapped his fingers. "I must've hit my head when I fell down! That has to be it!" Bobby smiled and sat back down at the desk. "None of this is real."

He grabbed the crown. "If I'm sleeping I guess the best way to wake up is to undo what I did." He placed the crown on his head and closed his eyes. Bobby imagined the warm Arizona air hitting his skin. He envisioned the sun resting on the horizon as Nicole stomped up to him and demanded that he "pick up the pace." Bobby was ecstatic to go home.

He opened his eyes and frowned. The desk, white walls, cabinets, and computer monitor reminded him that he was still in his dreamlike state. He retrieved the crown from his head and faced it. "Why didn't it work? What do you need me to do?" He placed it back down on the desk and sighed. Within a few seconds, Bobby's entire disposition changed. He still felt trapped, but in some strange way, the feeling didn't come with an overwhelming sense of urgency to head back to Arizona.

Sounds of voices from the other side of the filing cabinets made him freeze. He grabbed the crown and ducked under the desk. Bobby slapped his forehead as he made a startling discovery—the desk was made of glass. Before he could make a move to a better-suited hiding place, the filing cabinets shifted upward into the ceiling and downward into the floor. Bobby clutched the golden crown tightly, fearful of what may happen if he were to be found.

A man and woman emerged from the opening, folders and a tablet clutched into their hands and arms. They placed the tablets down onto the desk carefully before dropping the paperwork down with a loud bang, almost causing Bobby to shoot up and hit his head. The woman sat down in a chair as the man walked over to the door.

"Jonathan," the woman spoke. "I think you're not seeing the big picture. Starting a brand new initiative will bring other important developments to the forefront. You've spent so many years working on all these advancements, but we haven't had much success lately. Don't you think it's time for a plan B?" She typed a few commands into her tablet. "I'm sorry for sounding so insensitive, but we can't delay the inevitable. Your best bet would be to go back to Arizona, gather your key, say goodbye to your wife's family and make sure that this never happens again."

"That's heartless," he replied. "I always thought you cared about others."

"I do. Please believe me, none of my intentions or thoughts toward the Universe are bad. I just don't want them to suffer any more than they have to. They've been through so much."

The man she called Jonathan shook his head. "We are scientists, Sabrina. Our job is to test and observe their reactions so that we can learn from them and use that information to better ourselves. Our job isn't to destroy them, period. We are not monsters—we are merely curious minds who want to obtain more knowledge. We should be able to move onto another initiative without destroying their world. It just isn't fair for them."

What in the world are they talking about? Bobby thought.

The woman, Sabrina, sighed. "Our directive is to follow orders. The Ministry has voted. Our hands are tied." She stood up and pressed her hand to his back. "You have not failed, no matter what the Controller believes. I have worked side by side with you for a long time, and I have never lost faith in anything you have brought to the table." She smiled. "Take this new initiative as a means to prove all this to yourself and the rest of the world."

Jonathan pressed his hands to his temple. "I need some time to work. I've got to get this key reprogrammed so Meg and I can at least go visit her family before the end."

"Jonathan, you know you're not allowed to tell them anything about our plans."

"I have no plans to tell them anything. I merely want to say goodbye."

Sabrina nodded. "If that is the case, I'm back on board with your plans. I know how important Meg is to you."

"She's my wife. Of course she's important to me." Jonathan sighed. "It'll be nice to travel together instead of apart. It has been so long since I've been to Sedona." He leaned against his desk. "I miss the simple nature of the people there. Everyone is so friendly, and the food is very satisfying." Jonathan paused.

Sabrina pursed her lips. "Jonathan, you can't forget about the last time you were there. Surely you remember…"

Jonathan cut her off. "Sabrina, it was just a misunderstanding." He paused. "Besides, the Controller never found out about the incident which is a good thing, or else he would have stopped our exploration at once."

"Jonathan, don't get caught up in your memories too much." She grabbed her tablet and a few papers. "Remember which side you're on. The side of what is good for humanity as a whole." Jonathan ushered her out and slammed the door behind her.

Bobby stayed completely still, unsure of what to do. He listened to Jonathan bring his fist down hard onto the desk above his head. Jonathan dropped his body down into the chair Sabrina had vacated and placed his head into his hands. Bobby slowly eased the crown onto his head and gave transporting back another try. He closed his eyes and focused his thoughts. Breathing slowly and evenly, he meditated on the red rock of Sedona.

He opened his eyes and let out a huge sigh of relief. The sun was crawling down under the horizon, illuminating the red rocks and sand. Bobby pulled the golden crown from his head and placed it in front of him. He was still standing right where he was when he plucked the crown from its hiding place. His heart raced one hundred miles a minute, but yet his mind was still and free from all thoughts. He pulled his knees up under him while quietly watching the sun set in the distance.

"Bobby! How did you get all the way up there?" Nicole asked from below. She hopped from rock to rock until she was close to the ledge. She squinted to get a better look at him. A gasp escaped her lips. "Robert Walker! Is that the golden crown?"

Bobby looked down at the crown and then back up at her. "Yeah," he answered simply.

Nicole threw up her hands. "This is amazing! You finally found it! How does it feel?"

Bobby shrugged. "Eh." Truth be told, Bobby was still sorting out the last several minutes of his life.

Nicole snapped her fingers. "Earth to Bobby, what is the matter with you? You've been waiting for this moment for ten years! Ten years of crying and whining to all of us about how you were meant to have it. And here we are, in the middle of Bell Rock, and you have the crown in your hand, and all you can say is 'eh?'"

Bobby rolled his eyes. "I never *whined* about it, Nicole. I merely expressed my disdain for Faja's decision to keep me from coming after it."

"Whatever, Bobby, stop changing the subject. Come clean right now! Why aren't you dancing up a storm now that you've found it?"

Bobby grabbed the crown and held it up. "This thing is nothing like anything either one of us imagined." He paused. "It's sort of...magical."

Nicole sighed. "Bobby, I have no idea what you're talking about." Her eyes fell on the horizon. "The sun's going down. We need to get back to the car before it gets too late."

Bobby nodded and carefully placed the golden crown in his backpack. "Let me see it." Nicole said when he got back down to her. "What happened up there? Why are you so quiet? What do you mean *magical?*" She barked at him.

"Never mind." Bobby said as he began the hike down.

No matter how much Nicole nagged him on the car ride back to the hotel, Bobby didn't open up about the crown until they got back. Nicole threw her backpack on the bed and folded her arms. "Okay, Bobby, you've been unusually quiet. Spill!"

Bobby sat down on the bed and pulled the crown from his backpack. "This is gonna sound really crazy, but I think the crown may have transported me to some strange place."

Nicole stifled a laugh. "What? You're joking, right?" Bobby shook his head. "That's impossible. Things like that don't happen."

Bobby tapped the crown with his index finger. "I climbed up to the ledge where the crown was, and I put it on my head. I closed my eyes, and then I was in this really weird office."

Nicole narrowed her eyes. "What kind of office?"

"The desk was made of glass and everything was all white. The strangest thing happened. There were these filing cabinets, and they vanished into the ceiling and floor, opening up a secret passage to something." Bobby stopped to wait for Nicole's reaction. She motioned for him to continue, so he did. "All of a sudden this guy named Jonathan and a lady named Sabrina came into the office and started talking about all this crazy stuff."

"What kind of crazy stuff?"

Bobby thought for a minute. "They said something about experiments and some sort of initiative. I don't know, but it sounded a little crazy if you ask me. It seemed like they had to destroy some project that was really important to him."

She laughed at him. "You must think I'm a complete idiot. Transporting to a different place? Really, Bobby?"

It took him a good half hour to convince her he wasn't lying, and he wasn't crazy—it had really happened. Nicole's investigative instincts kicked in. She rushed over to the nightstand and retrieved the hotel pen and pad of paper. She quickly documented Bobby's account and looked up at him. "What else happened? Did they say who was involved with these experiments or what the purpose was?"

Bobby shook his head. "No, they didn't make any mention about anything, and I didn't stick around long enough to ask. I was hiding under Jonathan's desk as he reminisced about the project and..." Bobby paused. His eyes grew into giant saucers. "That Jonathan guy said something about Sedona and how much he missed it. He also mentioned something about saying goodbye to his wife's family. Sabrina mentioned someone named...Meg."

Nicole stopped writing down the information. "It's probably just a coincidence." She tapped the pen against her head. "If he was saying stuff about Sedona, he's probably been here before. It is a pretty well-known tourist destination." She pointed the pen at Bobby. "Did you see anything that reminded you of Arizona or any other place in the U.S.? Maybe you were in some other country?"

"No, I have no idea where I was, but it didn't seem like another country." Bobby said as Nicole wrote. "The way they were talking made me think I wasn't on Earth."

Nicole stopped writing. "Do you think that maybe you were in outer space?"

Bobby didn't respond. Instead he looked down at the golden crown. Nicole wrote a few more things then placed the pad on the bed. She reached out for the crown, but Bobby swatted her hand away. "I don't think that's a good idea."

"Why not?" She snapped.

"We have no idea what this thing is capable of. I don't want anything bad to happen to us."

"You touched it and teleported to another place, and nothing bad happened to you!"

Bobby grabbed the crown and shoved it back into his backpack. "I think this was all a bad idea. I shouldn't have taken this crown. Faja was right. I should have just left it where we found it." He tossed his backpack on the floor and laid back on his bed resting his head on one of the pillows.

Nicole came and placed a pillow under his left knee. "Bobby, I know what you went through was strange and usual, but that doesn't mean that the crown is bad news. Maybe we're just using it wrong. Or maybe you cracked your head when you fell. "

Bobby looked over at Nicole. "I'm not sure if I agree with that statement. I just have this really bad feeling about this whole crown thing."

Nicole put her hand out. "Well why don't I put it on my head and see for myself."

Bobby laughed and waited for Nicole to admit that she was joking. Normally Nicole would heed to Bobby's warning when he was so determined to keep her safe, but this time she didn't. She continued to hold her hand out firmly.

He had a change of heart. "Nicole, you're right about the whole crown thing. Maybe I'm using it wrong."

"That's fine but I still want to experience this whole other place myself," she hissed.

He shooed her away. "It's not yours. It's mine."

"Look, I'm not taking it from you! I just want to see this place myself. Once I come back, I'll give you your precious crown back!" Nicole negotiated. Bobby remained firm in his position to keep her in the dark. "Bobby, if it wasn't for me, you wouldn't be up here to begin with! You're acting like a selfish brat."

"I just don't want you to…."

Nicole cut him off. "Don't forget the true reason for our trip up here. We came to Sedona so we could get the crown and sell it online."

Bobby didn't want that. He wasn't ready to give it up just yet. Without any form of protest, Bobby took the crown out of his bag and placed it into Nicole's hand. "Maybe this is what needs to happen for you to see that we need to keep it" He took a deep breath. "Once you're on the other side it's pretty easy to get back. All you have to do is put the crown back on and think about where you want to be."

She nodded. "Got it."

"You better come right back!"

Nicole smiled and smoothed out her hair. "All right, here goes nothing." She positioned the crown on her head and closed her eyes. Bobby looked on, waiting for her to disappear into thin air. After several seconds, Nicole opened her eyes. "Nothing happened!"

Bobby took the crown from her head. "You're probably doing it wrong. Let me give it a try." He took a deep breath and slowly put it on his head. He closed his eyes and concentrated on Jonathan's office. He willed the tingles and vapors to transport him back to the place that had confused him beyond reason.

"Bobby, why are you playing tricks on me?" Nicole asked. Bobby opened his eyes to see her angry face. "I actually believed that the crown had magic powers."

Bobby pulled the crown from his head and stared at it. "That's so strange. Last time it worked."

Nicole put her pad of notes into her backpack and grabbed some clean clothes. "I'm going to take a shower, and then we'll go get dinner."

Bobby shook his head. "Nicole, you have to believe me! The last time I put the golden crown on my head, I travelled from Sedona to some strange guy's office." Nicole rolled her eyes at him. "It's true!" he said, desperate to have her in his corner.

"Fine, I believe you. Now leave me alone so I can get ready for dinner." She slammed the bathroom door in his face as he chased behind her.

Bobby took one last look at the golden crown before shoving it back into his backpack. Since Nicole always took way too long to get ready, Bobby pulled a few bills from his wallet and headed for the vending machine downstairs. The moment the door shut behind him, he had this incredible urge to head back into the room and retrieve the crown. Bobby unlocked the room and unzipped his backpack, freeing the crown from its hiding place. He set the crown on top of his pillow and grinned. "You're way cooler than I thought." He said before leaving the room again.

CHAPTER 13: WAS IT MAGIC?

Bobby returned back to the room and tossed his wallet in his backpack. He dropped down on the bed and placed his soda down so he could get a firm grip on his bag of honey-roasted peanuts. As Bobby opened the bag, he glanced over to see the golden crown and studied the symbols. Jumping up in a quick leap, he charged to the bathroom door and pounded on it uncontrollably.

"What?" Nicole hissed over the spraying water.

"What do you think the symbols on the crown mean?" Bobby yelled.

Nicole shut off the water. "What do you want, Bobby?"

"What do you think the symbols on the crown mean?"

"I don't know! Now leave me alone!" she snapped as she turned the water back on.

Bobby trained his eye on the crown and sat on the edge of the bed. "Where did you take me?" He asked it. The crown's symbols and tarnished surface didn't shine in the light which further perplexed Bobby. "What are you exactly? Are you simply just a crown, and I dreamed up the whole teleporting part?" Bobby waited to see if anything extraordinary would happen. He stared at the crown for several minutes, brainstorming possible reasons for its ability to take him out of Arizona and into another place within a matter of seconds.

Nicole emerged from the bathroom dressed in jeans and a blue T-shirt. Her eyes fell on Bobby's dusty hair and clothes. "Bobby, you're gonna shower before we go to dinner, right?"

Bobby ignored her, his eyes still stuck on the crown. She clapped her hands loudly in his ear. "Earth to Bobby! Are you gonna get ready for dinner or what?"

Bobby pointed his index finger at the golden crown. "What else do you think this thing can do?"

Nicole nodded her head and smirked. "Bobby, we've been out in the sun all day and you bumped your head. I'm sure you're just imaging the whole transporting thing."

Bobby looked at her. "I know what I saw, Nicole. I distinctly remember being in another place." He shifted his eyes back to the crown.

Nicole grabbed the crown and put it back on Bobby's head. She sat down on the bed with him. Nothing happened. Bobby took it off, laid it on his bed and prepared to get ready for dinner. When Bobby stepped out of the bathroom, Nicole was reviewing her notes. "Anything weird happen?"

"Nope." she said.

They went over Bobby's account a few more times. Eventually they gave up. Before they headed off to El Rincon, Bobby placed the crown in his backpack and shoved it under his bed. He ushered Nicole out of the room first to make sure she couldn't play tricks on him.

***

During dinner, Nicole took the time to bring up a very pressing matter. "Bobby, I've given it a lot of thought and I think we should keep the crown. Also, we can't tell Mom or Faja about what happened, no matter what."

Bobby nodded. "I totally agree. We need to figure this out before we say anything to anyone." He paused. "We have to find a safe place to store it until we know what to do next."

"I can always take it with me. Faja will never think to come over to my place and snoop around." Nicole suggested.

Bobby shook his head. He trusted his sister but not completely. "No way. I'll hold onto it and hide the crown so it won't have a chance to do anything strange. In the meantime, can you do some research at school and see if you can find anything about this crown?"

Nicole laughed. "Bobby, where is your sense of adventure? Why not start our search here in Sedona? I'm sure there's gotta be someone around here who knows a thing of two about the golden crown."

Bobby narrowed his eyebrows. "I don't know about that. What if we come across the real owner of the crown?" He leaned in. "What if the crown leads us to some dark wizard or something?"

"You have a point." Nicole tilted her head to the side and seemed to ponder his idea. She snapped her fingers. "I've got it! Let's pose as NAU students and pretend that we're researching the crown as a school project. If we come across anything weird or crazy, we won't run the risk of someone thinking we actually have it."

Bobby agreed, and they made plans to do their inquiry into the crown the following day. Early the next morning Bobby and Nicole woke, dressed in a hurry and hit the streets of Sedona looking for anyone who could shine some light on their new discovery. After an hour of visiting a few stores, they came across a small shop selling keepsakes from Sedona and a few books regarding the various harmonic portals Sedona was said to have. Nicole entered the shop first and held the door for Bobby.

Once Bobby set foot into the store, a wave of dust hit his nose causing him to sneeze very loudly. A short man hunched over a glass case filled with several old books raised his head. He watched Nicole admire the dusty shelves filled with books, maps, almanacs, and trinkets before clearing his throat to get her attention. She spun around, her fluffy blonde hair sending a cloud of dust into the air and straight for Bobby's nose. He let out another loud sneeze.

"Sorry kids, I haven't gotten around to cleaning." The man said with a crooked smile. "What are you two in the market for? Aliens? Witchcraft? If you're looking for weird or fascinating, I've got it here." He pointed to the shelves and displays spanning from the floor to the ceiling.

Nicole approached the counter and looked over a few books. "I'm a student at NAU, and I'm doing a research project on weird and strange things found in Arizona."

The shopkeeper chuckled. "Well you've come to the right place! I've got all sorts of information for you. How weird are you looking to go?"

By this time Bobby had cleared his sinuses. He approached the counter and stood next to Nicole. "We're not looking for witchcraft or aliens. We're looking for strange artifacts."

"You mean like rocks or minerals?" The shopkeeper asked.

"Nothing like that. Just things that don't seem to belong." Bobby scanned the room, hunting for something that he could use as an example. "Like Egyptian artifacts or things out of place like that."

The shopkeeper laughed loudly and snorted. "Son, I think you're in the wrong country if you're looking for Egyptian artifacts. You might want to try Egypt."

Nicole rolled her eyes at Bobby then turned to the man. "I think what my research partner means is, has anything been found here that doesn't belong? Like dinosaur bones or crowns or..."

The shopkeeper put up his finger. "There was something weird that happened around here a few years back regarding a crown."

Nicole smiled. "Great." She pulled her notepad from her backpack and grabbed a pen. "Tell me about this strange occurrence."

He leaned forward on the glass. "First things first, what made you think of bringing up a crown? Did you hear something?"

Bobby leaned in on the counter. "Why? Is there a crown around here that has sparked everyone's interest?

The shopkeeper drummed his fingertips on the glass case. "Only legends and rumors. Nothing that you'd want to put in your research paper."

"Well, you've sparked our interest, so please tell us more," Nicole said.

The man left the counter and disappeared behind a flimsy red curtain to the left of the glass case. Nicole tapped Bobby's shoulder and motioned for him to lean in close to her. "This seems really promising, but I want to use extreme caution. If something weird seems like it's about to happen we need to have some type of code or signal that it's time to go."

Bobby agreed. "How about you flip your hair three times if you see something strange? If I see something I'll scratch my nose three times."

Nicole accepted their plan and continued to scan the books in the case. Bobby ventured farther into the shop, mesmerized by all the junk that had been accumulated. He searched the titles on the shelves—Arizona history, aliens, witchcraft, ghosts, spells, portals, and *unusual.* He paused at the section labeled *unusual. With so many strange topics already listed, what could they possibly find "unusual?"* He lowered himself to the shelf to find only one book, a copy of the most recent phonebook.

"I have found something the two of you will certainly find fascinating!" The shopkeeper shouted as he pushed the curtain aside and reentered the room.

Bobby stood and quickly rushed back to the front of the shop. The man placed a notebook titled, *Unexplained* on the counter and turned several pages.

"What is this?" Nicole asked.

"I'm not the original owner of this shop. The man who I bought this place from gave me this notebook in case someone came in looking for something super strange." The shopkeeper continued to flip through several pages scribbled with notes and drawings. Bobby tried to focus on the information, but the man moved the pages too quickly. "Aha!" He stopped at one wrinkled page with a hand-drawn picture of the golden crown.

Bobby suppressed his surprised look. Nicole seemed to keep a straight face. "That looks like it doesn't belong here." She turned her head so she could attempt to read the entry about the crown. "What does it say?"

The shopkeeper turned the book towards himself and began to read the entry. "Today was a rather unusual day. A man came into town for a drink with a pretty red-haired lady. Normally that would not strike us here as anything strange except for the conversation they appeared to be having. The woman argued with the man to 'take her with him to wherever it was that he had come from.' Now I've been around some really peculiar relationships, but I have never heard a woman phrase leaving town like that. I took my findings to some of the locals who might find it interesting, and we decided to do some digging."

Nicole asked the man to pause so she could take notes. Bobby reflected on the passage. *Is this place referenced in the book the same place I had travelled to?* He thought. After Nicole had made her notes she asked the man to continue.

"We spoke with an expert who did a lot of research on portals, and he had quite the explanation for us. He firmly believes that we may have come in contact with an exploration team of aliens. These aliens use portals as a means to learn more about the human race. He was convinced that the invasion was upon us! The moment we heard this, we made arrangements to stop this alien race from attacking our planet."

"But they don't seem like aliens." Bobby slipped. Nicole stopped writing and glared at him.

"What are you talking about?" The man asked as he held the notebook close to his face.

Bobby struggled to backpedal. "What I mean is, it sounds like this man looked like a human and talked like one. Why would they automatically assume he was an alien?" Nicole gave Bobby a hard pat on his back. He assumed she was congratulating him for spinning the situation.

The shopkeeper skimmed through the rest of the page. "Here is a passage from a few days later." The man cleared his throat. "We came in contact with the man in town and convinced him to have a chat session with us. The alien sat down at the table and seemed to enjoy his coffee as we asked him questions. He told us he was from Ohio, just like his wife Meg, and he had gotten a degree from NAU in Geology. He went on to tell us stories about his childhood and how he had met his wife. Everyone wanted to believe he was innocent, but I couldn't."

"What did they do next?" Nicole asked.

The man turned the page. "I waited until the alien wasn't looking and took the liberty of searching his backpack. The moment I opened it, a golden crown with black marks and strange symbols fell out. The alien reached for the crown, but I snatched it up first. I asked him where he had gotten such a fine piece of work, and he became angry, demanding I give it back. I started to place the crown on my head, but it got very hot and I dropped it on the ground. The alien picked it up quickly and ran out the door, jumped in his Jeep and drove away".

"We chased the alien out of town and to the parking lot at Bell Rock. He jumped out of his Jeep and ran down the trail to the mountainous trails quickly, even though the sun was setting, making it impossible to see. We continued chasing the alien with flashlights until we lost him somewhere on the rock. Over the next two weeks we kept looking for any clues and came up with nothing. I will never forget what I saw." The shopkeeper closed the notebook.

Nicole wrote frantically. Bobby stood awestruck at what he had heard. He snapped out of his trance. "What was the name of the previous shop owner?" he asked.

"Nikolai Burns. He still lives in Sedona and loves to talk with others about his experience. He's committed to stopping the alien invasion. A little nuts if you ask me." The man wrote down an address on a piece of receipt paper. "Tell him Ernest from the shop sent the two of you."

Bobby took the paper from Ernest. "Thank you very much." Nicole gave Ernest a smile and headed for the door with Bobby trailing behind.

"Good luck on your research project." Ernest called after them as the door closed shut.

"Nicole, I don't know a lot about Aunt Meg, but I think this isn't a coincidence." Bobby said once they hit the sidewalk. "I think she was abducted by aliens."

Nicole placed her sunglasses on her face. "It's a possibility. First, we need to figure out whether or not this Nikolai Burns is telling the truth."

***

Bobby and Nicole arrived at the small sandstone home tucked away from the major roads near the edge of town. They wasted no time. Bobby led the way, climbing the three steps and knocking on the large brown door. No answer.

Nicole balled her hand into a fist and pounded a few more times. A young girl, no more than twelve years old, answered.

"Can I help you?" she asked Nicole.

"We're looking for Nikolai Burns. Is he here?" Nicole asked.

The girl shook her head. "That's my grandpa. He's out of town on business for the next month."

Both Bobby and Nicole let out a loud sigh. They said goodbye to the girl and headed back to the hotel. The moment Nicole sealed the door to their room, Bobby placed the golden crown in his hands. "I don't care what that guy says, I don't think the man I saw on the other side was an alien. And I don't think they're planning an invasion either. But the shop owner's journal did mention that this mysterious man had a wife named Meg. I'm convinced that this isn't a coincidence. It makes sense…right?"

Nicole took the golden crown from Bobby. "I need more evidence before I can believe that she was taken away to another planet. We should tread very lightly if we decide to continue our research."

"You don't really believe these people want to hurt us, do you?"

"There's only one way to find out." Nicole placed the crown above her head and slowly lowered it down.

Bobby pulled it from her grasp. "What do you think you're doing with my crown?"

"What do you mean *your* crown, Bobby?"

Bobby held it close to his chest. "I risked my neck trying to pull it from the rocks. It's my crown!" His eyes flashed red.

Nicole stopped pestering him at once. She seemed worried about him, but unable to find the right way to express her concern. She put her hands down. "Bobby, I'm not trying to steal the crown from you. I just thought it was something that both you and I shared."

Bobby put the crown in his backpack and zipped it up. "I've waited so long for the golden crown, I'm not letting anyone come between me and it."

Nicole laughed which eased the tension. "I would never take it from you, little brother. I'm on your side, Bobby. Don't ever forget that."

Bobby searched his sister's kind eyes. He let out a loud sigh. "I'm sorry, Nicole. I just have no idea what has come over me. I just get so emotional when I think about how much work it took to get to this point. I never thought I'd have a chance to get the crown again," he paused, "it might be something magical. It might be the key to something huge."

Nicole nodded. "I understand, just don't let it control you." She walked over to her bed and began packing her items. "I think our stay here is done. I'll see what I can find out when I get back to Tempe."

"I'll search the Internet some more and see if I missed anything. In the meantime, I'm gonna hide the crown somewhere until we can do more with it." Bobby said as he began packing his stuff. "I'll see what I can find out about this Nikolai Burns guy, too."

Nicole threw a few more clothes items in her bag before heading for the bathroom. "Bobby whatever you do, don't put that crown on unless I'm around. I don't want you disappearing forever without me at least knowing about it. I'm not sure what I would tell Mom and Faja."

Bobby agreed. They packed up and headed down to the lobby to check out. Once they were on the road, Bobby held his backpack tightly as he and Nicole shared funny stories from their childhood. As they entered the driveway, Gordy stood outside with a large smile. Nicole pulled up next to him and cut off the engine. Bobby and Nicole stayed completely still in the Jeep, fearing their father's massive grin.

"Do you think he knows?" Bobby asked Nicole.

"There's only one way to find out." Nicole opened her door and approached her dad, giving him a large hug. They talked for a moment as Gordy kept his wide smile and pointing at Bobby. Nicole started to cheer and gave her father another hug.

Bobby couldn't take it anymore. He grabbed his backpack and opened the door. "What's going on?" he asked.

Gordy gave Bobby a huge hug. "Bobby, your mom got a really good job with another insurance firm. We'll have enough money to take care of your hospital bills, buy a new SUV, and get the rest of the money needed for your college. Isn't that great?"

Bobby froze. He couldn't believe the change in his luck. He finally had the golden grown and didn't have to sell it. Gordy tightened his hug causing Bobby to lose his balance. His backpack hit the ground with a loud clink. Gordy looked down and let go of Bobby. "What do you got in there, Bobby? A set of bricks?" His laughter was cut short. "You didn't bring back any Lost Dutchman treasure, did you?"

"Um... well..." Bobby stammered.

"Faja! Come on, really? You think we'd disobey you like that?" Nicole asked as she hugged her dad. She gave Bobby a wink. "Now let's eat. I'm starving." She led Gordy into the house.

Bobby picked up his backpack and hurried into the house. Once inside, he wrapped his pinky finger around Nicole's and whispered, "pinky swear". They silently confirmed their agreement to never speak about the golden crown to anyone.

CHAPTER 14: ONE MORE YEAR

The thirty day waiting period to destroy the Universe came to an end. Jonathan requested a special meeting with the Controller. He had an important discovery to share with him...

Jonathan had spent the last thirty days examining the Universe II. He hunted for a reason to extend his project. He and Sabrina ran tests on the new habitat. Jonathan studied the projections regarding the sustainability that Senator Sergeev and the Russian scientists claimed would exist. Everything seemed correct, except for one thing. He made an immediate appointment with the Controller to discuss this issue.

Jonathan stepped into the Main room where the Controller was admiring the Universe II. He took a deep breath and stated, "The test subjects are under attack. We can't do our population selection until this war is complete."

The Controller turned to face him. "What are you talking about? What war?"

Jonathan placed a black file folder down on the glass table directly in front of the Controller's seat. "A biological war. There is an epidemic of a drug resistant bacteria that has made its way through Africa and into the Middle East. There are over 20,000 confirmed cases."

The Controller walked over and looked at the data. "Can't you give them a vaccine?"

"We're not sure exactly what it is or how to treat it. The test subjects think it's related to the Ebola virus, but they are not sure," Jonathan said. "Remember, I can't control them. I can only study their behaviors."

"I see. Do you think it can be spread to our people?"

Jonathan shrugged. "I don't know. But we can't risk sending anyone down to the Universe to investigate until it's contained."

The Controller cleared his throat. "What's the incubation period for this virus? Why didn't you bring this situation up sooner?"

"Senator Sergeev shut down this portion of the lab fourteen days ago. She didn't think it was necessary." Jonathan paused. "Sergeev also fired a third of my team which has led to efficiency issues in the lab. By the time we figured out that this was happening, the outbreak was beyond containment. The virus incubates for twenty-one to twenty-five days before the test subjects are able to see any symptoms. All in all, it's spreading because people with the virus are infecting others without knowing it."

The Controller put his hand to his chin. "I suppose you'd like to postpone the reaping for a few months." His eyes veered over to the Universe II. "I have to say, your timing is incredibly questionable. I thought you would have completed the selection process well before your thirty day deadline."

The Controller's astute observation sent a chill down Jonathan's back. "I won't lie about my intentions to extend the Universe. But I need you to understand my situation, Father." Jonathan pleaded. "Even if I told you about the virus sooner, there is nothing that neither you nor I could have done to change it."

The Controller stared in silence for what seemed like an eternity to Jonathan. "How long do you need?"

"One year."

The Controller retrieved the folder from the table. "I'll present this to the Ministry. I'm sure they'll agree with you findings." He put his hand on Jonathan's shoulder. "One year it is." The Controller left.

Jonathan found the Controller's easy surrender unusual. He came to the conclusion that he wasn't an observer convincing the Controller to see his point, but rather a son asking his father for another chance. A chance that seemed to be granted with kindness.

***

The next year flew by quickly. Bobby finished up high school and spent the summer before his first year of college preparing for the big transition. He chose MIT as the place where we was going to spend the next four years learning about nuclear science. Gordy and Kim reluctantly accepted his decision to move cross-country. Ashley got accepted to Texas A&M. She and Bobby shared a tear filled goodbye, and promised to stay in contact. Bobby was crushed, but his big sister reeled his focus back in.

Nicole took advantage of their last few months together investigating the golden crown. Bobby spent several hours a day doing research on the golden crown. Every search he and Nicole did regarding Nikolai's story led them nowhere. The golden crown, hidden inside a box, within another box and covered by several other boxes in the garage, continued to perplex them. It seemed as though the harder they worked to reveal its true identity, the more elusive the crown became.

At the end of the summer, Bobby quietly retrieved the golden crown from its many boxes and packed it inside his backpack to take with him to college. Gordy and Kim cried as they made the cross-country trip to drop their baby off in Boston at MIT. Bobby said goodbye to them and lugged his simple belongings into the dorm room he was to share with his roommate, Kermit "Kenny" Sergeev, who was originally from Russia.

Spending time in class and around campus with Kenny slowly tore Bobby's attention away from the golden crown. Pretty soon they became friends with a girl named Lindsay Churchill. The three college students spent hours poring over their science books while keeping up with the school's demanding curriculum. Bobby barely had any time to relax or phone home.

Then one day, a peculiar conversation with Kenny and Lindsay brought the golden crown back to the forefront of Bobby's mind. The three were in the library studying up on nuclear energy and fusion. Kenny had returned from a trip to the local coffee shop and placed three dark coffees on the table.

"You'll never guess who I ran into on my way back," Kenny said as he got comfortable in his seat. "Lindsay, remember that guy who dropped out of our physics class?"

Lindsay nodded. "That weirdo, yeah." She tossed her long black hair to the side and rolled her eyes.

Bobby's interest spiked. "What guy?"

Kenny sipped his coffee. "There was this guy in our class who was really weird. He believed in aliens and stuff. He wanted to build a spaceship to make contact or something."

Lindsay let out a loud laugh. "He was convinced that the invasion was upon us." She sipped her coffee.

Bobby's thoughts went back to the golden crown. "What was his name?"

Kenny opened his textbook. "I don't remember. Who cares?"

Bobby pulled out his phone to call Nicole. It went straight to voicemail. He focused back on his studies. "Hey, Kenny, can you help me with our last assignment?"

"Bobby needs all the help he can get." A familiar voice announced behind him. Bobby turned around to see Nicole walking up with a large grin on her face.

He jumped out of his seat and wrapped his arms around her. "I'm so happy to see you. What are you doing here?" Bobby asked.

Nicole shrugged. "I just wanted to see my little brother, that's all." Her voice was nervous.

Lindsay cleared her throat with a little hint of jealousy. "Bobby, who is this?"

Bobby pointed to Kenny. "Nicole, this is my roommate, Kenny." He turned back to Lindsay. "And this is my friend, Lindsay. Guys, this is my big sister, Nicole. She goes to Arizona State University."

Nicole gave them a wave. "Nice to meet you guys." She linked arms with Bobby. "Bobby, I need to talk with you about something."

"Sure." Bobby told her as she forcefully pulled him away from the table. Nicole didn't stop until they reached a corner of the library where only a few books and spider webs could be found. "Nicole, what are you doing here?" He queried. "Why didn't you tell me you were coming all this way?"

Nicole pushed some of her long blonde hair behind her ear. "I decided to do some more research on the golden crown to see what I could find."

"Did you find anything?" Bobby asked eager to get closure with his weird token.

"Nothing really interesting."

"And you came all the way to MIT to tell me that?" Bobby cracked a smile. "If you missed me that much all you had to do was say so."

Nicole smacked him in his stomach. "Don't be such a brat, Bobby!" She sat down Indian-style on the floor and motioned for Bobby to do the same. Once he sat down she pulled a notebook from her purse. "In one of my classes I was doing some research on our family tree, and I came across this." She flipped a couple pages until she landed on the

Walker family tree. Next to Gordy's name was Meg and the words *see police report.* "I got a copy of the police report and this is what I found."

She unfolded a sheet of paper and laid it out for him to see. The report stated that Megan "Meg" Walker had studied Geology at NAU and moved to Sedona about two years after Bobby was born. Her last known whereabouts were on Bell Rock with a strange man with dark hair. Several hikers recalled seeing the two hiking up Bell Rock but no one reported seeing her leave the location. Gordy and the rest of the Walker family reported her missing after she failed to show up for Bobby's fourth birthday party.

"Apparently Faja suspected something was up some time around your birthday that year. Aunt Meg had an unusual boyfriend that no one in the family ever met and they started hearing from her less often. Once your birthday came around, Faja started calling around in Sedona to Aunt Meg's friends and family. Eventually he realized that no one had seen her in a long time."

Bobby put everything together. "That Ernest guy mentioned that the alien had a wife named Meg and that the alien studied Geology at NAU. Nikolai Burns heard her ask the alien to take her back to his home."

Nicole nodded. "You were right, Bobby. All this can't be a coincidence. The golden crown had something to do with Aunt Meg's disappearance."

Bobby leaned back against the dusty shelf. "Aunt Meg was abducted by an alien." He said in disbelief.

"I know it's not likely, but we won't know the truth unless we go back." She paused. "You've got to put on the crown and see if you can find her, Bobby."

Bobby bit his lip. The seriousness in her eyes created a pit in his stomach. "Nicole, I don't know what to say. The people I saw on the other side weren't aliens. Aliens don't exist, we both know that."

"I feel the same way, but things just don't add up anymore. We can't ignore the obvious. We have to go back and put all these theories to rest."

"But the crown doesn't work that way. I can't just put it on my head and magically appear somewhere else."

She rose to her feet. "Bobby, no more excuses! We're doing this whether you want to or not." Nicole stuffed her notebook in her purse, stood up and put out her hand for Bobby to grab. She pulled him to his feet. "Where's the crown?"

"You can't make me put the crown on, Nicole."

She rolled her eyes. "If you're not going to do it then I am. Now take me to the crown."

He knew Nicole's determination would win. "Fine, I'll do it. I'll put the crown on."

Nicole smirked. "I'll be at the door waiting for you."

Bobby watched his sister leave before heading back to the table. Kenny and Lindsay were engulfed in a funny conversation, but hushed their voices once he neared them. Without giving either one an explanation, Bobby packed his school books into his backpack.

"I don't like your sister, Bobby. She seems pretty mean," Lindsay said.

He threw his backpack over his shoulder. "Somewhere inside she's got a heart. I'm convinced of it."

Bobby rushed to the door and met up with Nicole. They pretended to act naturally as they crossed campus and went straight to his dorm room. Bobby opened the door and dropped his backpack on the floor, taking each book out before returning it back to his back. After tightening the straps on his shoulders, he dug through his belongings. Nicole stepped over all the dirty clothes and lurked around his room. She grabbed a picture of the Walker family buried under notes and papers on Bobby's desk. The photo was from Bobby's seventh birthday.

Nicole sat down on Bobby's unmade bed and smiled. "It's so weird to see you here in college. I remember when you were a geeky little kid with a big nose and huge feet." she chuckled.

Bobby looked over his shoulder. "Yeah, you were bossing me around then, and you still do now."

Nicole put the photo on top of a stack of papers on the desk. "I don't boss you around."

"I'm putting the crown back on because you told me to."

Nicole got defensive. "You wanted to know what happened to Aunt Meg, right?" Bobby nodded. "See, I did you a favor. And most importantly, you putting on the golden crown is about you being a hero and saving the day, not me. I offered to do it. This is your choice."

"Whatever you say, Nicole, whatever you say." Bobby's hand grazed the top of the crown. He pulled it out and faced her. "Well, here goes nothing." He held it high above his head.

"Wait!" Nicole stopped him. "Bobby, I just want you to know that I don't think anyone can do this but you." She slapped his arm. "Now go be a hero!"

Bobby lowered the crown down slowly. Once it rested on top of his head, he smiled at Nicole and closed his eyes. He focused his thoughts on Jonathan's office.

Bobby envisioned himself passing through time and space. A feeling of excitement and adventure came over him as he waited for the process to begin. Too much time seemed to pass. He opened his eyes and sighed. Nicole shook her head.

"Nothing happened." She said.

Bobby took the crown from his head. "I don't understand why it doesn't work anymore. I tried to focus."

"Maybe that's the key to all this. You have to relax. Don't focus on travelling."

Bobby put the crown on his head and closed his eyes. "Okay, I'll keep my mind open, and maybe it'll work." He took several deep breaths. "I think I may have used up all my free trips," he joked. Nicole didn't respond.

Bobby opened his eyes. He sat in Jonathan's chair, facing the computer monitor. He pulled the crown from his head and placed it on the desk. "Here goes nothing." Bobby got up from the desk and opened the office door. Bobby poked his head out slowly and looked up and down the hall to see if anyone was close by. The hall was empty. He closed the office door and went straight for the filing cabinets.

Bobby spent several minutes pushing and pulling the cabinets, hoping to get the secret passage to open up. Exhausted and frustrated he gave up and plopped back down in the office chair. He looked at the crown. "So, what do I do now?" he asked.

Bobby sat back down, leaned back in the desk chair, and spotted two large desk drawers. He tugged on the drawers without success. It was useless. He decided to do more exploring. Bobby grabbed the golden crown, stuffed it in his backpack, and left the office.

Walking swiftly down the hall, Bobby passed an empty reception desk and stepped outside. The glass building climbing toward a perfect blue sky was the first thing he saw. Electric cars hummed down the clean and clear black paved streets. Pedestrians walked down the sidewalks, greeting one another with a warm smile and wave. There were people of all ethnicity, some dressed in traditional garb, others in formal *normal* clothes, and even others in jeans and t-shirts like Bobby. A hint of sugar was in the air.

Bobby chose to go left on the road and followed a stream of people. Two men, one red-haired with freckles and another wearing a turban walked in front of him. Bobby caught a few words of their conversation. The men seemed to be discussing a political situation in Jerusalem. The man in the turban shared his fears regarding strong government influence. The other man agreed and replied with, "We're lucky that we don't have to worry about that here." The two men shared a quick hug before the red headed man stopped at what seemed to be a bus station.

The man in the turban continued walking. He waved at what appeared to be an Indian man before heading into a tall building that resembled a vintage European church. "Where am I?" Bobby muttered to himself.

Each building he passed seemed to have been plucked from a different part of the world. White sandy structures stood next to sleek, tall glass buildings bordered with metal frames. Down the street, Bobby could see a brownstone planted next to what could only be described as a tree house. On the other side was a ranch style home. Bobby spotted horses traversing a large pen to the right side of the property. A quiet whooshing sound brought Bobby's attention to the above ground subway station. He remained perplexed.

"Good day, mate!" A young Australian man wearing a cowboy hat and white tee shirt said to Bobby.

Bobby grabbed his arm. "Excuse me, sir. Where am I?"

"You're on Unity Avenue. Where are you looking to go?"

Bobby rephrased his question. "What country am I in?"

The Australian laughed. "We got rid of countries a long time ago." A smooth silver train pulled up to a group of benches located next to the track. "Excuse me. I've got to go."

"Excuse me, mate." A short Australian woman with long blond hair walked past Bobby.

Bobby stepped off the sidewalk and stood under the shade of a tall eucalyptus tree hovering over the path. A river snaked across a patch of grassland to the east of him. Bobby realized that he was standing on a large cobblestone bridge that brought the two sides of the street together. The train was firmly planted on the other side of the road and in front of what seemed like a large university.

Australia is beautiful! Or what I think is Australia. Bobby thought. He didn't know much about Australia, so he took everything in as it came. Never before had he seen such a clean environment around him. The warm, crisp air felt good in his lungs. Everyone walking around him seemed so happy. Bobby clutched his backpack straps tightly and smiled to himself. He really liked this new place.

After walking around for some time, Bobby took a rest on a wooden bench in front of a completely glass building. The sun was still in the East. *It must be morning,* he thought. As he sat down and watched numerous people walk by, a familiar face passed him—Sabrina. Bobby figured that she knew Jonathan, Aunt Meg's alien captor, very well. Befriending her meant getting closer to finding his aunt.

Bobby shot up to his feet and caught up to Sabrina. "Hi, I'm sorry to bother you, but I'm new here, and I need some help finding things."

Sabrina gave Bobby a full grin. "New to Sydney? Sure thing! Where are you from?"

Bobby froze for a moment. "I'm, uh, from the country. I live in the woods. I've never been into the city before." *That should work. I hope.*

Sabrina patted his back. "I remember my first trip here. I got lost for a full day." She looked down the street. "There's a coffee shop down the road here. Why don't we grab a cup, and I can draw you a map."

121

Bobby smiled. "Thanks." This was a great place to start. Sabrina seemed to have an important role within the alien's hierarchy. Bobby hoped that she could lead him to Aunt Meg.

Sabrina and Bobby walked leisurely to the coffee shop, a wooden building with large windows. As they travelled, Bobby had trouble convincing himself that these people were aliens. They looked and talked just like he did. Besides, his current location resembled some place on Earth for sure. *Maybe I was mistaken about the whole alien thing.*

The smell of fresh-roasted coffee and baked pastries hit Bobby hard. Sabrina treated him to a low-fat whipped coffee drink complete with cinnamon and a shot of vitamins. Bobby's mouth watered at the double-baked chocolate brownies with chocolate almond butter frosting and a dash of minerals. "Do you want one?" Sabrina asked. Bobby nodded, so she added two to her order.

When it came time to pay, Sabrina pressed her palm to a key pad and grabbed the items. Bobby glanced at the keypad, trying to figure out its function. A small red laser scanned the person's palm and seemed to deposit the funds into the register. Bobby looked down at his palm, curious to place it against the scanner to see how it would be read. Before he could test the machine, Sabrina tugged his arm, sat down at a small wooden table and waited for Bobby to take a seat. He sat down across from her and placed his backpack next to him.

"Have you ever had one of these brownies before?" Sabrina asked as she took a satisfying bite.

"No." Bobby took a bite and enjoyed the sweet pastry. The light fluffy texture of the brownie was filling but not too heavy. "This is probably the best brownie I've ever had in my life." He said with his mouth partly full.

Sabrina laughed. "I've always liked this place the best." She sipped her coffee and laughed. "I got so caught up in our conversation that I forgot to get your name."

Bobby put his hand out for a handshake. "Bobby."

"Sabrina." Sabrina wrapped her hand around his and gave it a good shake. "What brings you into the city? Are you here to look into the University?"

Bobby nodded. "Yes. I'm thinking about attending in the fall."

Sabrina scrunched her eyebrows. "Why wait that long?"

Bobby was trapped. He thought hard about a clever response. "What's the normal school cycle?"

Sabrina let out a hearty laugh. "You really are from the country. You can set your own schedule, silly." Bobby grinned and nodded. "What program are you thinking of doing?"

"Exploration or something like that. What do you do?" He asked.

"I work on the Universe Initiative. I tried the Exploration team and travelled around for a few years until I found an opening in the lab. Have you ever thought about trying your hand at the Universe?"

Bobby sipped his drink slowly. "I'm not one hundred percent familiar with the Universe. What is that?"

Sabrina laughed. "You must be living under a rock." She pulled out a sheet of paper from her purse. "Come by the lab tomorrow afternoon at 3:00 PM, and I'll show you. In the meantime, here is a map of the city." She drew several streets and buildings Bobby would want to visit. Sabrina told Bobby about all her favorite places in the city and made recommendations of places for him to go.

As she spoke, Bobby secretly calculated the time difference between Boston and Australia. "I'm busy tomorrow afternoon. Can I come by in the morning? Around this time?"

Sabrina looked at her watch. "It's going on 9:00 o'clock right now. Let's say 9:00 tomorrow morning."

Bobby concurred. They continued chatting until Sabrina had to leave for a meeting. She said goodbye to Bobby and headed down the road. Bobby followed Sabrina a short way but lost her in the sea of people. With the map in his hand, Bobby ventured into the city to see what he could find out about these strange yet normal people he was encountering. Once complete, he would continue his search for Aunt Meg.

His first stop was at the museum. The building, made of glass and steel, housed years of evolution for what seemed to represent the human race. Bobby waltzed into the large main room full of icons including combustion engine cars, electric cars, shrines to different men and women, innovations in science and other technological advancements. Bobby first stopped at a large globe suspended from the vaulted ceiling.

He read the plaque. *Our goal is simple. Our focus is to create a world that is hospitable for everyone. Our mission is to help mankind evolve into a better species.* Bobby smirked as he thought, *Nice goal. Good luck with that.*

Bobby headed left toward a glass case covering several science models. Each model showed the transition between past samples and present day, improved samples. The first sample was soil. The second sample was water. Each sample of both soil and water showed how decreasing the use of toxins and pollutants provided better air, water, and soil quality. The plaque read *The Universe Initiative has helped us understand the importance of using biodegradable materials and resisting the use of pesticides. Because of this project, you can feel safe drinking and eating anything around you.*

Bobby moved on to another casing with mannequins holding hands, one was a black Muslim and the other a Hispanic priest—*Freedom of Thought and Mind. Our society has revolutionized the ideas and beliefs around religion and religious persecution. By understanding the crusades of various religions, The Universe has helped us develop a way for us to live in harmony without any uniformed belief system.* Bobby nodded. With the amount of religion-orientated warfare circling around the world, Bobby agreed with the idea of eliminating religion-related thinking from the general caucus.

Bobby was thrilled with what he was seeing. This group of enlightened individuals were not aliens, but merely a collection of people who wanted to make a difference. He continued on his path to the next exhibit—*warfare.* A mural of men and women laying down their weapons on the battlefield stretched across the wall. *By examining the effects of conflict on humanity, we have created a perfect utopia. We have overcome the need for warfare amongst one another as a means to solve complex issues.*

At the end of his tour, Bobby stopped at the final destination—*the Ministry.* Three men and two women stood arm to arm, wearing black suits. They ranged in age and nationality. *The Ministry has worked in the best interest of our people for over fifty years. We should rejoice in their tireless efforts for the betterment of our people. It is only through the Ministry that we find guidance and the support needed to make our society operate at its full potential. Thank the Ministry every day. If it weren't for them, we wouldn't have the world we enjoy so much.*

Bobby smiled as he headed out of the museum and back to the street. He had to share his finding with Nicole. Bobby found a secluded place behind a brick building. Once alone, he placed the golden crown on his head and closed his eyes, eager to share his good news with his sister.

CHAPTER 15: RULES

"So how was it?" Nicole asked as Bobby landed back on his bed.

He pulled the golden crown from his head. "Nicole, you wouldn't believe what I saw! I had the best coffee and brownies with someone from the lab. Her name is Sabrina, and she told me so many things about this place. She is the lady I saw the last time I was there. The food is wonderful. The air is perfect, and they've solved every single problem that's ever hit the face of the earth!" Bobby stopped talking long enough to take a breath. "I went to this museum and read up on these people."

"So are they aliens or what?" Nicole asked.

"I think they're human. And the place may have been Australia. I'm not sure. Anyways, they are the most civilized and the nicest people I've ever come across."

Nicole put up her hands. "What about Aunt Meg? The reason you went over there was to get her back! Did you find anything out?"

"Sabrina works with Jonathan. I think he's the one responsible for what happened to Aunt Meg. I tried to follow Sabrina to see if she was meeting with him, but I lost her in the crowd. After that, I figured I could spend the rest of my time at the museum learning about these people. You know, to make sure they weren't a direct threat."

Nicole punched Bobby's arm. "You know where Jonathan's office is, you goof! You could have waited for him!"

"And what was I supposed to say? Give me back my aunt, you crazy alien? He has the home court advantage—we have to tread lightly, Nicole." Bobby snapped his fingers. "Sabrina asked me to come by the lab tomorrow morning. I can do some digging once I go back." Bobby headed to his computer to look up the time difference between Boston and Australia.

Nicole grabbed the golden crown from his hands. "I don't know, Bobby. You and your ADD haven't gotten us too far. Maybe I should go instead."

"No, I can do it." Bobby took the crown back. "Besides, they expect me there tomorrow. If you show up, it might spook everyone."

"All right, I'll let you go back, but Bobby, you need to be smart. No more distractions!" Nicole said.

The door knob jingled. Loud knocking made the siblings jump. Bobby tucked the crown under his pillow and unlocked the door. "Come in," he said. Kenny came into the room. Nicole ran her hands through her hair, motioning to Bobby to address Kenny.

"Say something to him so he doesn't think we're being weird." Nicole said in a loud whisper.

Kenny threw his backpack on his bed and spied Bobby looking nervous. "You guys okay? You look on edge."

Bobby cleared his throat. "Yeah, just a family thing."

Kenny nodded. "So, ah, what was up with your sudden departure from the library?"

Bobby looked over at Nicole. She pretended to read a textbook. Bobby ran his hands down his face. "Nothing. Just needed to spend some time with my sister."

Kenny slapped Bobby's back. "Well, hang in there, brother." He jumped on his bed and propped his head up with his backpack. "Nicole, you came up here from Tempe to visit Bobby?"

"Is it a crime to visit your family?" She snapped.

"No, not at all." Kenny said, his voice cracking. "It just seems a little out of the blue."

Bobby's shoulders tensed up. Nicole approached Kenny's bed. "You shouldn't be concerned with things that have nothing to do with you."

Bobby got between the two. "Look guys, this is not something to fight about." He linked arms with Nicole. "Kenny, we're kinda in the middle of something that's really important. Can you give us a minute to finish it up?"

Kenny sat up straight. "Bobby, you look upset. Are you sure that everything's cool, man?"

Nicole put her hand up. "He's fine. Now find something else to do for a minute!" She relaxed her face. "Please?"

Kenny glanced in Bobby's direction. Bobby gave him a thin smile. Kenny slowly climbed off his bed and grabbed his backpack. "I guess I'll go *back* to the library." He headed toward the door. With his hand on the door knob he turned back to face Bobby. "Hey, Bobby, whatever it is that you're doing I hope it works out."

Bobby watched Kenny leave the room. The moment the door shut, he turned to Nicole. "Why were you so rude to him?" he asked.

She plopped down on his bed. "He was asking too many questions." She pulled the pillow back, unveiling the golden crown. "Besides, we can't risk anyone finding out about our treasure." Nicole marveled over the crown for several minutes. Her strange possessive behavior made Bobby really uncomfortable.

Bobby picked up the crown and hid it under a pile of clothes in his closet. She folded her arms. "Nicole, we should take a break from using the crown until we fully understand its power."

She rolled her eyes. "What do you mean by that?"

"I can't just throw the crown on my head and travel to this other world whenever I want. I think we should be more thoughtful and responsible with it."

Nicole was quiet. "Then we should make a set of rules for crown usage." She pulled out a pad of paper and a pen from her purse. "Rule number one, no travelling to Australia unless there is a specific mission that we both have agreed upon." She wrote down the rule.

Bobby nodded. "Rule number two, until we can figure out exactly where this other place is, no mentioning of our own world."

She paused. "Did you say anything about our world to this Sabrina woman?"

"No. I told her I lived in the woods."

Nicole laughed at his remark while writing the information down. "Rule number three, right now our main focus is to rescue Aunt Meg. If either one of us travels to Australia, or wherever it is you went, we have to go in and save her."

"Rule number four, no bringing anyone back with you except for Aunt Meg," Bobby added and Nicole recorded.

"Rule number five, no travelling to the other side unless one of us is present in the room when said person uses the crown." Nicole looked up at Bobby. "We can't run the risk of either one of us being trapped over there without the other's knowledge."

Bobby scratched his jaw. "How does that work, anyway?" Nicole paused and raised an eyebrow, implying that she didn't understand his question. "I mean, what do you do if I don't come back? How do I know how long I've been gone?"

"That's a good question." Nicole chewed on her pen cap. "How do we even know how long you were gone?"

Bobby thought things through. "It was evening when I left here and morning there. I felt like I was gone for an hour or two."

Nicole nodded. "That seems about right. Maybe an hour and a half."

An idea popped into Bobby's head. "So it's safe to say I was in Australia which means I should be able to use the timer on my phone to keep track of my time over there. I'll set it for an hour, and you do the same. When the phone rings, I know it's time to teleport back."

Nicole slapped his back. "Good thinking, little brother." She penned the information down. Once she had completed her task, Nicole set her notebook on the bed and rose to her feet. She climbed into Bobby's closet and yanked the golden crown from his pile of clothes. "The final rule. We both have to travel to Australia at least once. Since you've already been there twice, it's my turn."

Nicole sat down on the bed again and held the crown high above her head. Bobby planted his hand on top of her fluffy mane. "Nicole, I don't think that's a great idea."

"Why not? You've been there twice, and I haven't gone once." She shook her head back and forth until Bobby dropped his hand. "Besides I'm older, so I get to call the shots."

"This isn't a ride at an amusement park. If you don't know what you're doing, who knows where you'll end up?" Bobby said, worried about Nicole's wellbeing.

She shrugged. "It doesn't matter where you go, as long as you come back here, right?"

"That's not the way to look at it," Bobby protested.

Nicole dropped her arms down and placed the crown in her lap. "Bobby, you've been the only one having all the adventures with this thing. I disobeyed our parent's order and lied to them so *we* could hike through Bell Rock and find your precious crown. You owe me!"

Bobby sat quietly for a moment, reflecting on Nicole's words. She was right, if it weren't for her cooperation, he wouldn't have been able to capture the golden crown. This simple truth was unarguable, but he couldn't get past the fear of Nicole being in Australia alone—or not coming back. What if she got stuck over there? What if these people were actually hostile? Bobby couldn't leave either scenario to chance.

Nicole narrowed her eyes at him and clenched the crown tightly in her hands. She was feisty and strong, she could handle herself. It was inevitable—Bobby wouldn't be able to keep her from taking the trip.

"You're right. We're in this together. Part of us being in this means we both get to experience this strange world. So put on the crown."

Nicole didn't waste any time. She placed the golden crown above her head and took a deep breath. Lowering it slowly, she closed her eyes and waited to be transported. Bobby bit his fingernails and suffered from a mixture of fear and excitement for her. Both waited for several minutes before Nicole opened her eyes. She pulled the golden crown from her head and looked at it.

"I don't understand. Why doesn't it work?" she asked Bobby.

He placed the crown back on her head. "You have to open your mind and meditate. Once your thoughts are clear it'll transport you."

She followed his directions and closed her eyes. Bobby sat quietly and waited. Several minutes passed before she opened her eyes again. "Why doesn't it work?"

Bobby shrugged. "I have no idea."

"It doesn't make any sense." She pulled the crown off her head. "That weird Sedona guy used it and transported without any problems. Why am I the only one it doesn't work for?"

Bobby smiled. "Maybe it works like a genie in a bottle. What if I'm the crown's master because I found it before you did?" he joked.

Nicole didn't seem in the mood for comedy. Bobby figured that she felt left out of the adventure. She placed the golden crown in Bobby's lap. "I checked into a hotel room close to here. How about we go to dinner now so I can head to my room?"

Bobby picked up on her frustration right away. He nodded in response to her question and put his hands on top of hers. "Nicole, I'm sure you'll figure it out. And we'll keep working on it until you get a chance to go over there."

She gave him a weak smile and rose to her feet. Nicole headed for the door, and Bobby walked up next to her.

"Hide the crown before Kenny sees it." She said before exiting the room.

Bobby walked back over to his bed and picked up the golden crown. "What is your deal? Why didn't you let Nicole transport?" He paused, waiting for a response or flash of light. "Why do I seem like the only one able to travel between these two worlds?" Bobby realized he was having a conversation with an inanimate object and came to his senses. He tucked it away underneath his pile of clothes.

***

Bobby and Nicole headed over to a burger joint and caught up.

"I've loaded up on several classes, so I can finish my undergraduate and go straight to the graduate program," Nicole said, taking a bite of her burger.

Bobby dunked a fry into ketchup. "College is hard. I'm dying with my course load."

"Well, that's what your first year is like. You'll get into the groove of things next year."

Bobby nodded and ate his fry. "That Sabrina lady asked if I thought about joining the Exploration team."

"What's the Exploration team?"

"I'm not sure. I assume she'll tell me more about it tomorrow."

Nicole put her burger down. "Bobby, what if we were wrong about this place? What if these people are actual aliens?"

Bobby shook his head. "I got a really good look at them. They're not aliens."

"How can you know for sure?"

He paused. "I don't know how to explain it. They seemed like a group of smart, enlightened, and forward thinking individuals. They don't live within the confines of a complex government trying to take over their lives. They don't have war, religion, pollution, illness, or any of those things. These people embrace respect for others and working together as a strong unit."

Nicole nodded. "We need some of that over here. I mean, look at what's going on in our world today. That crazy virus that spread across Africa and the Middle East. The continuous conflicts between North and South Korea. Deadly earthquakes and tsunamis. The world's falling apart." She took another bite of her burger. Juice spilled down her chin.

Bobby sat back in the booth and admired his sister. Having Nicole at MIT with him seemed to ease the crown situation. "I'm happy you're here." Bobby thought about his family. Aunt Meg came to mind. "Nicole, what if Aunt Meg's happy over there?"

"What?"

He leaned in. "All the research we've done points to Aunt Meg willingly going over to the other side. What if she wants to stay over there?"

Nicole moved her food to the side and leaned in too. "It doesn't matter. We have a right to know what happened to her." She grabbed a fry and covered it in ketchup. "Tomorrow we find out the real story." She popped the fry in her mouth and gave Bobby a wink.

CHAPTER 16: THE TRUTH WON'T ALWAYS SET YOU FREE

The next morning Bobby waited impatiently for Nicole to arrive. His timing couldn't be more perfect—Kenny was in class and Bobby didn't have a class until much later. He felt lucky for a moment but dismissed it quickly. Bobby still wasn't entirely sure about the time zones. He hoped that his guesstimates were close enough.

Someone knocked on the door. *Finally!* He thought. When he opened the door, a frown covered his face. Both Kenny and Nicole were standing in the hallway. Bobby's heart started beating loudly as he desperately thought through different ways to get Kenny out of his room.

"Kenny, why did you knock?" Bobby asked.

Nicole spoke first. "He forgot his key!" she turned to Kenny. "Listen, Bobby and I need the room for the next hour or so."

Kenny looked her straight in the eyes. "This room doesn't belong to you." Bobby knew Kenny well enough to know that he was annoyed. "Normally, I'd let Bobby have his privacy, but I don't like you. Now please leave!" He put his backpack down on the bed.

Nicole folded her arms. "Look, I'm sorry for how I acted yesterday.

Bobby sped up the process. "Nicole is my older sister; therefore she's allowed to boss me around on occasion. And since she's older than you, she feels entitled to play big sister to you as well." He peeked at the clock. "With that being said, I hope you'll let her behavior slide."

Kenny folded his arms. "Not a chance, Bobby! I'm not leaving until you clue me in on your big secret."

Panic set in. Bobby took several deep breaths. It was time to bring out the big guns. "If you give us the next two hours in the room, I'll buy you pizza for a week." Kenny didn't budge. Bobby sweetened the deal. "I'll buy pizza for a week, and I'll let you photocopy my notes."

Kenny quietly deliberated for another minute. Nicole opened her mouth, but Bobby motioned for her to be quiet. Kenny cleared his throat. "Add wings, and we got a deal."

"Done!" Bobby shouted.

Bobby helped Kenny pack up his things. "Bobby, I just want in on your secret."

Bobby looked over at the clock "Let's talk about it some other day, buddy." He pushed Kenny out the door before slamming it shut and locking it.

Nicole had beaten him to the closet and retrieved the crown. She shoved it in his hands. "Set your alarm for one hour once you get there." She started to put the crown on Bobby's head, but he stopped her.

"Wait, what if the tour takes longer?" he asked while he put on his backpack. Nicole had already shoved the golden crown on Bobby's head. He was off before she could answer.

Much to his surprise, Bobby landed in an alley next to Jonathan's office building. No one saw him. He pulled the crown off his head, set his alarm, and placed the crown into his backpack. Bobby took a much-needed deep breath and headed for the office.

He stepped inside and was greeted by a short blonde lady with perfect teeth and a tidy white lab coat. Bobby explained to the front desk attendant that he had a meeting with Sabrina at nine o'clock.

The female attendant smiled. "Right on time." Bobby hid his shock. The woman picked up the phone. "I'll call Sabrina and see if she's ready for you." She motioned for Bobby to take a seat in a black chair close to the glass wall.

"Thank you." Bobby replied. He relaxed in his chair and watched the woman carefully as she said a few simple words into the phone.

She placed the receiver down and smiled at him. "She'll be right out."

Bobby took advantage of the moment. "Is Jonathan in?"

The woman frowned. "Not yet. Can I offer you a bottle of water?"

"No, I'm good." Bobby put his hands on his bag and scanned the room. Unlike most offices, the four walls surrounding him had no pictures or paintings. Everything seemed sterile and slightly cold with only a few *Innovator of the Year* awards to break up the monotony. A world peace poster encased in a brass frame hung on the wall behind the receptionist. Bobby noticed that the room was completely still. Unlike most office buildings he had visited, no one raced back and forth from the door to the hallway.

A few minutes passed, and Sabrina emerged from the hallway. Her hair was pinned back, and her white lab coat was immaculate.

"Bobby, it is very nice to see you again. I'm glad you were able to make it." She walked over to greet him.

Bobby threw his backpack over one shoulder, stood, and extended his hand to shake Sabrina's. "Thank you so much for allowing me to tour this place. I'm excited!" His enthusiasm was genuine. Yes, he was on a mission to find Aunt Meg, but Bobby wanted to learn more about this other world while he was at it.

Sabrina gave him a firm handshake and smiled. "You look exactly how I did when I walked through that door for the first time. I was about your age." Her mood changed to reflect fondness. "I was so young and unsure of what I'd do with the rest of my life. I knew I wanted to do something special, but I wasn't sure exactly how far that would take me. Then I landed here."

Bobby nodded. "Well, hopefully I'll learn a few things that will change my life."

Sabrina's eyes met his. Her mood had shifted again, but Bobby couldn't tell exactly what it was. "We're always looking for the right people to join our fantastic team." She leaned in. "There is something special about you, Bobby. I could tell the moment we first met."

Bobby felt out of place. He couldn't quite describe what he was experiencing, but it was unlike anything he had ever felt before. Sabrina's intrigue with Bobby gave him a sub-human feeling. It almost felt like Sabrina was...studying him, like he was an experiment. He brushed it off. She motioned to the hallway. "Shall we get started?"

Bobby nodded and followed her. He held onto his backpack strap tightly as they walked past several offices and rooms. "Everything seems so neat here. You must have an awesome cleaning crew."

Sabrina grinned. "We take cleanliness very seriously around here. It makes a difference between a good experiment and a great one."

Bobby looked over the glass walls. "How many labs do you have?"

"We have a total of thirteen. We only have time to tour one lab today." She stopped in front of a door. "This door will lead us to my boss's office. The lab where we conduct our Universe experiments in on the other side."

Sabrina swiped her hand across a black pad with a red dot. Once the dot turned green, she held the door open for Bobby. He recognized the office immediately from his past trips to the other side. Once he entered, she closed the door tightly. She motioned for Bobby to take a seat in a chair across from Jonathan's high back chair. As both parties sat down, she pulled out a stack of documents. Bobby swallowed hard. "Do I have to read all those?"

She shook her head. "No, Bobby. The only thing I need from you is a signature and your name printed on the last page." Sabrina flipped the stack over and removed the very last page. She reached back into the desk and placed a silver pen on top of the paper. "Bobby, what I'm about to show you is highly classified. This information is being used to promote life and sustainability for our entire race. Because of the important and fragile nature of our work, we ask that anyone touring our lab sign this agreement. Upon signing this agreement you are promising to keep anything you see a secret from others."

Bobby's shoulders tensed up. The hairs stood up on the back of his neck. "If it's so classified, why are you giving tours, especially to someone like me?"

Sabrina looked into his nervous eyes. "We're looking for interns to volunteer in our lab from time to time. If you like what you see, maybe you'll apply once an opening comes up."

Bobby was intrigued. "How often do you have openings?"

"We don't have formal job openings, if that's what you mean. The Ministry has a way of knowing who is an ideal candidate, and who is not. If I think someone would fit well in the lab, I let my boss, Ambassador Jonathan Lewis, know and he takes it from there. I can tell by your intent to learn that you are a prime candidate for this line of work."

Bobby looked down at the sheet of paper. The text was extremely small, making it impossible to read. Bobby wished that Gordy, Kim or Nicole would have been there to help him make the proper decision. On the other hand, Bobby was happy he had entered into this journey alone. Never before had an opportunity such as this one come into his life. He took a deep breath and grabbed the pen. Sabrina smiled and waited for him to sign the page.

"Will I be able to meet the Councilman?" Bobby asked.

"He's got a deadline coming up. I haven't seen him much so I don't know."

He gripped the pen tightly. A rush of nerves washed over his body. He put the pen down. "I can't do this."

Sabrina frowned. "What is the matter?"

Bobby shook his head. "It just doesn't feel right." He held on to the crown inside his backpack.

Sabrina pulled the paper back toward her. "I don't understand. My intuition is never wrong."

Bobby lowered his head and meditated on her words and his fear. Even though he didn't want to believe it, something inside him was slightly worried that he had fallen into a trap. What if they were aliens and this was all just a rouse to take over his world? Bobby didn't want to be responsible for endangering all of mankind.

"The first time I was in that chair, I had the same feelings you did." Sabrina muttered.

Bobby looked up at her. "What feelings are those?"

"Fear. Worry. I felt like I was in over my head. But then I realized that everyone probably felt that same way when they came into this office."

Bobby looked back down at the paper. Pushing his apprehensions to the side, Bobby released his bag and grabbed the pen. He reached across the desk and signed his name. Sabrina smiled and took the pen from his hand. "You are making a great choice, Bobby..." she looked down at the sheet, "Walker. You won't regret it." Sabrina put the papers and the pen back in Jonathan's desk.

"Now what?" Bobby asked.

Sabrina stood to her feet and motioned to Bobby to do the same. "I would like you to turn and face the door please."

Slowly, Bobby turned away and complied with Sabrina's request. He heard a number of things as Sabrina seemed to move about the office. Without receiving permission, Bobby turned back toward the wall and watched the secret entrance to the lab appear. He was awestruck. "That is the coolest thing I've ever seen." He walked around the desk.

Sabrina stopped him. "I'm sorry Bobby, but you're going to have to leave your book bag here. We can't run the risk of anything contaminating our workstations."

Bobby froze momentarily. She waited for him to put the bag down. He contemplated telling a lie, but settled on the truth. "All my most valued possessions are in this bag."

She shook her head. "I understand, but we have rules, and those rules must be followed at all times. Don't worry, this is my boss Jonathan's office—your bag will be safe."

Bobby's heart skipped a beat. "Can you put it somewhere safe?" he asked. "I don't want someone to take it."

She opened the bottom draw of the desk. "Here, let's place it in the drawer." Bobby slowly and carefully put the bag down, making sure the crown didn't make a sound. Sabrina locked the drawer and faced the entryway. "Are you ready?" she asked.

He nodded. Clenching his fist, he took his very first step into the lab.

***

Nicole paced the room nervously, wanting to jump through the portal and see where Bobby had gone. Her phone vibrated on the bed. She answered it without looking at the caller ID. "Hey Bobby, where are you?"

"It's not Bobby, it's Faja. How are you?" Gordy asked.

"Good." Nicole said stiffly.

"So your mom and I realized something the other day. Bobby turned eighteen a couple months ago and we didn't take that trip up to Sedona to Bell Rock so he could finally get that creepy crown. As much as I'd hate to reunite him with that thing, a promise is a promise. We were thinking of going the weekend after Bobby comes home for winter vacation."

Nicole chewed on her lip. She glanced at the time on her phone. Bobby would be back any minute. She wrapped up her phone call. "That sounds great, Faja. Listen, I gotta pee like a race horse! I'll give you a call later, and we can talk about it then." She disconnected the call right as her alarm went off.

Nicole was at her wits end. Bobby reappeared back on his bed with the crown tilted on his head. "We've got a problem, Bobby." She said as she braced herself against the door.

CHAPTER 17: NO RELIGION AND FLOATING PLANES

Bobby removed the crown from his head. "You'll never guess what I saw!"

"Faja and Mom want to take us up to Sedona to find the golden crown." Nicole said.

"We'll have to talk about that later. I've got something to tell you." Bobby headed for the closet with the crown in hand. Shoveling through several boxes and clothes, he hid the crown in a shoebox and threw several pairs of jeans on top of the box. He looked at the clock. "Kenny will be back soon. We should go to the library and talk about my trip."

Nicole agreed and they headed out. They took up residence in the same dusty corner of the library as the day before. "So, tell me all about it."

Bobby started at the very beginning; the moment the filing cabinets shifted.

***

Sabrina stepped into the lab and waited for Bobby to follow. He looked from side to side and slowly stepped through the opening and into the room. Several observers moved quickly from station to station, staring at TV screens, taking notes, and then moving on to the next station. Sabrina walked over to a large white cabinet and pulled out a lab coat. She handed it to Bobby. "If you're gonna be in here, you might as well look the part."

Bobby put his arms through the coat and pulled it around his body, feeling empowered. "What is all this?"

"This is the Universe." Sabrina walked over to the first station and grabbed two tablets. She handed one to Bobby. "This room is the life blood of our people." She powered on her tablet and did the same for Bobby. "Everything you see here is used to help us understand our people and how to better our world."

The screen flashed white for a few seconds before the words war, illness, religion, science, and a few others popped up. Sabrina tapped on the word *War.* She stepped up to the first station and looked into the little box. Bobby peeked into the box as well. A small picture of the earth spinning slowly appeared.

"How does this work?" Bobby asked.

"It's rather simple. We use these stations to observe the results of predictions we have made. On the tablet you can key in phrases like 'Ebola epidemic' or 'North Korea nuclear threat'. Once you put that information in and press the green button, a sample of test subjects affected by these issues will appear on the screen. We study these subjects based on several factors related to the given topic.

For example, let's look at nuclear war. War starts with some sort of conflict. We begin our experiment by looking at the conflicts that the test subjects are participating in. The next step is forming a hypothesis based on what we predict the likely outcome will be. This hypothesis is then tested in the field by examining the subjects as they make their decisions.

Let's say someone inside the conflict decides to use nuclear war to mitigate the problem. Once that decision is made, we'll monitor the situation until we reach the final outcome. In the end, the final outcome is recorded and our data is then discussed amongst our world's leadership. Our leadership will then make the necessary adjustments in our society so we are not affected by these problems."

Bobby leaned in close to the station. "Who exactly are the test subjects?"

"Everyone in the Universe." She pointed to the entire globe. "We watch them all on a daily basis."

"Do they know someone is watching them?"

Sabrina shook her head. "No."

Bobby's stomach was unsettled. Things weren't looking good. "Where do the subjects come from?"

"They are born, just like us. They live everyday just like we do. They have hopes and dreams too. They are just as human as we are."

Bobby's imagination kicked into high gear. "So, it's like we're their keepers?"

"Not at all, Bobby. They are free to live whatever lives they want. Our only goal is to observe them."

Bobby felt a tiny bit better. "I guess that's not so bad."

Sabrina flipped through pages in her tablet until she reached a page with a chart. "These experiments have changed our lives. Remember the drinks and brownies we had yesterday?" Bobby nodded. "Well, we found a way to add vitamins and minerals to everything in our diets by experimenting with Universe test subjects. Now we can enjoy our favorite treats and still have long life spans and healthier lives while still enjoying some of the good things in life."

"That's great." Bobby said. "Who would have thought to add vitamins and minerals to brownies to make them healthy?"

"That's just the tip of the iceberg. The reason we've learned how to fight obesity, cure cancer and prevent it all are examples of great things we have accomplished through the Universe Initiative. The reason you country folk have it so good is because of projects like this."

Bobby thought back to his trip through the museum. He approached the second station. "So each station studies a different topic?"

"Exactly. Here, I'll show you." Sabrina tapped Bobby's tablet several times until the main page showed. She tapped on *Religion*. She moved the cursor down the page until she landed on *Eastern religions verses Western religions*. "Bobby, you understand how much division can come with religion, right?"

"I'm not much of a religious person," he admitted.

"That's quite all right most of us these days are not very religious. We have studied this topic for many years ourselves and have come up with a similar conclusion." She typed in, *Controversy over the separation of church and state* then pressed enter. "By pressing this button I'll be able to examine a conflict among groups who believe that religion is a part of government. My objective is to see how both parties can come up with a reasonable solution."

"If you wanted to, could you create a new religion?"

"Yes, I could." Sabrina said confidently.

Bobby frowned. "I thought you said your main focus is to observe, not interfere."

Sabrina laughed. "We're not allowed to interact with the test subjects, however, we do have the ability to add and subtract elements from the Universe. I don't see it as interfering but rather as making a suggestion or pushing the test subject in a certain direction."

Bobby pondered her answer. "It sounds like you can control them if you want."

"You're open to your own opinion, Bobby," Sabrina replied. "Now, back to the observations. Our hypothesis, observations, and predictions are put through a series of theories called *substantial directives*. There are three phases of these directives: pre-work, current work, and post-work.

Pre-work is when we pick a topic, form our hypothesis, and gather our sample of test subjects. Current work is the phase where we observe the test subjects. Post-work is the final phase. This is the point when we make our assumptions and send our results to the Ministry for review and possible implementation throughout our world."

Bobby simply nodded. "That sounds like a lot of work."

"It is, but the work is well worth it. Take religion for example. By studying the way religion affects the test subjects, we decided it was best to no longer have any formal religion or religious creed for people to follow. Each person is allowed to believe whatever they like, but this is why we no longer have any mass religions telling us how to live our lives each day."

"And everyone is okay with that?" Bobby asked skeptically.

Sabrina smiled. "Absolutely. We all have the same moral code and law that helps us manage our lives. We respect one another and are encouraged to think openly about everything. Isn't it like that in the part of the woods you come from?" Sabrina moved away from *Religion*. Before Bobby could answer she continued. "Bobby pick a topic."

Bobby scanned the different topics, stopping on *Aviation*. He clicked on *Traveling*. "I've always had this theory that if they made a plane entirely out of the same material as the black box, no one would die."

"No one, including the test subjects, has figured that one out yet." Sabrina chuckled while she pressed on a few buttons until a command screen appeared. "If you were an observer, what type of hypothesis and observation would you like to explore?"

Bobby typed a few words into the tablet. "I'd have the Phoenix Sky Harbor airport shut down after a 747 missed its

landing and ended up in Tempe Town Lake and see how
people reacted."

Sabrina paused. "Bobby, that's oddly specific. How did
you know such a place existed?"

"Cause he's brilliant." A deep voice answered from the
other side of the lab.

Bobby turned around and came face-to-face with a man.
Jonathan, the man who took my Aunt Meg, He thought.
Bobby was hit with a wave of anger and fear. Act natural. He
quickly placed the tablet down on the station and put out his
hand. "Bobby."

Jonathan shook Bobby's hand. "Mr..."

"Just call me, Jonathan, please." Jonathan interrupted as
he shook Bobby's hand. He picked up Bobby's tablet and
keyed in a string of words before mashing the green button.
"We shall see how the Phoenicians handle a floating aircraft
in the desert." Sabrina remained quiet.

Bobby's phone beeped. He took off his lab coat and
handed it to Sabrina. "I'm sorry, I must go back."

"Back?" Jonathan asked. "Back where?"

"Home," Bobby stammered. "My ride is waiting for me."
He headed to the opening and waited for the filing cabinets
to open. Jonathan and Sabrina followed.

"Bobby, I overheard your questions and let me just say,
you are one of the most inquisitive students we've had in the
lab." Jonathan pressed several buttons on the wall and the
cabinets began to part.

"Thanks." Bobby walked through the opening and
headed for the office door.

"Bobby! You almost forgot your backpack!" Sabrina
called after him. She opened the desk drawer and handed the
bag to Jonathan. He paused and looked up at Bobby, his face
straight. "Boy this has got a ton of books in it." Bobby's heart
raced. Jonathan smiled. "Or is it filled with bricks?"

Bobby put his hand out. "No, just my school books."

Jonathan studied Bobby for a moment. "Are you considering joining the Universe Initiative? We could use someone like you."

"I'm not sure," Bobby answered shyly.

Jonathan placed the bag in Bobby's hand. "Perhaps you'll come back and see what happened to the plane?"

"Sure." Bobby gave Jonathan and Sabrina a weak smile before heading out of the office and down the hall. Once he hit the sidewalk, Bobby started running at full speed until he reached a deserted area. He threw the crown on his head and took a few breaths. The next thing he saw was Nicole.

***

Nicole didn't say a word, which never happened. Bobby waved his hands in her face. "Nicole, are you listening?"

She blinked a few times. "So they're not really aliens, but more like other humans who study us?"

Bobby shrugged. "I don't think they study us per se. It seems like they study a group of people that are similar to us. Maybe they study a subset of humans people somewhere in our world?"

"There's only one way to find out." Nicole pulled out her phone and searched Google for any articles regarding a plane floating in Tempe Town Lake. Before she pressed *enter*, Gordy had sent a text with a picture of a Boeing 747 half submerged in the manmade lake. She turned the phone around so Bobby could see it. "You've got a lot of explaining to do."

Bobby sunk down to the floor. "What have I done?"

Nicole read a few articles. "Apparently the plane malfunctioned during its landing and the pilot had no choice but to land the plane in that nasty water. The good news is no one was hurt in the crash." She read further into the article and started laughing. "One witness stated that the airlines

149

should start making the planes out of the same material as the black box to ensure the safety of passengers and crew." She became excited. "Bobby, this is you! You punched a few buttons on a clipboard and caused a plane to end up in the lake!"

Bobby remained still on the ground. "Nicole, we're the test subjects. Don't you get it?"

Nicole calmed down. "Bobby, you're right. Let's think this through." She paused. "You did say they are just observers. They normally don't try to control us. Maybe this is a onetime thing."

Bobby pointed to the picture of the floating 747. "I did that, Nicole. I pressed a few buttons on a screen and put that plane in Tempe Town Lake." Reality set in. He stood. "I think it's time I told Mom and Faja the truth."

Nicole shot up to her feet. "Bobby, are you sure? Faja's gonna murder you and bury your rotting corpse behind the house once he finds out you cost a major airline millions of dollars in damages."

"Don't you understand? This type of power shouldn't be taken lightly." Bobby started breathing heavy. "We need to think of the consequences. What if Jonathan and Sabrina start World War III?"

Nicole grabbed onto his shoulders. "Robert Walker, you are overreacting." She took several breaths and motioned for Bobby to do the same. "Bobby, you have to be realistic. I don't think these pod people have the ability to cause mass destruction in our world. I don't think they'd want to."

"Regardless, it's not safe to keep the crown here with me. You never know who might find it. I'm taking it home during Christmas and giving it to Faja for safe-keeping."

Nicole patted his back. "I think we've got it under control. Let me have the crown and I'll hold onto it until you come home."

Bobby gave her the crown, even though he wasn't sure if that was the best idea.

CHAPTER 18: DO MOTHER AND FAJA KNOW BEST?

Bobby couldn't get over his trip to the other side. He read several articles regarding the Tempe Town Lake incident. Each picture created a pit in his stomach. The guilt was almost too much to bear.

Bobby sailed through his finals and left on the first plane back to Phoenix after school let out. As the plane neared Phoenix Sky Harbor Airport, he gripped his seat. He closed his eyes and prayed to the plane gods that his aircraft wouldn't end up in the murky waters of Tempe Town Lake. Much to Bobby's pleasant surprise, the plane landed safely without as much as a hint of turbulence. He emerged from the aircraft and almost kissed the dirty airport carpet.

Gordy and Kim laid eyes on Bobby and wrapped their arms around him, holding onto their son tightly. Bobby let out a sigh of relief. He spent the entire car ride home sharing his college stories with his parents. Once they made it to the house, Nicole left her apartment and travelled home. That night at dinner the family celebrated Bobby's first semester of college and Nicole's top of class GPA. After Gordy and Kim said their goodnights, Bobby snuck into Nicole's room.

"Did you bring it?" Bobby asked.

Nicole rolled her eyes. "Of course, I did." She unzipped her suitcase and pulled out the golden crown.

Bobby took it into his hands. "You didn't put it on, did you?"

"Don't be a cheese-head, Bobby. I made you a promise, and I plan on keeping it."

He gave her a smile. "In some strange way, I feel good about giving the crown to Mom and Faja."

Nicole dropped her suitcase on the floor. "Bobby, I think you're forgetting a very important part. Faja's gonna kill you once he finds out that you risked your life for the crown after he told you not to." She sat down on the bed.

Bobby ignored her comment and sat down next to her. "What about Aunt Meg? Don't you think he'll be happy to know that we found evidence that she might be alive?"

Nicole smacked his arm. "Not really. The whole reason you went over there for a second time was to get her and you came back empty handed!"

"Don't get mad at me! I kind of got distracted once I realized that I had the key to our universe in my hands!" Bobby snapped.

Nicole folded her arms. "Bobby, all I'm saying is this thing might not go as you planned. If we give the crown to Faja how do we know he won't destroy it before we can get Meg back?"

Bobby detested her idea. "Let's say we keep the crown and go back to retrieve Meg. What am I supposed to do, ask Jonathan to hand over our dad's sister? He did refer to her as his *wife*. You don't just give up a life with your wife. What if they have children? Besides, I'm sure the crown is made of some type of weird alien rock that's impossible to destroy."

"Are you starting to believe they're aliens?"

He crossed his legs and faced her. "I don't know what they are." He took a deep breath. "Nicole, you're missing the entire point. We're in over our heads here. If you ask me, I think ridding ourselves of this curse is the best thing that could happen at this point."

Nicole laughed. "Bobby, you're freaking out over nothing. You have to think this through completely. *We* can't say for certain that this group is after our world. *We* can't know their true intentions unless we confront them. *We* can't do that unless we have the crown."

"Should we go back over there and ask Jonathan about his diabolical plan to take over our universe?" Bobby wanted no part of Nicole's scheme. "If that's what you're thinking then count me out."

Nicole twisted her hair. "I don't know if I would go that far, or where we should start, but I think we should be smart about it."

Bobby sighed. "Didn't you hear a single word I just said? I'm not going over there again, Nicole."

She folded her arms. "*Robert Walker.* I can't believe what you're saying. How can you be so selfish?"

"Selfish? I'm not selfish!"

"We may be Aunt Meg's only hope. Did you even think about that?"

Bobby leaned in. "Nicole, this isn't about Meg anymore. You have to open your eyes to the truth. We're playing with fire now, and I can't have all this weighing on my conscience anymore. I'm telling Faja tomorrow and giving him the crown. I don't care about how much trouble we're both going to be in."

"I think you should reconsider." She put her hand on his shoulder. "Listen, I support your need for parental intervention, however, I don't agree with you retreating from this situation just because you're scared. You're overreacting, Bobby. If you take a deep breath and look at all our options you'll see everything exactly how it is."

"And how is that?" he scoffed.

She smiled. "In my opinion, I think you're special. The fact that the golden crown was there and we managed to find it when we went back to Sedona means something. It's almost like the crown was waiting for you to return."

He raised his eyebrow. "And that's a good thing?"

Nicole opened her mouth but paused. "I don't know. I don't know exactly what it means. All I know is we can't just give Mom and Faja the crown and pretend that our lives will just go back to the way they were. We're a part of this, whether we like it or not."

A knock on the door made Bobby freeze. "Yeah?" Nicole stuffed the crown under a pillow and picked up a magazine.

Kim opened the door. "Keep it down, you guys." She pointed a finger at Bobby. "You better get to bed, young man. We're leaving really early in the morning for Sedona."

Reluctantly, Bobby stood to his feet and joined his mother at the door. Kim closed Nicole's door and ushered Bobby into his room. "Bobby, you seem troubled about something. Do you want to talk about it?"

Bobby held his breath. He wanted so badly to share his secret with her and rid himself of the golden crown. However, he couldn't do it. Bobby couldn't tell her just yet. "I'm just tired from a really long semester at school."

Kim rubbed his back. "Well, it's a winter vacation. Before you know it, you'll be back in Sedona." She leaned in. "And there will be a surprise waiting for you."

Bobby kissed his mom's cheek. "Love you, Mom."

Kim gave him another hug. "I love you, Bobby. I am so glad you are home and happy to have us all under the same roof again. Now go to bed." She kissed Bobby's cheek and shut the door.

Bobby changed into a T-shirt and basketball shorts. He pulled back the sheets and climbed into his bed. Once the lights went off, he stared at the dark ceiling. Over the past few weeks since Bobby had traveled to the other side, he had followed several stories surrounding tragedy and loss in the news. Train wrecks claiming lives, devastating weather destroying homes, and nuclear bombs looming in the distance in places like Iran.

Each time Bobby saw something tragic in the news, his thoughts travelled back to the golden crown and the lab. He wondered if Jonathan and his team had planted another threat in *the Universe*, only to watch defenseless people suffer. He turned over and hugged his pillow, breathing slowly. "What is going to happen next? Another killer earthquake? Are we on the brink of World War III?" These questions floated around in Bobby's head as he drifted off to sleep. He hoped for the best and couldn't wait to give the power of the universe to his father.

***

The next morning, Gordy, Kim, Nicole, and Bobby piled into the family SUV and headed for Sedona. Once the truck hit the highway, Nicole started a conversation with Gordy and Kim about her plans to achieve her goals. She had become excited about the prospects of her future and the possible jobs she could get. Her passion was journalism and she had every intention to use this skill in any way she could. As she carried on her conversation with Kim and Gordy, she moved her eyes toward Bobby.

Bobby sat quietly in his seat with his ear buds inserted deep into his ears. He stared out at the fast-moving desert passing by his window. His mind was in a whirl. Having the golden crown in his possession seemed to make him more and more confused. He took a deep breath and attempted to organize his worries. After several minutes of trying to think rationally, only one thought remained.

The world was coming to an end. This race of super humans was using our world as a means to control us and put our lives in danger for science. Why weren't they using their power to fix the problems in the world? His world. Bobby felt conflicted with knowing the truth. But if Bobby had never found the golden crown, he would have never discovered this other world. A small part inside of him was grateful for knowing the truth. Even with this knowledge, Bobby still questioned his future with everything he had been exposed to. He couldn't shake what Nicole had said about him. *Was he special?* Was the golden crown hiding undiscovered until *he* found it?

Nicole pinched Bobby's arm, leaving a large mark. "What's with you? Why are you being so quiet?" She smirked then whispered, "Did my speech last night about you and the crown change your game plan?"

"No, not at all. I'm thinking about unrelated things," he whispered.

"Are you sure giving Faja the crown is our best option?" she asked. Bobby paused. "Think about Aunt Meg and the universe, Bobby."

Gordy glanced in the rearview mirror. "Bobby, what was that? Why are you so quiet today? Usually we can't get you to shut up."

Bobby looked up. "I'm just trying to relax on our trip, that's all."

Gordy narrowed his eyebrows. "I figure you'd be screaming out the window right now, letting the world know that you were on your way to claim your forgotten treasure." Bobby shrugged, hoping to throw Gordy off the trail. "You know, Bobby, if you don't want to head up to Sedona I can turn the truck around."

Nicole's eyes widened. She pinched his arm. Bobby ignored her and continued to speak with his father. "Faja, I'm not sure exactly what to do. I mean if you think about it, there are so many awesome things in Sedona other than that crown."

Gordy's eyes veered to the road and then back. "That's one way to look at it. On the other hand, you made such a production about that thing in the past. Why the sudden change of heart?"

Bobby stayed calm. Nicole took a deep breath. He knew she was preparing herself for the moment that he would reveal their big secret. "I'm older now. I have other things to worry about." He winked at her, hoping she would take the hint. "Basketball was my real golden crown anyway."

Bobby didn't want to tell his parents until they were on Bell Rock and in the exact spot where the crown had originally been found. He bent over and unzipped his backpack to check on it. He ran his fingers across the T-shirt that encased the crown, pressing down on the pointy edges. He let out a sigh, zipped up his bag, and sat back in his seat.

Kim turned to face Bobby. "So you don't want to go up to Bell Rock?" She looked down at his knee from the front seat. "Any pain?"

Bobby shook his head. "I feel fine. And we're going to Bell Rock. I just want you guys to know that the crown is not my entire reason for going up there. No biggy if we can't find it. I'm here to spend time with my family and enjoy as much of Sedona as we can."

Gordy looked over at Kim and then back at Bobby. "If you say so. Did you have a lobotomy when you were away at school?" He chuckled. "Maybe caught that Lime Disease? We'll see how calm you are once we find the crown." He turned on some classic rock and roll music and began speaking with Kim about the family's weekend budget.

Nicole pulled Bobby's face close to hers. "Bobby, what's your problem? Your mood swings are giving me whiplash," she whispered loudly.

He pulled his face away from hers. "This is not the right place to tell them. We should wait as long as we can."

"Remember, I don't support your plan." Nicole said. She pulled out her iPod and a magazine to read. Bobby faced the window again and turned up the volume.

The Walker family reached Sedona mid-morning. Gordy pulled into the parking lot of El Rincon so he could rearrange the hiking gear. Bobby stepped out of the SUV and admired the red rocks. The cool desert air felt good against his sweaty forehead. He was nervous. This was the moment he had been waiting for since he got back from MIT. Even though he still had every intention to tell Gordy and Kim about the golden crown, Bobby couldn't get Nicole's concern for Aunt Meg out of his head.

Gordy peeked his head around the SUV and broke his thought. "Hey, Bobby, can you help me with the hiking gear?"

Bobby nodded and aided his father. After everything was reorganized, the family did some touring of Tlaquepaque before having lunch at El Rincon. With satisfied bellies and high hopes, Gordy and Kim led Bobby and Nicole up Bell Rock and toward the crown. Bobby held onto his backpack tightly while Nicole continued to talk him out of his plan. He debated the topic with her, hoping she would see things his way.

As they argued, the two fell behind their parents on the trail. Gordy waited for Bobby and Nicole to catch up before he called for a break. The family stepped over red rocks and followed up the trail until they found a nice shady spot under a few trees. Kim passed Bobby and Nicole some trail mix.

Gordy took a gulp of water before turning his attention to Bobby. "Okay, son. We have to talk about something."

Bobby's shoulders tensed up. Sweat poured down his forehead. He looked over at Nicole who had adverted her eyes toward the landscape. "What's up, Dad?"

"Dad? You never call me Dad." Gordy replied.

Bobby stopped breathing and gulped some water. Nicole began staring at Bobby before cracking a smile. "So you do like your nickname, Faja?" she asked.

Gordy turned to her and then back to Bobby. "Kids, you two have been acting strangely since you got back from school. As a concerned parent, I'm worried about what's going on."

"I'm just worried about the hike," Bobby said.

Kim shook her head. "Bobby, it seems like more than that. Are you worried about your grades?"

Bobby took the bait. He lowered his head and nodded. "I hope I did okay." A sense of relief washed over his body. He patted his backpack and smiled.

Gordy turned to Nicole. "What's going on with you? I've noticed you've been really hard on your brother lately."

Bobby smirked at Nicole. She rolled her eyes and threw her hands up in the air. "We're siblings. We're gonna fight!"

"You remind me so much of your Aunt Meg. You're just as headstrong as she was." Gordy said.

Bobby watched Nicole carefully. She placed her water bottle down on the red, dusty ground. "What's the real deal with Aunt Meg? Did she just disappear or is there more to the story?"

Gordy stood to his feet and threw on his backpack. "Let's not talk about that." He looked up the trail. "Let's get moving so we can find that crown before the sun goes down."

Nicole darted a look at Bobby. "Your father doesn't like to talk about her," Kim said. She pulled herself up. "Now come on, kids."

Bobby jumped to his feet and got into Kim's path. "Mom, were Faja and Aunt Meg close?" Nicole stepped close to him. Bobby assumed she wanted to hear the answer, too.

"They were the best of friends. He misses her a lot." She sighed. "Now let's catch up to your father before he makes it up the mountain without us."

Nicole started to say something to Bobby, but he sprinted up the trail and joined his father.

***

Several hours passed. The Walker family managed to hike up Bell Rock and reach the general area of the golden crown's original resting place. Gordy began looking above the rocks as Kim looked closer to the trail. Nicole pretended to look for a few minutes before she joined Bobby at the base of the rock where the crown had rested.

"Well this is your magic moment, Bobby." She patted his back. "It was nice knowing you."

Bobby stared at the empty crevice in the rocks. He placed his backpack down and knelt down beside it. With his hand on the zipper, Bobby hesitated. Heaviness entered his heart. All the work he and Nicole had put into finding the crown was going to be lost. Gordy missed Aunt Meg, and Bobby had the key to getting her back. He didn't know what to do.

Gordy stepped up behind Bobby. "Is this where the crown should be?" Bobby nodded. Gordy squinted. "I can't see it. Do you see it, Bobby?"

Bobby stood to his feet and looked up. He turned toward Gordy. "Faja, there's something I have to tell you." Nicole narrowed her eyes at him.

"What is it, Bobby?"

Bobby pointed to the crevice. "Someone took the crown."

"How do you know?" Gordy asked.

"Because it's not there. Nicole and I have searched all over this rock, and we didn't see it."

"Are you absolutely sure it was in this spot?"

"Positive." Bobby picked up his backpack and threw it over his shoulders. "I'm sorry I drug everybody up here for nothing."

Gordy pulled Bobby into a hug. "Oh thank God! I was hoping we wouldn't find that thing." He pulled away. "That crown still freaks me out to this day."

"If that's how you feel about it, why did you agree to climb up Bell Rock to look for it?" Bobby asked.

Gordy explained. "You were so darn adamant about getting that thing. I didn't want to disappoint you any longer. Besides I made a promise and…"

"…a promise is a promise." Gordy, Nicole, and Bobby said in unison.

"No offense, Bobby, but I don't want that thing anywhere near our family." Gordy started to hike toward Kim, more than likely to tell her the good news.

Nicole turned to Bobby and smiled. "What changed your mind about telling Faja?"

Bobby threw his arm around Nicole. "You were right about everything. How do we know exactly what these crown people are up to unless we snoop around? And we need to find Aunt Meg."

Nicole nodded. "You made the right choice, Bobby. Now let's plan our next trip to the other side!"

CHAPTER 19: WAR AND PEACE

Jonathan sat quietly at his desk. His one year extension was up. A special meeting had been called to discuss the Universe Initiative. He had grown tired of the constant debates surrounding the destruction of his most valued project. After the Phoenix Sky Harbor plane incident, the Council called a meeting to discuss Jonathan's conduct. When Jonathan had arrived at the Depot Hall for the meeting regarding disciplinary actions against him, he was surprised to see no other members from the Council present. He walked through the building cautiously, worried that the meeting was all just a plot to get him out of the lab. Fearing the fate of his experiment, Jonathan headed for the door.

"Don't leave, Jonathan," the Controller called after him. Jonathan stopped and turned around. The Controller smiled at him and pointed to the Main room. "I have arranged for us to have a chat session."

"I have work to do." Jonathan replied.

The Controller laced his hands together and dropped them to his waist. "I'm aware of that. Our meeting won't take too long."

Jonathan marched up to the Controller. "I don't have time for this right now. I need to get ready for the destruction of my greatest work."

The Controller nodded before heading into the large meeting room. He travelled across the room and sat down in his chair at the head of the spacious table. Jonathan watched him sit patiently for a few moments before he entered the room and threw his body down in a chair next to his father.

"I'm sure you know why you're here?" the Controller asked.

Jonathan pointed to the other empty chairs. "Where is the rest of the Council?"

"This conversation didn't require their attendance." He leaned in. "You and I are going to talk off the record."

"Is this some sort of father and son moment you're trying to have with me?" Jonathan scoffed.

"You allowed a young boy to put a commercial airplane into a manmade lake in Arizona's most populated area. Why did you do something so careless?"

"It was a prank. A prospective intern wanted to understand how the Universe Initiative worked so I showed him. Besides, he was the one who elected to put the plane in that location, not me." A small laugh slipped from Jonathan's lips.

The Controller narrowed his eyes. "You find this situation comedic? You think allowing an unknown boy from the country access to our most important projects is a wise thing to do?"

Jonathan placed his hands on the cold table. "Father, you have every intention to destroy this universe. Why does it matter?" he paused. "Why do you suddenly care about what happens to these test subjects?"

The Controller exhaled loudly. "Jonathan, I'm not the evil man you think I am. I am not void of all emotions when it comes to the test subjects." He pointed to his heart. "Their hearts beat just like ours do. They have endearing relationships amongst themselves just like me and my loved ones do." He put his hand on Jonathan's. "Son, you have to keep things in perspective. Our action to terminate the project is merely a means to end their suffering."

Jonathan lightly grabbed his father's hand and placed it back on the table. "I am not a child—you don't have to treat me like one."

"Why do you feel I'm treating you like a child?"

"I don't need an explanation for your indisputable decision. You don't have to hold my hand like I'm upset over spilled milk." Jonathan leaned back in his chair and folded his arms. "Now let's get back to business. Are you going to reprimand me? If not, I need to leave."

The Controller slammed his fist down. "What has gotten into you? It's almost as if you have absolutely no concern for anything. Your negligent attitude has to change before you make a huge mistake."

The two were silent. Jonathan placed a hand against his chin and stoked his stubble. "I can't do this anymore." He paused. "I don't have the energy to create a brand new initiative from scratch. I've worked way too hard on—"

"Now you listen to me, Jonathan," the Controller interrupted. "You have been given the gift of science. I've raised you to approach every situation and project with the ability to overcome it. Everything you are telling me does not reflect the appropriate conduct I expect from you. The Universe Initiative will be destroyed, and I expect you to continue your extraordinary work on The Universe II!"

Jonathan no longer wanted to speak about the issue with his father. He rose to his feet and walked toward the door. Before exiting he turned back. "Mr. Controller, we have evolved from these types of fights. Our people have grown to have more respect for one another. We owe these people and their ancestors for all we have. You should think about that before you chastise me." He walked out the door without another word.

***

"You're going to be late to your meeting, Jonathan," Sabrina said. She had stepped out of the lab and placed a stack of papers on his desk.

Two days had passed since Jonathan and the Controller had their showdown. The Ministry had instructed the Council to review the latest projections from Jonathan's team. If all the key pieces were put together, the Universe would be set for destruction. Jonathan had lost all his energy. He had accepted his defeat and carried on with his team's plans, just like the Controller had directed him to.

"Are these the preliminary reports from the Universe II?" Jonathan asked Sabrina.

She nodded. "We're in the final stages of adding the finishing touches to the blueprints. Once the current Universe is destroyed, we'll take DNA from sample groups throughout the real world so that the Universe II would start off basically with the same population they currently have."

Jonathan ran his hand through his hair. "I wish I had more time."

She sat down in a chair and faced him. "When do you plan to tell Meg?"

"I'm not sure. I don't know how someone tells the person they love most in the world that their family is about to be destroyed." He stood up and grabbed a few papers. "You know how she is. She'll try to go back over there and save everyone."

"That is true, but I fear what her reaction will be if you never tell her. That will put a lot of strain on your marriage."

Jonathan picked up a file folder and tucked the papers inside. "I work long hours and hate what I do—my marriage is already strained."

Sabrina stood. "Perhaps you can take some time off once the Universe Initiative termination is complete. A brief sabbatical will rejuvenate you and your work."

Jonathan gave no reverence to her comment. "I have to attend my meeting now." he patted her shoulder. "Thank you for the concern, my friend. At this point in time, I need to apply as much effort to this project as I can before the Ministry terminates it ahead of schedule."

***

Jonathan entered the Depot Hall and passed the other Council members without a word. He sat down in his chair and pretended to review the notes Sabrina prepared for him. Everything was in order for the Universe II: a suitable habitat was complete, a list of initial predictions was being complied, and the test subjects were selected. Senator Sergeev took a seat next to Jonathan.

"This is a very dark day for you, I assume," she hissed.

Jonathan tilted his head. "Depends on your definition of the word dark."

"Have you had a change of heart? Did you decide to side with the Council?"

"Some battles are won on the field while others are won in a lab."

The Senator raised her eyebrow. "What are you implying? Have you defied a direct order and plan to proceed in saving the Universe?"

Jonathan closed his folder. "We both know that is not a possibility."

"Then what are you referring to?"

The Controller entered the room and took his place at the head of the table. Everyone stood and waited for him to call the meeting to order. After this was completed every member took his seat. The room was completely silent for several long moments. The Controller made eye contact with Jonathan.

"I have called this special meeting to go over The Universe II. Jonathan, please share the lab's progress with us."

Jonathan stood and held onto his folder. "The new initiative has made favorable progress. The new world was just completed a few days ago. Sabrina and her team have gathered all the necessary concerns from the Council and plans have been updated accordingly. At this moment, we have compiled a list of elements needed to begin our brand new experiments."

"And what about the test subjects?" the Controller asked.

"The test subjects have been selected. We will reap them once we have monitored the progress of the habitat for a few days."

"Tell us about the test subjects. Are they as loveable as the current ones?" Senator Sergeev scoffed.

The room rumbled softly with laughter. Jonathan looked straight into the Controller's eyes. "These test subjects will come from different races, ethnicities, religions, ages and social groups from our current society, including people from your region of the world Senator. They will replicate us. They will live in families, just like we do and just like the current subjects we are observing today do. They will be us and we will be them. I anticipate that these people will bond together and attempt to problem solve as a group. They will think like us and act like us. The only difference is that they will live with different experiences than we do because we will force them to." He paused and took a deep breath. "They will worship peace and do anything to attain it."

The Controller looked downward. "Thank you for your report, Jonathan." Jonathan dropped the folder onto the table and sat down. The Controller picked up his head. "My fellow council members, something has been puzzling me for the past several weeks. During a conversation with one of our valued members, my integrity was placed in jeopardy." The room buzzed with chatter. No one would dare question the integrity of the Controller except one person; Jonathan.

Jonathan clenched his sweaty fists and held his breath. "It is because of this conversation that I have changed my position on the Universe Initiative. I have decided that we will not destroy the Universe."

Jonathan let out a sigh of relief while the other council members seemed disgruntled about the idea. Senator Sergeev stood to his feet. "Mr. Controller, I must interject. On what grounds have you made this decision?"

"My decision stems from a long period of meditation and deep thinking. I reflected on the state of our world and the Universe which led to a startling discovery. As we continue on our path to self-enlightenment and peace among us, each member of our society must understand the negative effects of complete world destruction."

Senator Sergeev turned to the others around the table. "But Mr. Controller, that is the point of terminating the Universe. Everyone in our world will see how putting these pathetic test subjects out of their misery will benefit us. We can move on to more advanced technologies by putting our new test subjects in a new updated environment. This new group of 'people' will unlock the hidden mysteries that baffle us today, plus a long list of other benefits. I say we maintain our current schedule and terminate the Universe as planned."

Applause engulfed the entire room. The Controller banged his gavel several times until the members gave him the floor. "The fact that we are having a debate over the fate of a project is the whole basis for my concern. I understand that living in a life without conflict is almost impossible. However, we as a collective must prepare ourselves for the possibility of war."

"Can we move forward with the Universe II?" Senator Buckingham of England asked.

Another senator nodded. "I motion that we put it to a vote."

169

The Controller shook his head. "The Ministry and I have discussed this matter and it has been decided that no vote will take place among the Council. I have made my ruling, and we will not destroy the Universe."

"And wait for the war to come upon us." Senator Sergeev muttered. The Controller's face became worried.

A cramp grew in Jonathan's stomach. War was never something the Controller had worried about. His father's words and attitude set off alarms. Jonathan stood up. "Mr. Controller, our people have conquered war. There hasn't been any conflict between citizens that we haven't been able to resolve as a result of the Universe."

"That is true, Jonathan, but we do not have complete peace like I had hoped. The only way we can obtain paradise is by studying the effects of a massive world war. The war I'm speaking about is not like World War I or World War II, but rather a war where the entire species of test subjects completely destroys one another beyond repair."

"That is absurd. The only way the test subjects will do that is by declaring nuclear war on one another." Jonathan argued.

The Controller sat up straight in his chair. "Precisely. The only way we can fully know peace is by knowing what total destruction looks like. If the test subjects are programmed to create nuclear conflicts amongst one another, we can find ways to keep that from happening to our people. I recommend that we introduce a new conflict within the Universe that will result in a massive war amongst all its members. Once this has been completed, *the test subjects* will destroy their own world and we will gain the ultimate data to protect us from the same fate."

Senator Sergeev's eyes lit up. "We'll let them destroy one another. I'm in favor of that." The rest of the Council cheered along with him.

Jonathan placed his head in his hands. He closed his eyes to stave off the headache that began to grow in his temples. The Controller banged his gavel three times. "Jonathan, it is no mystery to me about what you are thinking. We are not barbarians, my son. The test subjects do not know the misery they are in. We have caused them so much pain by putting them through these strenuous tests. Why not allow them a chance to die by their terms?"

"Can you really say that you are doing them a favor? We have all the resources needed to create the new world. We can leave them alone, without support and interference from us. Is it really important that we use the existing universe to prove our points about war?" Jonathan asked.

The Controller nodded. "We must plan for every single possibility. We created this experiment, and we have to see it to the end."

Jonathan shook his head. "Then you are, without a doubt, a soulless man, Mr. Controller. If you want to be responsible for the death of an entire group of people, I will not stand in your way. But you have lost my respect."

The room was silent until Senator Sergeev spoke. "When would you like this super war to take place?"

"Jonathan and his team will administer the project in phases. We will start setting the stage for the war as soon as possible."

"Consider it done." Jonathan's voice was mute of any emotions.

The Controller approved the new proposition and the remaining members of the Council seemed beyond content with his decision. Once the meeting was adjourned, Jonathan climbed onto the solar train and travelled back to his office. Sitting next to him was a young teenage boy who seemed somber. Jonathan had a mind to start up a conversation, but decided against it since he enjoyed the quiet.

171

"Sir, I don't mean to bother you, but do you happen to know the time?" the boy asked.

Jonathan flashed his watch so the boy could see. "Almost noon."

"Thanks." The teenager paused. "You just came from the Depot Hall. Are you a member of the Ministry?"

Jonathan abandoned his reservations about continuing the conversation. "No, I'm on the Council. We report to the Controller who reports to the Ministry."

He smiled. "Well you tell them thank you for me? My dad just got released from the hospital after being sick for a couple weeks." The train came to a stop. The boy sprang to his feet and put out his hand. "I'm Paul. Tell the Ministry that I appreciate all the work they have done to help my family."

Jonathan shook Paul's hand and watched him jump off the solar train. Bobby came to his mind. Jonathan thought about talking Bobby out of joining the Universe Initiative. He pulled out his phone and dialed Sabrina.

"Hello, Jonathan. How did your meeting going?" she asked.

"I'll bring you up to speed once I return to the office. Can you do me a favor?"

She chuckled. "I work for you which means nothing I do for you is considered a favor."

He smiled. "I'd like to take a trip out to the country today. Can you provide me with Bobby's home information?"

The phone was silent for a moment. "Bobby, as in the young man who toured the lab?"

"That's the one. Can you give me his information?"

"I apologize, but we didn't gather any information about him."

"Sabrina, we work in a highly classified area! Anyone who sets foot into our lab must provide their personal information and sign all the waivers. You know that!"

She sighed. "Of course I know that. I guess I got caught up in my conversation with him that I forgot to follow procedure." She paused. "Jonathan, there is something special about Bobby. I knew it the moment I met him. We need him on our team."

Jonathan clutched the phone tightly. "Let's talk about that later." He rubbed his throbbing head. "I'm taking the rest of the day off. Tomorrow I'll bring you up to speed on everything the Ministry wants us to do."

Sabrina began to ask questions regarding the meeting. Jonathan provided short, unclear answers before disconnecting the line. He lay back in the seat and stared out the window, admiring the beautiful landscape. Jonathan couldn't leave anything to chance. He knew what he had to do. He had to finish his key to the Universe and retrieve his lost crown. His lost crown—the failsafe. Jonathan let out a sigh of relief.

CHAPTER 20: ALTERNATE PLANS

Jonathan walked through the door of his home, grabbed a pastry from a clear glass bowl and then headed straight for his home office. Dropping everything down in one loud thud, he chomped on the sticky, sweet dough as he rummaged for his notebook. Meg materialized in the doorway, knocking softly.

"Hey, you. The sun's still up. What are you doing here?" she teased. Jonathan glanced up at his wife before diving back into the pile. Meg stepped over a stack of papers on the floor and placed her hand on his back. "Jonathan, what are you doing here? Did something happen in the lab?"

"Things always happen in the lab, which is a good thing," he joked. Jonathan moved a heap of papers from a book-shelf and dropped them onto the large glass desk taking up most of the narrow room.

Meg locked eyes with him. "Jonathan, what is happening? Is it the Universe?"

He weighed his options. He could tell Meg everything, or he could keep it hidden. The Universe was her home. It was a direct attachment to who she was. Sharing confidential information with his wife on the matter would create several issues for everyone. Meg was a fighter. Jonathan knew he couldn't keep her from trying to stop the destruction of her home world. She raised her eyebrow, implying to Jonathan that he needed to provide an answer, fast.

"Every day something happens with the Universe." He turned back to his piles of paper and produced a notebook. He grabbed the file Sabrina had created for him and dashed out of his office.

Meg grabbed his arm right as he set foot in the kitchen. "Jonathan, you have to tell me. If it's something that will affect my loved ones you have to tell me the truth."

"There isn't much to say. Our initiative is performing exactly the way it's supposed to." He grabbed another pastry and sat down at the kitchen table.

Meg sat across from him. "You're really good at dodging questions."

"I learned it from you." He smiled and took a large bite.

Meg narrowed her eyes at him before grinning. Jonathan opened his notebook and the file folder. Inside both items were pictures and dimensions for the golden crown. Meg leaned and glanced over each page as Jonathan turned them at a rapid pace. "Are you thinking of making another key?" she asked.

"Yeah." He paused. "I'd like to go back down there and gather some samples."

Meg's eyes lit up. "If you were able to create another crown, could I travel with you?"

"The crown doesn't really work that way."

"How does it work?"

Jonathan leaned back into the chair. "My key is programmed to work for me. No one could use it to enter our world. If I were to retrieve it I'm not sure if I can undo what I've already done."

"I see." Meg leaned back in the chair and folded her arms. "You know, you've never told me exactly what happened that day you lost the golden crown."

Jonathan hunched over his work. "There's nothing to talk about."

"I think it's relevant."

"Well, it's not," he snapped. Meg nodded and stood. Jonathan put his head in his hands. "That was the single worst day of my life."

"You've been holding onto that story for so many years." Meg sighed. "The truth is, I'm worried about you."

"You're always worried about me," he muffled.

"This is different. Even the girls are worried," Meg said. Jonathan looked up at her. "They ask me about you all the time. They see the constant anger and fear all over your face. You're not very good at hiding it. They want their daddy back."

Jonathan sat back in the chair, his tired eyes searching his wife's concerned face. "I had to go back. I had to return to the Universe to gather some samples and do some field work. When I crossed over the threshold someone saw me."

Meg lowered her body back down into the chair. "Someone saw you teleport?"

"I don't know what they saw for sure, but they made a point to give me reason to believe they saw something. As I continued doing my work, I noticed a few people taking special interest in me. The more I tried to conceal my identity, the more aggressive the test subj— people became."

"My people are curious about anything that seems unfamiliar. You can't blame them for taking a special interest in you." Meg protested.

"I understand that. This time I couldn't risk anyone seeing my presence."

"What were you studying at the time?"

Jonathan looked down at this paperwork and fanned through each document. "Bell Rock in Sedona has the most incredible soil samples I've ever seen." He pulled out another picture of the crown. "When I landed on Bell Rock, I wanted to observe a few individuals up close. As I watched the people, I got careless."

"How?" Meg asked.

"I got caught up in my research. I had introduced a toxin that was supposed to eat through the bedrock and augment the soil's composition until all the organic substances deteriorated. Once this happened, the soil would become an airborne neurotoxin that could be used in biological warfare." Jonathan smiled. "Every time I introduced the toxin to the soil, the soil remained unchanged. It was fascinating."

Meg began to flip through Jonathan's notebook. "I just don't understand why you have to poison and blow up my people for science."

"It's more than just science, Meg. This is how we grow to understand exactly how our people will react to negative and positive elements. Your people have given me so much insight on how to protect our people. I'm extremely grateful for them every day."

"And yet you torture and destroy them!" Meg started to breath heavily. "Jonathan, these are people, *my* people. They are not just some mindless lab rats that are here for you to throw bombs and toxic potions at!"

"I understand that!" Jonathan's voice cracked. "Meg, every time I travelled to the Universe, I met so many wonderful, interesting people, including you. It pained me so much when I had to turn my back on them after my crown was lost."

Meg took a deep breath. "So, how did you lose it? How did your crown get left behind?"

"The people of Sedona had become suspicious of me, so I fled. They chased me out of town and up Bell Rock. It was extremely dark out when I finally found the perfect place to travel back. I was preparing for transport when I noticed the flashlights closing in on me. Afraid of what they might see, I shoved the crown on my head and waited."

The emotions caught up with Jonathan. He climbed out of his chair and grabbed another pastry. Meg got up and stood before him. "We've really gotta work on your diet."

Jonathan smiled and kissed her lips. "I like my sweets." He took a bite and continued his story. "As I stood there, waiting to transport back home, a flash of light caught my eye. In one instant, I felt myself being propelled out of Sedona as the crown fell beneath my feet."

"It fell off your head?"

Jonathan nodded. "That's never happened to me before. But even without it, I managed to arrive back safely without my key."

"But, I thought you couldn't transport without it on your head. How on Earth did it fall off?" Meg was full of questions.

Jonathan thought for a moment. "When I transport to our world, I'm lifted up into the atmosphere and carried over to our world. I was in a hurry so when I put the crown on my head, I didn't secure it all the way. The force of my body being pushed upward caused the crown to fall off my head and land somewhere on Bell Rock."

Meg's eyes widened. "So you only needed the crown to start the transportation process? Why didn't the crown get caught in your 'travel waves?'"

"I'm not sure what you mean by 'travel waves,' but I think I understand your question. The truth is I don't know why it didn't come back over with me. It's one of the very few mysteries that plague me."

"What mystery plagues you the most?" Meg asked.

"Why none of the test subj…" Jonathan corrected himself, "…why none of your people have found the crown yet. I'm sure it was just lying on the ground in plain sight."

"Maybe it got stuck somewhere," Meg offered.

"Maybe," Jonathan said. He smiled. "I'm happy I managed to get back over to this side to you and our daughters. The entire time I was down there I couldn't stop thinking about you guys."

"I never understood exactly how you were able to transport both of us at the same time."

Jonathan put his finger up. "I was perplexed by that too until I discovered this." He scurried back to the table and pulled out another document. "The day we left Sedona was the same day an anomaly crossed our path. On that day, Sabrina accidently created a new frequency that caused the perfect environment for someone other than me to cross over to our world."

"So, when you grabbed my hand and put on the crown you didn't know if it would bring me over here?"

"Not exactly. I designed the crown, Meg. I'm linked to it. When I put the crown on, it reads my DNA and thoughts, like a super computer. The day we left Sedona, I put the crown on and hoped that I could manipulate it to bring you here. Once it worked, I went straight into the lab to figure out what had happened. That was when Sabrina explained what she had done and we put two and two together to figure out what had happened."

"I see," Meg said in agreement although her voice was not too convincing.

Jonathan chuckled. "Basically, she made a mistake in one of the experiments which created the perfect condition for you to travel with me."

"So, this perfect condition was the only reason why we could be together? Otherwise, we would have been separated for the rest of our lives?" Meg stared at the picture of the golden crown. "If I were still down there, would you have continued your research?"

Jonathan placed the pastry on the table. This question was not easy to answer. His father had brought up the same point. Jonathan's judgment and extreme emotional commitment to the Universe and its people created the perfect breeding ground for destruction. He couldn't remain committed to conducting experiments while the love of his life remained subjected to them. When the time came for him to choose between Meg and his calling, he sought the advice of his mother.

Jonathan's mother, an even-tempered, caring woman, was shocked when she heard of her son's bizarre attachment to Meg. She questioned his motives and their relationship for several weeks before eventually giving him her blessing. Once Jonathan professed his love to Meg and made arrangements to somehow bring her back with him, everything changed. His mother became ill, causing her health to deteriorate quickly. The lab had no idea how to control the flu-like epidemic that had stricken a significant portion of the population.

Jonathan had a choice to make. He finally understood the importance of his research. With the fate of so many sick and near-death people, including his mother, in his hands, he had no choice but to continue with the project. In the end, he managed to save several lives, but not his mother's. On the day of her death, he teleported back, crownless. Later, the Universe would be exposed to the H1N1 flu and Jonathan would learn how to keep his world safe from similar diseases.

"The day I lost my crown and my mother changed everything for me. I can't answer that question without putting someone on either side at risk." Jonathan dove back into his work convinced that Meg didn't like his answer.

She sat down next to him. "I want what's best for everyone. I understand the burden you bear, however, I can't just sit back and be silent about it any longer. These people, or test subjects as you so adequately call them, are my people, my family. I can't live in two worlds at once—you know that, Jonathan."

"Which is why I want to make another key." Jonathan placed his hand on the pile. "Meg, this is my one and only chance to do something about the problem. The Council and the Ministry haven't acknowledged the fact that we can co-exist in one way or another. I'm going to create another crown, travel back to your world, and bring back documented proof that we can have an alliance."

"They're going to destroy it, aren't they?" Meg placed her hand over her mouth and held in her grief and anger. Jonathan's shoulders tensed up. He never meant for her to figure it out this way. "That's why you want to make a crown." she paused. "You want me to go back and say goodbye to my family before it's too late."

Jonathan couldn't allow that. He knew the Universe could embark on war at any time. It was too dangerous. "I want to make this crown so I can bring our two worlds together."

"You never answered my question which means I'm right. They are going to destroy it. I want my family. I want you to bring my family over here." Meg wiped a tear that fell down her face.

Jonathan shook his head. "That is not a good idea, you know that. No one from that world can come over here."

"I'm here. I was from that world, and you brought me over."

"That was different."

Meg leaned into him. "No, it wasn't. You are the Controller's son. You made your father bend the rules for me. I'm sure you can make him bend the rules for the rest of my family."

"Under no circumstances can anyone from that world come over here." He took a deep breath and tried to relax. "Our world is not equipped for the war that would ensue."

Meg chuckled. "My family isn't dangerous."

"I'm not talking about your family; I'm talking about the Ministry. The Ministry will imprison anyone who sneaks into our world."

"But you can talk with your father and maybe he can—"

Jonathan slammed his hand down. "Enough, Meg! There is nothing I can do to help you. The Controller has made his decision, and that's it. Your family must stay over there."

Meg climbed out of her seat. "I see." She lowered her head as she left the room, leaving Jonathan completely devastated.

CHAPTER 21: OBSESSION

Jonathan sat quietly for a couple minutes. He wanted to try another attempt at having a conversation about the issues at hand but decided against it. There was absolutely no way he could convince his father to allow Meg's family to come live in their world. The fact that the Controller allowed Meg to come over was just the beginning, the fact that he did not let the Ministry know was a true miracle.

Jonathan jumped right into action. He had to attach a new pass code to the replica golden crown—the key. He advised the lab that he was taking some time off to prepare for the transitions in the Universe Initiative. He poured over his journal and the files, writing down instructions. Something was missing. Jonathan needed to break into the software and write the pass code.

"This crown is going to be different," Jonathan said to himself. He nodded and smiled.

Meg reentered the kitchen with Sabrina close on her tail. "You have a visitor."

"Sabrina? What are you doing at my home?"

Sabrina looked over at Meg and then back at Jonathan. "I wanted to drop something off…may I have a word with you?"

Meg left the room, keeping her head low and her eyes away from Jonathan's. He pointed to the chair across from him. "Please, sit down."

Sabrina lowered herself down. "I need to get your opinion on how to administer the super war."

"That is not a priority on my list at the moment." Jonathan continued his research.

Sabrina began to fidget. "I understand. It's just that Senator Sergeev wants to get started with the new research." She paused. Jonathan remained focused on his task. "She needs this war to begin sooner rather than later."

"What's Sergeev's big hurry? Why is she so anxious to watch innocent people spill one another's blood?" Jonathan asked without looking up.

"She's ready to pull the trigger on the Universe II. Everyone is, including all your colleagues at the lab." Sabrina sighed.

"At the cost of billions of lives," he muttered.

Sabrina seemed to be taken aback, "Is that the way you see it? Do you think what we're doing is mass murder?"

The stress of the situation was getting to Jonathan. He looked up at her. "I'm done talking about this subject with you or anyone else. Now unless you have some other pressing issue you'd like to discuss with me, I suggest you get back to the lab."

"It's not that easy, Jonathan. You have to give the go ahead."

Jonathan sighed. "I can't give the go ahead, I'm in the middle of making history." He pointed toward the window. The sun was beginning to set. "It's getting late. I think it's time for you to go." Jonathan felt pressured to complete his key as quickly as possible.

"No." Sabrina laced her hands and placed them on the table.

Jonathan raised his eyebrow. "Excuse me?"

"The Senator told me not to leave until I got your approval." She sat back in the chair. "I'm ready to sit here all night if I have to."

"Sabrina, I don't have time for juvenile games."

She looked across the table. "I can see that. How's your progress going with your key?"

"I'm taking my time. I can't seem to break out the system." He turned his computer around in her direction. "Wanna take a stab at it?"

She slowly studied the screen. "I'm not good with hacking into computer systems."

Jonathan frowned. No one understood the process of making a key for transporting like Sabrina did. She was there in the lab when he made his first one. They spent hours together, measuring and then re-measuring until it was absolutely precise. She helped him with each transport to the other side. When he came back from his travels, he told her all about Meg and the land that he had discovered.

"What should I do?" Jonathan asked. "Should I give up?"

Sabrina sat back in the chair. "I'm not sure. Maybe you should create another way in."

Jonathan contemplated her observation. "How would I do that?"

"Find a way to get it to work without needing a pass code."

"Hmmm." He paused. "Instead of using a pass code, what if I created a backdoor?"

"No, I don't think it's that. It can't be something so simple."

They both let out a loud sigh. Jonathan's eyes drifted toward the window. The sun was moving steadily behind the countryside close to his home. He imagined relaxing in the crisp air and taking a break from his draining work. Deep inside he wanted to give up his job and enjoy hopping from place to place on a whim. He wanted to be an explorer, a traveler, just like Meg.

"That's it! I've figured it out!" Jonathan's energy level rose. "Maybe I can program the crown to work independently from the software."

Sabrina leaned back. "That would solve your problem but can you be certain you could get back if you do that?"

"I need to figure out how I can pull this off." Jonathan offered.

"Your DNA hasn't changed. That's a benefit. Start there and see what you come up with."

"True, but I think there might be more to the computer programming than I thought. I might have to re-design the entire thing." Jonathan said.

Sabrina shook her head. "The crown is a computer; we have complete control over it. You can make it work."

"We have to look at the facts. The crown's computer could reject my DNA or something about my commands. This might be the end of my road."

She hid a smile crawling across her face. "Jonathan that is not the case. Your crown will never reject your DNA. It's impossible."

Jonathan felt the stress and tension leave his body. The main mystery of why the crown wasn't working seemed to be solved. "So then it's solved. I'll get the crown to work. But I need you to help me."

"How would you like to proceed?"

"I want you to go back to the lab and gather everything you would need if you were going to do a field test. We're going to check the crown's computer circuitry and make observations. By the end of the day we should know what is going on with this."

Sabrina didn't move an inch. "So, let's say we run this test and figure out what is wrong with the crown. What happens if the Ministry finds out about our plans? Is this a risk you're willing to take?"

Sabrina seemed apprehensive. "You think I'm prolonging the inevitable?" he asked.

"Senator Sergeev is on a mission. She is going to destroy the Universe and there is nothing we can do to stop it. I suggest we use this key so Meg can say goodbye to her family. Don't try to save the day."

Jonathan could not heed to Sabrina's warning. His obsession with his new plan to save the Universe was far from over. No one, including Sabrina, would keep him from his directive. "This is the road I'm travelling. I have to exhaust all options before I can give up. There is absolutely nothing else left except for fighting the good fight."

"What fight is that?"

"I have to make this key and travel back, one last time. I need to come face-to-face with the test subjects so I can understand what went wrong. If I can learn something from them, I can keep all the future Universe Initiatives from being destroyed. That is my fight."

Sabrina shook her head. "Jonathan, nothing *went wrong*. The Universe performed exactly how it was supposed to. We learned so much from them, more than anyone could ever have imagined. You didn't make any mistakes or do anything wrong. It was designed for this day, whether done intentionally or not."

"The people in the Universe are smart—they should have learned to overcome their inadequacies. I think we can still learn a great deal from them." Jonathan said.

Sabrina sighed. "What you are planning is not logical. We have passed the point of no return with the Universe. It would cost too much money to correct all the issues the test subjects are having."

A thought came to Jonathan's mind. "We are scientists. Our job is to introduce a hypothesis and build irrefutable theories based on what we have found. I believe gathering any remaining data from these test subjects will help us maintain the Universe II and keep it cost-effective. I want to finish what I started and complete my work."

Jonathan's admission of his plans was merely half true. After observing Sabrina's attitude towards his ideas, he realized that she wouldn't help him without a good reason. Putting science first and abandoning Meg's plea to save the Universe was the only way to bring Sabrina onboard. He watched her closely, hoping that she would take the bait.

Sabrina put out her hand and embraced his. "If that is what you want to accomplish, count me in. I'm willing to do anything I can to further our scientific advancements." They shook hands and made arrangements for the following day.

Shortly after walking Sabrina to the door, Jonathan took a shower and climbed into the bed next to Meg. She was awake and reading an article on her tablet. He stared at her, waiting for her to start a conversation. She continued to ignore him.

He brushed his fingers against her arm. "Usually it's me who's the one up late reading articles."

"I'm plotting out exactly what I need to do to overthrow the Ministry." Meg said proudly.

Jonathan sat up in the bed. "You shouldn't joke about that."

She put the tablet down. "I'm not joking. Everyone in this world we live in except me seems to be afraid of this weird group." Meg moved her face close to Jonathan's. "I'm not going to let them destroy my family."

"I'm going back to your world, Meg. I'm going to take samples and gather evidence to prove to the Council and the Ministry that your world should be saved," he pleaded.

"What about the future of my world? What if the Council decides to destroy my world in the future? I'm not just doing this for my family—I'm doing this for all of my kind." Meg placed the tablet on her nightstand. "Jonathan, this place needs a real leader. We need someone who wants to help everyone advance, not just the fortunate people who were born here in your world."

"I hear you, Meg. I want change too. You have to understand that it doesn't happen overnight." Jonathan leaned over and kissed her cheek. "Things will work out, just trust me." He turned off his lamp.

Meg reached over his body and snapped the light back on. "Why don't we have a conversation with your father about this?"

"Let me get my research done first, and then we'll talk with him." He groaned. The light went back off.

Meg turned it back on. "I can always go talk to him."

Jonathan's full attention went back to her. "We should go together, *after* I complete my research."

"Fine." Meg turned the light out and snuggled next to Jonathan. "Will you bring the other golden crown back with you?"

"Of course." Jonathan wrapped his wife in his arms. He inhaled sharply. "Do you think I've changed?"

Meg chuckled. "We both know the answer to that question."

Jonathan remained focused on the question. "How have I changed?"

"You seem a lot more stressed these days. It's almost like you've lost all joy in life." She patted his chest. "But don't worry, honey. I'm sure you'll find something to be excited about after I overthrow the Ministry."

"Meg, you're not really going to overthrow them."

"If you say so," she replied.

Jonathan's heart sank. "No matter what happens, I want you to know that I love you and the girls with all my heart."

She kissed him. "If that's how you feel, you should show it."

He knew there was no turning back from this point. Jonathan closed his eyes and fell asleep instantly.

***

Jonathan had breakfast with his family for the first time in several months. His daughters peppered him with questions about the lab while Meg made comments under her breath about taking over the world. After breakfast was over, Jonathan kissed his family goodbye and ushered them out of the house to school and work.

He sat down at the table and looked over all his notes. Sabrina was set to arrive at any moment. Even with the prospect of being able to return to Sedona, Jonathan worried that he was wrong about his theory. *What if he wasn't the problem? What if the only key that could open the portal was laying on Bell Rock, far away from him and his team?* Jonathan munched on several pastries.

The doorbell rang. When Jonathan answered, he spotted Sabrina with two boxes, one under each arm. He grabbed as much as he could and opened the door wide for her to come in. "Did anyone ask you about anything?"

Sabrina headed for the kitchen table and dropped a box down on the floor. "Everyone in the lab is on pins and needles, waiting to see where all this will go."

Jonathan closed the front door and headed to the kitchen. "You didn't tell them what we're up to, right?"

"Of course not." She opened a box and pulled out a tablet and some wires. "Senator Sergeev would go ballistic if she knew what you were trying to do."

Jonathan began pulling more wires out. "This is our little secret." Jonathan got out the replica golden crown. His hand grazed across the smooth, metal object. "Once we get this entire issue fixed, I'm heading straight to Sedona to do my research."

Sabrina nodded in agreement. "I'll be here on this side, waiting for you to come back."

Jonathan and Sabrina laid each item out. In her toolkit, Sabrina had brought a large metal machine, a tablet, and several cords of wire. He pulled a chair away from the table and sat down in front of Sabrina. "Where shall we begin?"

She powered on the tablet. "I'm going to start by doing a complete scan of the crown for any anomalies. The slightest hint or clue can help us." Sabrina plugged one side of the wires into the metal box and the other side into her tablet. Jonathan took a deep breath. "Usually, this isn't done on a key, but we'll see where it takes us."

Before Jonathan requested that Sabrina spend all her time in the lab, she was the head of field research. She travelled into the Universe and did studies on the test subjects without their knowledge. The task was simple—enter their homes as they slept, carefully attach the leads to their bodies, gather data, and head back to the lab. No one could do this job like Sabrina.

Just like Jonathan, Sabrina found the people within the Universe very compelling. She had fallen in love with a young man named Dimitris who lived in Greece. Dimitris had just joined the Greek military. He travelled from country to country, meeting Sabrina in various locations around the world. She was a young girl, in love for the first time and ready for whatever adventure would come next.

Sabrina and Dimitris continued their relationship until the Ministry ordered that all observers stay away from the Universe until further notice. Just like Jonathan, she contemplated what to do about her situation. Unlike her friend and colleague, she couldn't imagine her life without their world. As much as she loved Dimitris, Sabrina couldn't give up her research. She abandoned him and took up her post in the lab.

Soon after everyone returned back from the Universe, a war broke out among the test subjects in Yugoslavia. Sabrina watched as many men in Dimitris's NATO platoon were shot down. Fearful about what might happen to her love, Sabrina observed him from her post. It wasn't enough. She felt guilty for leaving him behind. On a whim, Sabrina grabbed her key to the Universe, a small silver charm bracelet, and prepared to teleport back to the other side.

It was too late. Without anyone's knowledge, the Ministry had decommissioned each key, one by one, with the exception of Jonathan's. The Controller had put in a special request for Jonathan's golden crown to remain active so that he could assess the damage after the war. Sabrina begged Jonathan to allow her to use his crown to travel over to the other side. Jonathan painfully declined due to the severe danger of the war. Sabrina was forced to stand and watch as Dimitris and a few others disappeared into the mountains of what now was known as Slovania, never to be heard from again. Jonathan tried to ease her pain by giving her several proactive assignments in the lab.

Sabrina was never the same after Dimitris. She excelled in the lab, but her attitude toward the people in the Universe had changed. Instead of seeing everyone as individuals, she began to call them test subjects. Jonathan knew Sabrina envied him and Meg, but he wanted her to understand that the Controller was behind the war. It didn't matter. Sabrina seemed to have realized that the Universe was there to help her people. She bought into the Ministry's decision to keep everyone grounded. Jonathan, on the other hand, believed that Sabrina should have chosen Dimitris. But she always remained loyal to the Universe Initiative and its leader, Jonathan.

"Normally this is all done digitally." Sabrina said.

"Why are we using this machine?"

"I want a clear reading." Sabrina replied. She synched her tablet in with the machine and typed several codes across the screen. "Okay, Jonathan, let's see what we can learn about this crown."

Jonathan took several deep breaths. "Sounds good."

The machine let out a light humming sound as Sabrina continued to type. She scanned the crown with her tablet. After a few minutes, she put the tablet down. "Let's look over the data." she paused. "We'll have to wait a few moments for the results."

"Okay." He smiled.

Sabrina pulled out a clipboard and a checklist. She scratched off a few boxes. "This is a new frontier for us."

Jonathan narrowed his eyes. "What frontier?"

"Your key will be completely independent from the lab." She moved her attention back to the tablet. "I think I've figured it out!"

Jonathan sat up straight and gave Sabrina his full attention. "What did you find?"

Sabrina placed everything down and took a long, deep breath. "I don't think you're going to like this."

Jonathan sensed her serious concern. He relaxed his body. "I'm calm, Sabrina. Now, tell me your news."

"In order to transport, you'll have to connect your key directly to—"

A knock on the door caused Sabrina to pause. Jonathan rose to his feet and approached the door with caution. He let out a sigh and motioned for Sabrina to head upstairs.

"Who is it?" she whispered.

Jonathan didn't answer but continued to motion for the stairs. Eventually Sabrina received his warning and took each step carefully. Jonathan pried the door open and looked his visitor up and down from head to toe.

"I take one day off from work, and you come looking for me at my home?" he asked.

CHAPTER 22: OBSTRUCTION

Jonathan held the door open partially and blocked the view into his home with his body. The Controller narrowed his eyes at Jonathan. "My son, I sent a message over to the lab requesting a meeting with you. They told me you were at home."

"I'm taking a brief break from my work."

The Controller motioned to the living room. "Can I come in?"

Jonathan stepped outside and shut the door behind him. "Now is not a good time. Can we have a discussion when I return to the lab?"

"We'll go out then." The Controller walked over to an electric car. The sedan was black with dark tinted windows. The driver jumped out and opened the rear passenger door. "Are you coming, Jonathan?"

Jonathan wrestled with his conscience. Sabrina opened the door slightly. "What are you going to do?" she asked.

He turned to her. "What is it that you wanted to tell me about my crown?"

She pointed to the car, making sure that the Controller couldn't see her. "Your father has planted a virus in the crown's binary code."

That was all Jonathan needed in order to make his decision. He advised Sabrina to keep on working on destroying the virus and closed the door. The driver opened the rear car door for Jonathan. The Controller curled his lips into a tight smile. "Now, where would you like to go?"

The pair ended up at the same coffee shop that Sabrina and Bobby had visited on their first meeting. The Controller ordered a black coffee with a shot of energy. Jonathan gave into his sweet tooth and ordered two pumpkin-spiced donuts, and a caramel iced coffee with extra whipped cream and a shot of vitamins. Jonathan recommended that the two take a seat in a secluded table close to the window.

The Controller rejected Jonathan's request and sat in the middle of the coffee shop. Jonathan followed. Several other patrons recognized the Controller and whispered among themselves. Jonathan chuckled. "I almost forgot about your need to make others known of your presence."

"My presence in establishments such as this brings our people peace and rest. They feel assured that things are running smoothly."

Jonathan didn't like the sound of that. "Are things running smoothly?"

The Controller's face became stern. "I was made aware of a situation in the lab last night."

Jonathan shifted his weight in seat. "What type of situation? Did one of the experiments suffer some sort of difficulty?"

The Controller leaned in. "You know exactly what I'm talking about. I was given a report that clearly showed your attempts to make another crown for transport."

A blonde waitress stepped up to the table and placed the food and drinks down. She smiled at the Controller. "Sir, I just want to say that it's an honor to serve you today. I truly appreciate everything you've done for the world."

Jonathan buried his face in his mug. The Controller nodded at the girl. "Everything I and the Ministry have done is for the benefit of people like you."

"Or so they say," Jonathan muttered before taking a drink. He looked up to see his father's angry eyes. "The Controller and his amazing team of geniuses have created our utopia. We should always be grateful for everything they do," he added.

The waitress excused herself.

"Why must you always try to undermine my authority at every moment?" the Controller asked.

Jonathan focused on the main reason for their conversation. "So, you're spying on me now? How are you doing it? Did you have my office bugged with cameras and microphones?"

"Listen up. I want to give you one last chance." The Controller narrowed his eyes. "We are going through with the full destruction of the Universe. Having said that, let me make something extremely clear. Under no circumstances can you or anyone else travel to that world."

"Meg's family is down there. She has a right to see them before they are gone forever."

"No, she does not. Meg gave up her rights when she chose this life. You cannot allow her to leave and travel back there."

"You have absolutely no right to take that away from her!" Jonathan slammed his hand down on the table. A couple seated close to their table turned around. This sparked a thought in Jonathan's mind. "These people have a right to know. We should ask the civilians for their thoughts on what you're proposing."

The Controller took a long sip from his coffee. "Jonathan, don't make this difficult. I just need you to relax and do your job. Don't try to be a hero or a rebel. Just keep your head down and work."

Jonathan stroked the stubble on his chin. "You're right, I should do that. But I think a little bit of public awareness around the matter is also in order."

"You are impossible sometimes!"

Jonathan pointed to the window. "I love our home. I truly do. I'm very happy and grateful that nature selected me to live here and not in the Universe. With that, you have to respect my current position. It's okay for us to disagree on this topic."

The Controller shook his head. "We cannot have division in our household, nor can we divide the Council."

Jonathan bit into his pastry. "Don't worry—no one in the Council is on my side."

"A few members have expressed an interest in seeing how your ideology about leaving the Universe alone would play out. Some members have gone as far as voting to keep the project running for another ten years."

This was an incredible development. "How long has this been going on?" Jonathan asked.

The Controller straightened out his suit. "You have succeeded in touching the emotions of our elite membership. In the end, everyone has come to their senses, but I still worry."

"Are you telling me that you're losing ground with the Council's decision to end my work? Have they voted to keep my project active?"

"I would never say that. I'm merely letting you know that you have created a bit of a ruckus amongst the members." The Controller paused to take a long drink. "This small victory was short lived. I wouldn't spend too much time dwelling on it."

Jonathan moved his plate and cup to the side. "Father, you can clearly see the value in all this. We are finally operating like a complete unit. If the Council makes a decision independent of the Ministry, we will have complete freedom. When the Council was first founded, the goal was to make sure there was balance amongst our leadership. The Ministry should not have the power to override our desires so freely."

"We are not prisoners to the Ministry. We never have been. Our founding fathers created the Ministry to provide leadership to our people. As our population grew in size, the Council was created to be a voice of our populous and later for the Universe. We govern the rights of all our people and promote their wellbeing by making the best decisions for them. The Ministry works with us, not against us. You can't allow your mind to believe that the Ministry, the Council or anyone in this world is your enemy. You are an invaluable addition to the Council, Jonathan, and the Ministry is very pleased with you." the Controller smiled.

Jonathan raised his eyebrow. "Mr. Controller, are you trying to manipulate me? If your goal is to derail my thoughts, you have another thing coming."

"No, my son, I would never do that." He placed his hand on Jonathan's shoulder. "I will always have your best interests at heart."

Jonathan sighed. "I will take everything you have shared with me into consideration."

The Controller nodded. "I'm happy to hear that." The driver approached him and whispered into his ear. "I'm afraid I'm needed back for a conversation with a senator. I have sent for another car to take you back home."

Jonathan remained seated. The cold goodbye bothered him, but he wasn't in the mood to play pretend with his father any longer. The Controller seemed to let Jonathan off the hook, which was the only thing Jonathan was grateful for. He watched his father exit the coffee shop, leaving his half empty mug behind. Jonathan sat back and enjoyed his pastries. There was no way the Controller would keep him from making Meg's wish come true.

***

Jonathan opened the door to his house and spotted Meg and Sabrina sitting at the kitchen table. Meg marched over to him. "Why did you tell your father about our plans to build another crown?"

He took a step back from her. "What are you talking about? I didn't tell him anything."

"The Controller had a team of men come in and take everything," Sabrina stated. She handed Jonathan an envelope. "Before they left, one of the jerks gave me this."

Jonathan opened the letter and read it out loud. "Jonathan, it has been brought to our attention that illegal contraband has been stored at this residence. We, the Ministry, have confiscated such contraband. In accordance with our bylaws, we have noted your conduct in our files. We encourage you to understand our position in this matter. Cordially, the Ministry."

Meg snatched the letter from Jonathan's hand. "Jonathan, we have to do something about this! We can't let these dictators rule over our lives any longer. We have rights! We must stand up for what we believe in!"

Sabrina looked between the two. "Jonathan, what is Meg talking about?" she placed her hand over her mouth. "Meg, you aren't thinking of challenging the Ministry, are you?"

Meg kept her eyes on Jonathan. "You can't just stand by and wait to see what will happen. I want to see my family! I want them to be safe. As my husband, you have to do your best to make that happen."

"There is nothing I can do at this point. I'm lost without my original golden crown. If I could do something to help you, I would." Jonathan pleaded.

Meg stomped off. Sabrina walked to the door, followed by Jonathan. She turned back to face him. "The lab will be under surveillance. You and I are on temporary leave of absence until the Ministry tells us otherwise."

He chuckled. "I put myself on leave of absence so it's not a huge issue." Jonathan wasn't as concerned as Sabrina seemed. "I'm sorry about this. I will let the Controller know the full details of what happened. I'll make sure your suspension is lifted." Jonathan reassured Sabrina.

Sabrina gave him a stiff hug. "I managed to remove the virus from the crown's computer hardware. I programmed it with the pass code 817. Not that it matters—they took it with them."

"We did our best." Jonathan said, "I appreciate everything you've done for me."

"All your research is gone and the replica crown is gone. What will you do now?"

Jonathan opened the door. "Spend the rest of my time making this catastrophe up to my wife."

Sabrina patted Jonathan's back. "Don't worry, things will work out. You are a good man and she is a very understanding and good woman."

The moment Sabrina closed the door behind her, Jonathan raced off to his office. Amongst the mess of papers and notebooks, he searched for any remaining documents or clues to his project. Everything was taken. Jonathan fell back into his chair.

Meg appeared in the doorway. "The girls have been asking questions about my family. What should I tell them?" Jonathan never knew that Kathleen and Emily had mentioned anything to her.

"I have no idea." Jonathan sank deeper into his chair. He wasn't shocked when Meg shared her big revelation but rather defeated. "I truly am sorry about what has happened here. Part of me wishes that we just stayed down there in the Universe. It's so hard watching these people every day, seeing them suffer…"

Meg's eyes lit up. "Can I go to the lab and see my family through your looking glasses?" she blurted.

"We don't use looking glasses, Meg." Jonathan laughed. He got up. "The lab is under surveillance. I'm not allowed back in until after my suspension is over."

Meg was uncharacteristically quiet. Jonathan kissed her cheek. "I'm sorry for being so hard on you." She laced her fingers in his and walked him over to the bedroom. Sitting on top of the comforter was a shiny, golden crown.

Jonathan grabbed onto the doorframe for support. "Meg! What? How? Where did you get that?"

"Sabrina was upstairs when the girls and I came home. I ventured into the kitchen and found this. Shortly after I discovered it the door flew open, and the Ministry's minions came into the house. I hid the crown in the cupboard until they left. Sabrina didn't know anything about it, so don't tell her. I did not want anyone to know but you and me."

Jonathan threw his arms around Meg. "You are the best wife any man could ask for." He kissed her. "I need to get over to the other side and get my original crown so we can travel together."

She placed her hand on his arm. "You're okay with me going to the Universe?"

"I've given it a lot of thought. You should see your family." He grabbed the crown and punched in the pass code. He disarmed the security sensors. "We're running out of time. I need to go."

Meg nodded. "Hurry back."

He handed her the crown. "Will you do the honors?" Jonathan closed his eyes as Meg placed the crown on his head.

He felt a surge of energy as his body was teleported out of their home and to his destination. He concentrated on Sedona. Within the blink of an eye the process was over. Jonathan took a much-needed breath to calm his nerves and opened his eyes.

A panel of three men and two women sat quietly at a glass table. The room was cold, with no windows and a steel metal door. Each person seated at the table had a tablet in hand and a stern look. Their grey suits gave away their identities. Jonathan pulled the crown from his head. He walked over to the table and placed the crown down softly.

"Jonathan, the Controller advised us of your plans to return to the Universe. We hoped you wouldn't be foolish enough to sacrifice yourself in this way." One of the men stated.

Jonathan bowed his head down. "I'm sorry I let you down. I'm sorry I disobeyed the Ministry."

The members looked back and forth at one another. "We, the Ministry, have thought long and hard about your punishment. Truth be told, your crime is considered an act of treason against us." A woman stated.

Jonathan raised his head. "I only wanted to take one final trip down to the Universe before it is destroyed."

"Your decision has cost you greatly. We have no choice but to imprison you for your crime."

Jonathan fell to his knees. His family was no longer safe. No one was safe.

CHAPTER 23: PLOTTING

Bobby and the rest of his family left Sedona a few days after their hike across Bell Rock. Once they were in the safety of their home, Bobby was ready to confront Nicole about the golden crown situation. He had done a lot of thinking and came up with what he had considered to be an ideal plan.

Bobby grabbed his sister and together they raced off to his room, shutting the door quietly. "Nicole, now that we have decided to keep the golden crown, I think we should use it to our advantage."

Nicole seemed intrigued. "How would you like to do that?" she asked as she sat down on his bed.

"I've been giving it a lot of thought, and I think we can program that lab to help us in our world," Bobby said. Nicole opened her mouth but paused. He continued. "Here's what I mean." Bobby stepped over his dirty laundry and hunted for a pen and paper.

"So, you want to travel to the other side to change our world?" Nicole had saved him the trouble of explaining himself.

Bobby turned back to her. "Exactly!" he abandoned his previous task. "I put a plane in the middle of Tempe Town Lake. Imagine what we can do if we actually tried."

"I don't want to play God."

"We wouldn't be 'playing God' at all, Nicole," Bobby stressed. "If these monsters are out there messing with our planet, we should fight back. We should be the ones controlling our planet, not some weird alien race."

"Still sounds like we're playing God."

Bobby wanted to pull his hair out. "You're not listening to me! We have the power of the universe in our hands, literally. We could save all of mankind from disease and hunger and war. These things are ruining us, day by day."

Nicole pulled Bobby down to the bed. "Bobby, I understand what you're saying, however, you have to look at all the facts. You became super upset once you realized that everything that's happening in our world is the doing of this super alien race. What about our people? Don't you think everyone on planet Earth would see your plan as the same thing? People don't want to be programmed to do anything. They want to make their own choices."

Bobby was completely surprised by Nicole's position. Normally, Nicole was the one talking Bobby into taking risks and trying to save the world. Bobby pondered Nicole's words for a moment. She did have a point. "Everything you're telling me makes sense."

"Great!" Nicole retrieved the golden crown from Bobby's bag. "Now let's talk about—"

"However," Bobby interrupted. "You have to ask yourself, Nicole, what else could we do with a crown like this? I believe the universe selected us to use it for the greater good of mankind. You said it yourself. What do you believe?"

Nicole rolled her eyes. "I was getting to that, moron," She placed the crown on her head and Bobby flinched. Nothing happened. "I'm not entirely against your plan. I think using the crown to our advantage is a great idea, but we have to be strategic about it. We need to do more research."

Bobby liked the sound of that. He hopped onto his feet and reached out for the crown. "Let's get started!"

Nicole shielded the crown from Bobby's fingers. "Not so fast. Before you get a chance to travel to the other side, we have to make one more trip."

"Where?"

"Remember that old guy from Sedona who saw the crown and Jonathan?"

Bobby nodded. "Yeah. What about him?"

"I think we should go back to his house and see if he's there." Nicole gave him a sinister grin.

Bobby sighed. "We just came back from Sedona. Why didn't we go by there when Mom and Faja were with us?"

"Because Mom and Faja were with us," Nicole reiterated. "Bobby, we have to be very careful and tread extremely lightly when it comes to all things crown related."

"How do you propose we sneak back up there?"

***

Nicole had plotted out the perfect plan. She and Bobby came down for dinner that evening, dressed in their best clothes, with smiles on their faces. Kim was in the middle of setting the table while Gordy was seated and reading a newspaper. Gordy lifted his eyes up from the paper. "Okay, what do you two want?"

Nicole sat down. "Faja, I just wanted to start off by saying that Bobby and I are truly grateful for the trip to Sedona."

Gordy put the paper down. "Nicole, what did you two do?"

Bobby sat down on Gordy's other side. "It's not what we did, but what we want to do."

Gordy leaned back in his chair and folded his arms. "As you are well aware, Bobby didn't find his precious crown. He's lost his sense of adventure because of it," Nicole started. "Bobby and I got to talking, and we decided that it would be cool if he spent some time down in Tempe with me. We're working on a project."

Kim stopped setting the table. "During Christmas break?"

Nicole looked over at Bobby and motioned for him to answer. "Well, not really." he said.

"What do you mean by 'not really?'" Gordy asked.

"We're thinking of going back down after Christmas and coming back this way for New Years." Nicole smiled.

Gordy laced his fingers and laid his hands on top of the newspaper. "So let me get this straight—you two are going back to Nicole's apartment in Tempe to work on a project?"

Bobby nodded. "Yes, Faja, we are."

Gordy let out a laugh. "Are you two asking for permission? You're both adults."

Kim sighed. "But it's Christmas. We never get to see you two." That was the response Bobby and Nicole had feared.

Bobby's shoulders tightened. "I know, Mom, but this is really important."

Gordy sat up straight. "Can't you work on your project here?"

"No, we can't." Bobby asked.

"You two are lying to us," Kim said before vanishing into the kitchen.

"You've been hiding something from us for months." Gordy pointed to his nose. "I can smell it. Now spill your guts."

Bobby was a horrible liar, but he did his best. "It's a special anniversary present for you two." Kim and Gordy were married the first weekend in January and were celebrating their 35 wedding anniversary this coming year. He paused to look at his sister. She smiled. "We didn't want to say anything until it was done."

Kim reappeared. "Bobby, that is so sweet," She kissed his forehead. "I'm okay with that."

"So am I." Gordy chimed in.

Nicole pointed her finger in Gordy and Kim's direction. "You guys can't come by! It'll ruin the surprise."

Bobby watched as Nicole gave him an approving smile before starting a conversation with their parents about a guy she had met. He envied her confidence. Everything seemed so easy for her.

That night, Nicole snuck into Bobby's room. She raised her hand in the air for a high five. "That was painful, but we got the job done. You and I in Tempe will make everything so much easier."

Bobby left Nicole hanging. "We're not out of the woods yet. We've got to get over to the other side and save the world."

Nicole dropped her hand. "Don't look at it like that, Bobby. I figure we got the hard part done."

Bobby grabbed more clothes and threw them in his suitcase. "I guess you've got a point."

"We'll go to Sedona first and then back to the other side," Nicole said.

Bobby felt uneasy about the plan. He stopped packing. "Nicole, maybe we should just forget about this whole thing."

Nicole grabbed the golden crown. "You can stay here if you want, Bobby, but I'm taking the crown back with me."

Bobby grabbed a corner of the crown and tried to pull it back from Nicole. "No, the crown and I go together."

They continued to struggle. Bobby wrestled the crown away from Nicole. She tackled him to the ground and grabbed it. They both climbed to their feet. As Bobby reached for his treasure, Nicole held the crown above her head. Everything happened fast. Bobby lunged for it, Nicole tripped, the crown slammed onto her head and within a few seconds, she was gone.

CHAPTER 24: MISTAKE

Meg waited up for Jonathan to come home. Over an hour had passed since he had put the crown on. She racked her brain on what to do. Every reasonable option led to a dead end. Sabrina had no idea that Jonathan was missing, so she had no one to turn to. She couldn't break into the lab either. She sat down on the bed and tried to sort through her thoughts.

"Mom, where's Dad?" Emily asked. "All his research is gone."

Meg felt a sense of hope. Emily wanted to be an observer too and had paid close attention to everything Jonathan did. "Honey, how much of your father's research did you read?"

Emily was silent. Meg tried to wait patiently for her to say something. Anything. "He didn't keep his work out for me to read. Why?"

Meg's nerves were shot. She took a deep breath. "Your father is working out in the field, and I'm trying to get a better understanding of where he might be."

Emily wrapped her arms around her mother. "I'm sure he's okay. I wish he would have taken me with him."

Meg held onto her daughter. "What your dad does is very dangerous." she let go of Emily. "I hope you'll choose a different profession."

Emily shook her head. "Daddy changes the world. I want to do that."

Meg bit her tongue. She kissed Emily good night and sent her off to bed. She checked on Kathleen who was completing her homework. Meg sighed. "Where's Dad?" Kathleen asked without looking up from her work.

"He's working," Meg replied.

"Okay." Kathleen muttered.

Meg was saddened by the fact that Kathleen had given up on having a relationship with Jonathan. The only time Kathleen acknowledged him was on the rare occasions they saw each other. She seemed content with a simple, *Hi, Dad,* to hold her over until the next time they met again. Jonathan wanted to spend more time with her, but trying to save the Universe became his entire focus.

Kathleen was smart. She excelled in school, making her a prime candidate for a career with the Council or the Ministry one day. Meg desperately needed help. After Emily, Kathleen was her next hope. "Your father travelled back to the field, and I haven't heard from him. I need your help. We have to find him before the Ministry finds out."

"Why would the Ministry care if Dad's doing his job? Isn't that what he's *supposed* to be doing?"

"I understand this doesn't make any sense, but you and I are the only two people who can help him right now."

Kathleen continued to work. "What about us? We've all had to sacrifice because he wants to work all sorts of crazy hours, Mom. He doesn't care about us, obviously."

Meg grabbed the pencil out of Kathleen's hand. "I understand that you're upset with your father. Believe me, I'm upset with him too. But at the moment, I need you to help me get him back."

Kathleen's interest sparked. "Mom, what's going on?"

Meg sat down on Kathleen's bed and motioned for her to do the same. "Kathleen, there's something I need to tell you about me and your father." Meg explained the entire story to

Kathleen. She first started with how she and Jonathan had met. Meg shared everything about where she had come from. At the very end, she expressed her fears with her world being destroyed.

"So you are one of these test subjects from the Universe? They are human too?" Kathleen asked.

Meg nodded. "Yes, I'm one of them. So is the rest of my family. I left them all behind so I could live here."

"Why does Dad want to destroy the place you come from?"

"The Controller wants to destroy my world. To him, my people are just a bunch of lab rats to be used in an experiment. We were manufactured to help move this world forward."

Kathleen fought back the tears. "Mom, I'm so sorry for what's happening to you. I never meant to be so difficult. I had no idea that you and Dad have been trying to save your world."

Meg kept a strong face for her daughter. "It's okay. Right now you and I have to work together to stop the Controller." Emily came to the door. "Honey, you're supposed to be sleeping." Meg said. She got up and walked over to Emily, hoping she hadn't heard the conversation between her and Kathleen.

"I was sleeping, but someone kept knocking on the door." Emily admitted. "There's a man downstairs who wants to talk with you."

Meg froze in her tracks. She quickly sent Emily back to Kathleen's room. Meg took a deep breath and walked down each step slowly. Her visitor had taken a seat at the kitchen table.

"What do you want?" Meg asked.

"I wish you and Jonathan would let me spend time with my grandchildren. Emily doesn't even know who I am." He motioned for her to sit across from him. Meg folded her arms and refused to sit down. "Suit yourself," he shook his head. "I'm pretty sure you've figured out that something has happened to Jonathan."

"What have you done with him?'

"I warned Jonathan not to disobey my orders," the Controller stated. "I'm sorry to disappoint you, Meg, but there is nothing I can do at this time to help him."

Meg processed the situation. "You didn't have anything to do with what happened to him?"

"The Ministry has taken Jonathan prisoner for trying to escape to the Universe."

"He wasn't trying to escape. I just wanted to see my family again for one last time before you destroyed every single memory and person I love."

The Controller folded his arms and sat back. "That was very sweet of him. Unfortunately, Jonathan's misconduct has cost you and your entire family a great amount."

Meg finally sat down. "You didn't destroy it yet, did you?" Her soul was crushed by the mere thought that everything in the Universe was gone. "Chandler, I beg of you, can you at least try to see things the same way I do?"

Referring to the Controller as Chandler, his first name, was forbidden. Meg didn't care. She had placed all her formalities aside. Her husband was missing, that was the only thing that concerned her. Meg hoped the Controller would admire her devotion to Jonathan. She reminded him of Jonathan's mother. He seemed to let down his guard to connect with her.

The Controller unfolded his arms. "Meg, think what you may about me, but I do not rejoice in the destruction of your home. I appreciate your love and care for my son and your children. Nothing I have done in the past has been directed towards you. Every decision I have made has been to help everyone in our world survive."

"You're dodging my question. Did you destroy Earth?" she asked again.

The Controller inhaled deeply. "To answer your question—no, we haven't."

Meg sighed.

"However, we have sent out the program to begin destruction. It's only a matter of time until the collapse begins."

Meg threw her head into her hands. "Bring me my husband."

The Controller stood to his feet. "Jonathan's going to be gone for a while. He has been arrested." he placed his hand on her back. "I'm sorry, Meg. Truly, I am."

She swatted his hand away. "No, you're not sorry. If you were, you would have done something to convince the Ministry to let my family be. How can you just sit back and allow your only son to be held captive? You are the most prideful man I know. Clearly you haven't shown the slightest bit of care for Jonathan!"

The Controller seemed unaffected by Meg's blatant disregard for his possible feelings for Jonathan. He paused for a long moment before reaching under the table and removing something from the chair next to him. He placed the shiny gold crown down in front of Meg. "When you and my son married, both of you knew that something like this would happen. You two came from completely different worlds; your path would not be easy. Meg, you saved Jonathan a world of pain and suffering the moment you decided to move here and set up your home. I appreciate that."

A tear ran down her face. "If you appreciate me so much, why are you continuing with your plans to destroy both of my families?"

"The course the Ministry and I have chartered cannot be stopped, not even by someone as special as Jonathan." He placed his hands on top of the crown. "I give you my permission to travel back to the Universe, your home, and say goodbye to your family. It's the least I can do given the circumstances."

She wiped her face and steadied herself. "What? Why are you allowing me to go back?" she asked in complete shock.

"I have a heart, just like you. If I were in your shoes, I'd like to go back and say goodbye to my family, too." He held back a smile.

Meg shook her head. "If you were in my shoes, you'd do whatever it takes to get the Ministry to stop the destruction of your home." The Controller lowered his eyes to the floor. Meg sighed and accepted the Controller's act of kindness toward her. "Thank you for allowing me to see my family again, but what about my husband? I will not rest until he is brought back to me."

The Controller retrieved a tiny paper from his coat pocket and put it down next to the crown. "One miracle at a time, Meg. One miracle at a time." He walked over to the door and placed his hand on the handle. "I'm just as worried as you are about Jonathan, but at least I know he's safe."

"Wait!" Meg shouted. The Controller paused. "If I make it over to the Universe and can't find my way back, will you make sure your grand-daughters are safe?" The Controller nodded.

The door opened, and he left. Meg opened the paper. Pass code 817. She ran her fingers across the top of the crown. She took a deep breath, put in the pass code, and placed it on her head. Nothing happened. Full of anger and frustration, she pulled the crown from her head and tossed it onto the table. Meg knew she couldn't get it to work without Jonathan.

***

Bobby grabbed his chest. Nicole was gone. A knock at the door made him jump. "Son, you and your sister need to give it a rest!" Gordy yelled.

"Yes, Faja." Bobby's voice cracked. He waited until he heard Gordy's feet stomp down on the stairs before he moved. "Man, oh man, what have we done now?" His heart raced. Nicole's trip to the other side was completely unexpected and neither one of them was prepared. *How long should I wait for her to come back before I really freak out? What if she gets into trouble over there?* Bobby's head was spinning.

Petrified with fear, he sat on his bed and impatiently waited for her return. After an hour, Bobby felt the need to do something. He opened his door partially and scanned the hallway. No one was in sight. He dashed to Nicole's room and hunted for her notes on the golden crown. This simple move was all that came to mind.

Lying in a notebook deep within her purse was a lead. Nicole had wanted to visit the crazy old man in Sedona. *That's a start!* He thought. Bobby raced back to his room—his knee tingled slightly. He ignored it and dropped down in front of his computer to look up Nikolai Burns on the Internet. He retrieved a phone number and called it at once.

"Hello?" an old, raspy male voice asked.

"My name is Bobby Walker, and my sister is missing, and I think you might be able to help me!" Bobby stopped to take a deep breath. "We went to your shop a while ago to ask about the golden crown, and Ernest, that crazy guy who works there, said you knew things about the crown and that you had travelled to the other side!"

The man was silent. "Sonny, I missed half of that. You've got to slow down and start from the beginning. Your sister is missing?"

Bobby rolled his eyes. "Yes, she's lost over in that alien world that the golden crown took her to. I need your help. You're the only person who's been over there besides me."

More silence. Bobby checked the phone to make sure he still had a connection. "So you're telling me that you found that golden crown?"

"Never mind." Bobby was at his wits end. "I thought you could help me but I was completely wrong. Have a great night." He pulled the phone away from his ear.

The phone crackled as the voice on the other end begged Bobby not to hang up. He placed the phone back up to his ear and caught the man in the middle of his sentence. "...most of the time people call me with pranks. I believe you, and I want to help you out."

"How can we help her?"

The man cleared his throat and lowered it by a few octaves. "First things first, I need proof that this isn't a prank."

"How do I give you proof?"

"Come to Sedona and show yourself! That will be your first step."

Something seemed a little off with the man's voice, but Bobby was willing to do anything to help Nicole. "Tell you what. If my sister isn't back by morning, I'll be at your house by 8:30. Fair enough?"

"You've got yourself a deal. Oh, and before I forget, my services are not cheap. Bring five hundred dollars with you."

Bobby slapped his forehead. "Five hundred dollars? You're really going to make me pay you to help me?"

"Do you want to see your sister again or not?" the man snapped.

Bobby raised his eyebrow even though the caller couldn't see his face. "I'm having trouble believing you. Are you sure you're Nikolai Burns?"

The phone shuffled. "Young man..." At first the man's voice was high, but he cleared his throat. "Bobby, I am here to help you. I want to do all that I can. In order for me to do so, I need payment. You have to understand."

Bobby weighed his options. Five hundred dollars was all the money he had in his savings, but that wasn't the main issue. The entire scheme felt like a trap. On the other hand, the caller was probably Nikolai Burns, the man Bobby was certain had travelled to the same strange place he had. "Okay, fine. If I don't hear from her, or if she doesn't come back tonight, I'll head up to Sedona, and I'll bring the money."

"Good. I'll see you tomorrow, Bobby." The man hung up.

Bobby stayed up until past midnight, hoping that Nicole would show up eventually. She never did. There was no sign of her. Bobby finally fell asleep, worried about his sister and afraid to tell Gordy and Kim the truth about the crown. The moment the sun was up the next day, Bobby checked for Nicole without finding her. He hopped into Nicole's jeep and headed toward Sedona.

CHAPTER 25: LIAR, LIAR

Jonathan opened his eyes and looked up at the metal ceiling. He guessed the sun had risen, but had no way of knowing. The entire room was a metal box. No windows and just a small door. Jonathan jumped to his feet and walked over to the door. He balled his hand into a fist and proceeded to knock until someone opened a small window.

"Please stop knocking." The man in a red uniform answered.

"I demand to speak with my father, the Controller." Jonathan said.

The officer looked around the room. "If you're in here that means you've done something incredibly wrong. You are not permitted to speak with anyone until your legal representation comes."

"When will that be?"

"Let me check." The man closed the window. Jonathan could hear footsteps and muffled voices. He concentrated on the voices, one young and one old, but he couldn't make out a single word. All of a sudden the door opened. "I guess your legal counsel is already here."

Jonathan shook his head. "I haven't asked for any counsel."

The man slapped a metal device on Jonathan's wrists. "Well, someone has come to visit you, nonetheless." He stepped behind Jonathan and pushed him to walk forward.

The hallway was cold. Jonathan walked quietly as he pondered who could have been his counsel. He was certain that the Controller wasn't there to help. But if it wasn't the Controller, who else could it have been? Meg? Jonathan thought about his wife and the fear she was more than likely facing. He felt sorry for the decisions he had made.

The guard pushed Jonathan towards another hallway. At the end was a door with a window. Jonathan could see lights on the other side. He smiled. Things might go better than he expected. The guard pulled Jonathan to a stop and unlocked the door. On the other side was a room with a large glass table and six chairs. Jonathan was instructed to take a seat at the table and wait.

A few minutes later, the Ministry walked into the room and sat in the remaining five chairs. Jonathan sighed loudly. Things had gone from bad to worse. Each member of the Ministry opened a folder and placed their glasses on their faces. The eldest gentlemen in the group cleared his throat and looked up at Jonathan.

"Are my wife and children okay?" Jonathan asked. "I was told I was meeting with my counselor—where is this person?"

"Jonathan, you have been charged with the act of treason against the Ministry and our entire world. How do you plead?" The gentleman asked.

"Does it matter how I plead? The five of you are going to euthanize me anyway." Jonathan snapped.

The members glanced at one another before resting their eyes back on him. "Your father, Chandler, has asked that we consider alternative punishments. He is under the impression that your misconduct was not an act of treason, but a misunderstanding. He explained to us that your wife, Megan, is a member of the Universe Initiative, and you wanted to give her one last chance to see her family before its destruction. Is any of this true?"

Jonathan nodded. "Most of what you have said is true. What my father, the Controller, has failed to mention is my disdain for the destruction of such a valuable project. I believe you, the Ministry, have made a terrible mistake. If you saw what I see every day, you would fight to protect this amazing habitat and its high-functioning test subjects."

Another member, a woman with white hair, cleared her throat. "We have been informed of your crusade to protect and save your project, Jonathan. You don't need to defend yourself to us. What you fail to understand is the nature of our decision. We have insight into where our world is going. You may think you know everything about the test subjects, but you have no idea what they are truly capable of."

Jonathan raised his eyebrow. "What do you mean?"

The woman continued. "Last night we had your colleague, Sabrina, administer the first installment of the destruction plan. She's been helping us ever since you told her about the replica golden crown. She implemented a conflict amongst Russia and the United States in Ukraine. Other countries in the Universe are being pressured to choose sides. China has sided with Russia. The Arab nations have created their own defense. Europe is at a stalemate. Canada is unsure if it will aid the US. It's beginning. "

Sabrina? Her betrayal was unanticipated. Jonathan's heart sank. "Have the test subjects started threatening nuclear warfare?"

"It doesn't matter." Another member, a middle-aged man in his late forties, said. "The day has finally come for all this to end."

Jonathan had a startling thought. "My key was left behind and abandoned in one of the locations within the project. I was always told that it was the fail safe to keeping the Universe from being destroyed. How did you override that function?"

The Ministry was silent. Eventually the eldest member spoke. "Jonathan, we had no idea that your key was still in the Universe. If we knew that, we would have demanded someone to travel to the other side and get it."

"Well that is exactly what I was trying to accomplish." Jonathan retorted. "So you're saying that the golden crown malfunctioned on its own?" Jonathan was completely confused. And then it hit him... *Or it's not in the Universe any longer.*

***

Bobby made it to Sedona in record time. He slammed the Jeep door, hopped up the steps and pounded on Nikolai's door until he answered. The man squinted and frowned as he wrapped his robe around his body. "Who in the blazes are you, and what in the blazes do you want?"

Bobby put out his hand. "I'm Bobby Walker. We spoke last night about my missing sister." Nikolai raised an eyebrow. "You told me to come to Sedona in the morning, and we would talk about the golden crown."

Nikolai folded his arms. "Is that so?"

Bobby reached into his pocket and pulled out the five hundred dollars. "You told me to bring this, and you would help me get my sister back from the alien race that might be holding her hostage."

The man looked down at Bobby's hand and let out a loud sigh. "Hold on one moment." Nikolai closed the door, leaving Bobby on the porch desperate and confused. The door flew open and Nikolai clutched the ear of a young boy. "I believe this may be the explanation we are both looking for."

Bobby narrowed his eyes. "I don't understand. The person I spoke with over the phone sounded like I imagined you would sound like."

"Peter is my grandson. He wants to be an actor and has been using my website as a way to make some extra money.

You're one of two people who have come to my home with a handful of cash, looking for a family member who was taken by aliens." Nikolai pressed down on Peter's ear. "Now tell Bobby you're sorry."

"Sorry!" Peter shouted.

Bobby wanted to throttle Peter. "I drove all the way up here for nothing?"

Nikolai glared at Peter. Peter shrugged. "Like I said before, *I'm sorry.* I didn't think you would take me seriously!"

"My sister is missing! I'm trying to do whatever I can to get her back!"

Nikolai muttered a few words in Peter's ear. The boy fled into the house as Nikolai closed the door behind him. "Bobby, I'm sorry to hear about your dear sister, but I'm afraid there is nothing I can do."

"So you have never seen or heard of the golden crown?" Bobby huffed.

"Golden Crown? Is that what this thing is about? I've heard of it, and I've seen it. The last time I came in contact with that thing was over ten years ago. Unfortunately that's all I can tell you."

Nikolai reached for the door. The moment his hand hit the handle, Bobby intercepted him. "There has to be more. You're the only other person I know of who has made it to that side and back other than me. You have to help me."

Nikolai released the handle. "Bobby, I don't know what to tell you. I put the crown on my head and ended up in Australia. Then I was brought back here as quickly as I had teleported. That's all I can give you."

Bobby raised his eyebrow. "You know, for someone who has been traveling the world talking about aliens, you seem very uninterested in everything I'm telling you."

The man sighed. "I've spent the last decade of my life trying to make sense of what I experienced. As my career comes to an end and I approach retirement, I have come to one very important conclusion. Aliens don't exist. Whatever happened to me was a fluke." He placed his hand on Bobby's shoulder. "Young man, I was like you once; full of questions about the unknown and searching for answers. But at this point in the game, you have to open your eyes to the truth. Whatever you think happened is not real. It was all a figment of your imagination. Your sister probably ran away."

Bobby removed Nikolai's hand from his shoulder. "I know what I saw. I've been to the lab and seen the experiments." He pointed to the sky. "My sister is up there, or wherever this place exists, and she might be in danger. You may not want to help me, but I'm not going to stop looking until I find her."

Without another word, Bobby stormed off the porch and headed for the jeep. The moment he hopped inside his phone rang. It was Gordy. "Hey Faja, I'm sorry I left this morning without waking you and Mom up first."

"Is your sister with you?" Gordy asked.

Bobby's shoulders tensed up. "She's in the store buying something." He slapped his head.

"Well, hurry home! You'll never guess whose here!"

"Nicole?" Bobby asked before he could stop himself.

Gordy paused before laughing. "You're such a kidder! No, your Aunt Meg!"

The phone fell out of Bobby's hand as he fired up the Jeep and raced back to Phoenix.

***

Jonathan was escorted back to his cell against his will. He overheard some valuable information. The moment the Ministry found out about Jonathan's mistake with the golden crown, they sent out guards and enforcers to check every home. A test subject, a threat, was loose in their world. Jonathan smiled to himself as he watched the leadership of his world scramble. Everything was going awry, which is exactly what he wanted. He wanted to see revenge for what they had done to his wife's family.

But deep inside his heart, Jonathan understood the concern the Ministry had regarding the test subjects. The test subjects had grown to become amazing, innovative people with a desire to be free. If anyone from the Universe knew what was happening to their planet, they would revolt. Any group would have done that. He feared for his wife and children's well-being. Jonathan crossed over the threshold into his cell and set his eyes on his new "cell mate."

"My, my, Jonathan. Everything you have done in the past few days has elevated our situation from bad to worse," the Controller said.

The guard removed the metal wristbands from Jonathan's arms. He rubbed his skin. "I didn't do anything intentionally. If you ask me, it seems as though the Universe and nature are finding a way to co-exist. Everything happens for a reason, Father."

"I gave the crown back to Meg so she could say goodbye to her family."

Jonathan couldn't hold his feelings back. "The world is in the process of being destroyed! The Ministry has administered the beginning stage of the eradication process. You just sent my wife to her death!"

Jonathan fell down to his knees. The Controller crouched down next to Jonathan and placed his hand on his back. "Now is not the time for you to be defeated, my son. We must get you out of here so you can save her."

The Controller pulled Jonathan up to his feet. "You want to help me?" Jonathan asked.

The Controller retrieved a small black tube from his coat pocket. "You are my son. I would do anything to help you." He pressed the tube against the door jam and waited for a few seconds. The door opened without resistance. "Now, let's get you back into your lab so you can save Meg."

Jonathan walked out of the door with the Controller close on his heels. As they walked down the hall, side by side, Jonathan took this time to get a clear confession from the Controller. "So, in your opinion, are we bad people? Do you think everything the Council and the Ministry are doing is inhumane?"

The Controller threw his arm in front of Jonathan. A set of footsteps approached. The two men changed direction and stepped into an empty room. "Jonathan, we are not inhumane people. We are not the villains. Our objective is simple—we study the people in the Universe so we can better understand our own people. Their world no longer reflects ours. You keep explaining to us that we control the test subjects, but that is not true. They are their own people." The Controller was silent as footsteps drew closer.

Jonathan pressed his body against the wall, hoping that no one could see him. "Is that what you really think?" he whispered.

The two guards' footsteps neared the door and stopped. Silence. Jonathan held his breath and concentrated on Meg. *Was she okay?* he thought. The footsteps moved away from the door and in the direction Jonathan and the Controller had come from. Jonathan felt a hand on his back.

"Son, you have to understand something very important about our people. We never intended to destroy the Universe when we first built it. Due to the amount of problems and peril the test subjects have endured, we feel that we are acting in their best interest. I want you to believe me when I say that." The Controller said.

Jonathan looked out into the hallway. "Okay, Father, this is our chance to leave." The Controller took a step into the hallway, but Jonathan stopped him. "Once I get out of here,

I'm going to stop the destruction of the Universe. If you want to help me succeed, please, come with me. If not, don't stand in my way."

Jonathan put his hand out. The Controller grabbed his hand and shook it. "I'm with you on this."

Jonathan smiled and ran down the hall. Both he and the Controller escaped.

CHAPTER 26: SOMEONE HAS SOME EXPLAINING TO DO

Bobby rehearsed his speech over twenty times before he felt it was right. He pulled into the driveway and shut off the jeep engine. "Anything's possible if you just try," he muttered to himself as he opened the car door and made his way to the house. He took a deep breath and opened the front door.

"Nicole?" he asked as his eyes fell on her.

She smiled. "No, it's your Aunt Meg." Meg said as she wrapped her arms around Bobby.

He hugged her back. "If it weren't for the red hair, I would have believed that you were an older version of my sister."

Meg chuckled. "Or maybe she's a slightly younger version of me? You're so big now."

Bobby laughed. He peeked his head around the house. "Where are my parents?"

"They went out to get pizza for lunch. Your parents and I spent a long time talking about me."

Bobby didn't waste any more time. "Aunt Meg, Nicole and I found a golden crown in Sedona awhile back, and we've been using it to go to this other world. Actually I'm the only one who was using it to go to this other world. Anyway, to make a long story short, I think that's where you were, and now Nicole is over there in that world while I'm stuck here, worrying about her."

Meg paused. "You and your sister have the golden crown?" Bobby nodded. "And Nicole is trapped on the other side?"

"It was an accident. Normally she can't do it, and I can. I'm worried because she's been over there for a long time, and I don't know what to do." Tears fell from Bobby's eyes.

Meg pulled him into a hug. "Take a deep breath, Bobby. It's going to be okay. So you know the truth about me? You used the crown? Well I'm here right now, and we'll figure this out together."

Bobby had an epiphany. He finally had a chance to put he and Nicole's theories to rest. "Aunt Meg, you seem to be quite comfortable with what I'm telling you. Some weird guy in Sedona said that someone by the name of Meg fell in love with someone from that world and left with him. You've been missing for a long time now. Are you the one they were talking about?"

Meg guided Bobby to the couch and took a seat. "Everything you know about me is true. I met Jonathan several years ago while I was in college. He told me the story about where he is from, and I chose to go back there with him."

"What is that place, anyway?"

"I'm not sure, but it's like our world except completely different." Meg sighed. The time had come for her to tell Bobby the truth. "Bobby, my husband, Jonathan, and his team are in charge of using science to impact our planet so they can improve their world, my new world, by studying your world, my world...you know what I mean. We are their test subjects."

Bobby nodded. "Believe it or not, I already knew that. I teleported into the lab and wound up getting a tour of the entire thing. Jonathan and Sabrina showed me how to program the test subjects."

Meg's eyes widened. "You were the intern Sabrina met? You know how it all works?" He nodded. Meg grabbed his hands. "Listen to me very closely, Bobby. There is this group over there called the Ministry, and they have set up a program to destroy our world."

The color left Bobby's face. A flood of emotions ran through him. "They're going to kill us?"

"Not if we can help it," Meg said. "Bobby, you know how the lab works! You can stop them!" She yelled.

Bobby scrambled for a moment. "Wait a minute, I'm not sure if I can do that. I only went to the lab once, and Jonathan is the one who set everything up. I just pressed a few buttons, and the plane was in the water. Besides, they typically just set things in motion and let us do the rest on our own. Are you referring to what is going on in the Ukraine?"

Meg squeezed Bobby's hands. "Bobby, you can do this. I believe that you have everything we need to take care of this problem."

"But I don't have a way to get over there." he said. Meg jumped up from the couch and grabbed a paper bag from the kitchen table. She pulled out a golden crown. "Where did you get that?" he asked.

"Jonathan made a replica. At first it didn't work, but eventually I found my way over here. I don't think the Ministry can track it either." She placed it in his hands. "Bobby, please take this key to the Universe and use it to stop the Ministry. You are special. You're the only one who can."

He was floored. "I don't know." Bobby heard a key being inserted into the front door lock. He grabbed Meg's hand and pulled her up to his room. Slowly and carefully he closed his bedroom door. "My parents don't know that Nicole and I have the original crown or the fact that Nicole is missing."

Meg pulled the crown into her hands. "Bobby, I'll hold your family off while you travel to the other side. In the meantime, I want you to break into the lab and do everything you can to save all of us."

She started to place the crown on his head but Bobby dodged it. "What if I fail and Earth is destroyed? If you stay here, you'll be gone."

Meg smiled. "Bobby, I believe you can do it. I'm not worried." She raised her hands above his head. "Now go over there, and save all of us!"

Bobby closed his eyes and allowed Meg to put the crown on his head. He held his breath and waited to transport to the other side.

Kim knocked on Bobby's door. Meg turned as the door opened. "Hey, Meg, I saw Nicole's jeep out front. Have you seen my kids?"

Meg smiled. "No." She turned back and looked around the empty room. Bobby had made it.

***

Jonathan and the Controller set foot outside the Holding Hall used to detain anyone who was considered a disruption to society. They managed to make it to the solar train minutes before the warning went out. A voice came overhead, advising everyone that a test subject was loose inside their world. The passengers looked back and forth at one another, confused as to what they should do.

"Most of these people have no idea what's going," Jonathan whispered to the Controller.

"I'll handle this." The Controller stated before addressing the crowd. "Ladies and gentlemen, a suspected intruder has come into our world. There is no need to panic, just keep an eye out for anyone who seems out of place."

One of the passengers, a young man in his mid-twenties, shouted. "You're the Controller! We were warned that you and another dangerous criminal escaped prison today!"

The Controller froze, but lucky for him, Jonathan was prepared. He grabbed the emergency stop lever, pulled it down, and braced himself and his father for impact. The train came to a screeching halt, shoving the passengers forward and into one another. Jonathan and his father regained their balance and pushed the doors open, jumping out before the man could grab them. They headed toward the lab as a group of bystanders began to chase them.

Jonathan ran as fast as he could, keeping his focus on the distance between themselves and the lab. As he passed people on the street, one person in particular, a woman, grabbed his attention. "Meg?" he shouted as he stopped.

Nicole shook her head. "No, I'm not Meg."

The Controller caught up to Jonathan. "Son, we have to keep going!"

Jonathan looked down at Nicole's hand and spied the golden crown. "Where did you get that?"

Nicole looked back at the crowd closing in on them. She took off running, afraid of what seemed to be going on. Jonathan ran after her, followed by the Controller. "Where did you get that?" Jonathan yelled again.

Nicole didn't answer. She dodged the people on the street and headed away from Unity Avenue. Jonathan ran faster to catch up to her. Nicole managed to evade Jonathan as she disappeared into an alley. She crouched down behind a large recycle bin. Jonathan passed the alley and continued down the street with the Controller trailing behind him shouting for him to slow down.

Nicole counted to ten and popped up from her location. She came face to face with two guards. They reached out to grab her, but Nicole was quick on her feet. She took off running with the golden crown in her hands. Nicole cleared one corner and ran down another alley at full speed. When she turned around, no one was chasing her. She smiled to herself and rounded another corner.

"Stop!" a loud voice shouted. Nicole froze.

A line of guards surrounded her on both sides. Nicole threw the crown on her head and closed her eyes. She felt it being removed. "Get away from me!" she demanded.

The guards were cautious as they continued to approach her. This was her only moment to act. She kicked the shin of the man closest to her and broke her way through the crowd. Nicole kept running down the alley, unsure where to go or what to do.

***

Bobby appeared in the lab. He pulled the golden crown from his head and placed it on one of the stations. "Okay, Aunt Meg, here goes nothing." Out of instinct, he grabbed one of the lab coats from the rack and placed it on his body. Bobby picked up a tablet and powered it on.

He approached the first station: *War.* "I can do this." he muttered to himself as he pressed a slew of buttons on the tablet. After several failed attempts to log in, Bobby managed to arrive at the main screen. He clicked the button labeled *War.*

"What are you doing?" a voice asked.

Bobby clenched the tablet and turned around. The Controller stood before him. "I'm saving the world." Bobby replied.

The Controller looked down at the golden crown and then back at Bobby. "Are you the test subject that escaped from the Universe?"

Bobby was confused until he realized that the man was more than likely referring to Nicole. "I didn't escape. I'm not a prisoner."

Jonathan stepped into the lab. "Bobby? What are you doing here?"

The Controller looked between both Jonathan and Bobby. "You know this boy?"

"He's the local boy from the country that I thought would make a great intern. He is the one who toured the lab with me a few weeks back. Bobby, again, what are you doing here?" Jonathan asked.

This was a pleasant surprise. Bobby realized that neither Jonathan nor the Controller know who he actually was. He thought for a moment and looked down at the lab coat and tablet. "I'm here to stop you from destroying the Universe. I realized that these are wonderful, amazing people who deserve a chance at a life. It is not our place to stop them from having that."

The Controller put out his hand. "Bobby, give me the tablet."

Jonathan whipped his head around. "Father? I thought you were here to help me save the Universe?"

The Controller grabbed the replica golden crown. "Jonathan, I'm here to save you from yourself. If you stop the destruction of the Universe, you will be executed." He put his hand on Jonathan's shoulder. "Please, son, don't do this."

Jonathan immediately began to argue with the Controller. Bobby looked down at the tablet. He slowly moved his fingers over the commands and typed in the word *Peace*. Taking in a deep breath, he entered in the code *End War* and completed the task. He looked up at Jonathan and the Controller. "It's too late."

Jonathan broke his concentration and focused on Bobby. "What did you do?"

"We don't have the power to destroy and kill people. It's not our right." Bobby said.

The Controller shook his head. "You really shouldn't have done that."

233

The doors to the lab opened and a fleet of guards entered. As one guard grabbed Jonathan by the arms, another retrieved the replica golden crown. Bobby slowly placed the tablet down. "Am I under arrest now?" he asked.

The Controller took a few steps forward. "Young Bobby, you are not allowed to administer such commands. Only the Ministry gets to decide the fate of the Universe."

"I apologize, but I don't agree with your logic."

"Bobby, this is not a game. What you have done is a very serious crime, an act of treason."

Bobby lowered his eyes to the ground. Inside the Controller's coat something metallic glistened. He looked up and spotted the other crown in the guard's hands. "What is my punishment?" Bobby asked as he bit back a smile.

"You will have to go before the Ministry, and they will decide what to do with you." The Controller put his hand on Bobby's shoulder.

"He's just a young man!" Jonathan shouted. "You can't arrest him!"

The Controller turned to Jonathan, putting the crown in Bobby's reach. "This *boy* has broken the law. We must make an example out of him."

This was Bobby's only shot. In one quick, fluid move, he reached into the Controller's coat and grabbed the golden crown. Within seconds the crown was on his head. He closed his eyes and waited for something to happen. When he opened them, Meg was standing inches away from him.

"What happened?" she asked.

Bobby pulled the crown from his head and tossed it into his closet. "Well, I met your husband for a second time. And his dad."

Meg's eyes widened. "What did you tell him?"

"I got into the lab and was about to stop the destruction of Earth when they caught me. All these guards showed up, and they arrested Jonathan."

Meg grabbed onto Bobby's arm. "No!"

"During the commotion I managed to stop the whole process of the world coming to an end. Jonathan's father was about to arrest me when I grabbed the original golden crown and teleported back." Bobby rushed out.

Meg let go of his arm. "So the other crown is still over there?"

"Yes." Bobby slapped his forehead. "And so is Nicole! I only had a short moment to escape. I had to leave her behind!" Bobby was crushed. He threw his body down on the bed. "Now what am I going to do?"

Meg sat down next to him. "Bobby, I will take the crown, transport back over and find your sister."

Kim poked her head into Bobby's room. "Bobby, Meg, we're drooling for some pizza! Hurry up!"

Meg gave Kim a brave smile. "Just a moment. Bobby and I are catching up a bit."

"Don't keep us waiting too long." Kim started to shut the door. "Can you tell Nicole, too? I knocked on her door, but she didn't answer."

Bobby nodded and waited for Kim to close the door. Once Bobby and Meg were alone, he continued. "Aunt Meg, things seemed pretty bad when I left. I think Jonathan's on his way to jail."

"Don't worry about that. Jonathan is the Controller's son. Chandler won't let anything happen to him. The Controller is the whole reason why I'm here. He gave me the crown so I could come say goodbye to you guys. He was already jailed and I was wondering how Jonathan got out of jail in the first place.?" Meg said with confidence.

235

Bobby narrowed his eyes. "What if he was trying to get rid of you?"

Meg's lifeless expression said it all. "I have to go back." she rose. "Let me say goodbye to your parents, and then I'll go back to the other side."

Bobby got up and they went downstairs. Kim had set five places at the table. A knot grew in Bobby's throat. Now was the perfect time to tell Gordy and Kim about his big secret. But before he could begin, Meg opened her mouth first. "This looks great, but I'm afraid I can't stay."

"You just got here. We haven't seen you in forever. You can't leave yet." Gordy pleaded.

Meg shrugged. "Something came up, and I have to head back to the hotel."

"At least let us know where you are living so we can keep in touch," Kim said.

Meg looked over at Bobby. He felt a hand on his shoulder as Nicole joined the conversation. "Come on, family, Aunt Meg has people to see and things to do."

Bobby was awestruck by Nicole. So was Meg. Gordy clapped his hands to get everyone's attention. "Come on, you can't have a little pizza before you go? I got pepperoni and pineapple, Meg, your favorite."

Nicole motioned for Meg to take a seat. "I guess one slice won't hurt." Meg sat down at the table.

Nicole linked arms with Bobby. "We'll be right back." She pulled Bobby into the kitchen.

The moment they were out of sight, Bobby threw his arms around her. "Oh my gosh, Nicole, I thought you were a goner! I saw both golden crowns over on the other side, and I thought one of those people took you hostage or something."

Nicole pried herself away from his grasp. "You saw the golden crown?"

Bobby quickly told Nicole everything that happened. Nicole high-fived him. "I knew you had it in you!"

Bobby smiled. "Aunt Meg is amazing! She explained everything to me. All our hunches about the other world were true! They are trying to hurt us, but her husband, Jonathan, is trying to keep us safe." His shoulders tensed up. "Nicole, the bad guys captured Jonathan. Meg has to go back and save him. But if she does that, we'll lose the crown."

Nicole hushed him. "Don't worry about it, little brother, we'll be just fine." She headed off to the dining room.

Bobby pulled her to a stop. "Wait a minute. Nicole, how did you get back?"

"Man, have I got a story for you!" she smiled. "There's a lot more to all this then we previously imagined."

"Tell me everything!" Bobby tried to sit still.

Nicole began her story. The tale she had for Bobby left his head spinning. She was right—there was a lot more to the golden crown than he had ever imagined.